T0369241

THE KILLING KIND

A NOVEL BY
JACK NEBEL

Order this book online at www.trafford.com
or email orders@trafford.com

Most Trafford titles are also available at major online book retailers.

Printed in the United States of America.

ISBN: 978-1-4269-3736-1 (sc)

Library of Congress Control Number: 2010910302

Trafford rev. 12/06/2010

 www.trafford.com

North America & international
toll-free: 1 888 232 4444 (USA & Canada)
phone: 250 383 6864 ♦ fax: 812 355 4082

Prologue

A white, windowless van drove by at what he was sure to be half of the speed limit until it disappeared over a rise in the road ahead. He slugged down some beer and tried to force the thought out, but it insisted. It never really went away. It would just fade out when he tired of the sorting and figuring process that came with his wiring harness. He was again thinking about that day a few months ago, maybe it was a Wednesday, blue skies above, walking out to get the mail, opening an envelope addressed to him in the handwriting of a young child. Inside, by the same reluctant black pen, it read:

> Now that we know where you are, know this-
> You will never escape us. We will be with
> You always. In our time, it will be done.

He had thrown the letter down on the kitchen table. "Bring it the fuck on," he had told the kitchen cabinets. What were they waiting for? Part of him, the part that flipped fear into workable realities, figured it was the work of State Department *operatives*. Could he still trust Dragon, his mission chief for all these years? He had to think so. Had to.

Now that Colonel Jake Parker had become Sam Castle, real estate investor from West Des Moines, Iowa, this might have been somebody just giving him a reminder just how dangerous it was for him out there and lest he become weak at any given moment, his life and that of many others could be at risk should he give in to the need to act out, or worse, speak out. If it was Dragon, he wasn't about to give him the satisfaction of an acknowledgement. Let the old wizard spin around just for one uncalculated moment wondering if he hit his mark or not. Then again,

Dragon would figure he might do just that. And on and on it would go, into oblivion, if Dragon worked it right.

Nonetheless, Parker was convinced West Des Moines was a good place for people like him in CGOP- Covert Government Operatives Program, a lesser-known, never existing cousin to the Witness Protection Program. Its main purpose for *not* existing was to protect uniquely gifted assassins like Parker while awaiting the next *engagement opportunity*, as they liked to say. West Des Moines was an up-to-date, but small suburb, always under the radar, with quiet people and quieter neighborhoods.

Parker was sure no one knew he owned a black Explorer. He always drove a silver Acura TL. The Explorer had been covered by a tarp in the garage for over a year. Just in case he and Karen needed a quick escape. Turned out she found hers another way. So it would figure the Explorer would buy him some time to at least get out of Iowa. And there were a shit load of white windowless vans on the roads of America. Only one of them hid the arsenal they had readied for him. Moments of paranoia came to him and tried to set up shop but he never completely bought in.

Then he would laugh and shake his head, maybe think about the best days with Karen, or the worst, when the heroin destroyed her so quickly it almost seemed like a deliberate poisoning. The logic that tried to follow up became lost in a search for beginnings. His mind would hover, then fast forward through the shattered dreams and promises that became the only worthy footnote on his unofficial State Department career- captured and terminated somewhere in the mountains along the border in Pakistan.

The dark. The DARK! He would come to know that he spent as much as four months at a time without seeing a sliver of light. He was alone, lying on his stomach, the unrelenting damp odor of feces and urine and a heavy sulphur burning into every air chamber in his lungs. He would lift his head only to bang up against a rock ceiling inches above him. He reached out in each direction to find more rock. He could not turn over, he could not stretch out, he could only move enough to find the rock perimeters of this living tomb. He could run his fingers over the narrow opening in front of his face. He would hear a door opening somewhere, muted footsteps, then a small round tray was shoved through the slot that also provided the acrid air that kept him semi-alive. Though he could not see what he was eating, it mattered not. Initially it smelled and tasted like clumpy cold rice and soggy vegetables, but soon his mind convinced him it was nothing more than a scoop of rat innards, and worse as time went on. For days at a time, he would simply push the small tray back out the slot and listen to it fall against the rocks on the other side, each time to the echoing laughter of his waiter. He had learned to be patient. If he waited long enough, insects and worming larva from the belly of the earth would attempt to latch onto his body. If they seemed to want to bore in where he could not get a hand on them, he could usually maneuver his body enough to scrape them off against the side of the rock. Others, though, would slowly make their way up, knowing the easier way inside the body was through the mouth or nose. He had become adept at choosing those that were fit for consumption, preferring the cracking carcass of a large roach to the foul slop on the tray.

In almost pleasurable moments, when his body was too numb to move, he would assume he was dead, the body waiting to rot, the mind waiting to shut down completely. As the feeling crept back into his feet, then his legs and up, he would begin to sob into the grit beneath his face, occasionally laughing hysterically, but mostly just whirling in a delirium, waiting again to die, fearing most being unable to do so. He would feel his heart pounding into the rock beneath him, shaking his body, begging to explode through his chest. He would try to make it do so, urging it on, screaming at it to be done with it all. Then it would subside, and the exhaustion would bring on sleep. He never knew how long he slept, how long he was awake, and after a time he could not differentiate when he was awake, thinking or dreaming. It was the same nightmare either way, the sheer terror on him with the heat of fiery reptiles while giant prehistoric birds pulled the skin off his body an inch at a time.

It was always a blurry recollection, but he remembered being dragged from his cell from time to time. There were echoes of laughter, and he wasn't sure if the angels of either God or Satan were whisking him off to whatever and wherever the end was. They would push and poke and prod as deep Arabic voices yelled within inches of his ears. "Infidel!" They screamed. "Get up!" Men with large, strong arms picked him up and forced him upright and out of his cell, dragging him along until his feet caught up. He said nothing as they slapped at the sides of his head and swore in Arabic and spit on his bare, filthy skin. They forced him through a series of door openings as his eyes tried to adjust to flashes of light. Finally, they hurled him to the floor in the middle of a large room with dim amber glowing lanterns hanging from high rock walls. "Take off those filthy rags, you stinking waste!"

He curled in agony and slowly pulled himself up into a sitting position, pulled off his thin rags and tossed them into a small pile, waiting fully naked for the needles of icy water to begin hitting and spinning him like a toy from a box of Cracker Jack. The red welts would come, some would bleed, but all would heal well enough before next month's bath.

Back in the protection offered by his tiny cell, a day or night came, not unlike any other, blending and droning on, when the cave suddenly began to shake and vibrate and rumble like it was on the verge of collapsing. It seemed of no consequence given his mental state. Then his jailer was suddenly tossed to the ground while on his way back out the door carrying the bucket of human waste. He tried to get to his feet only to have a boulder three feet in diameter land directly on his head, pinning him to the ground next to Parker. The only thing Parker could see was the jailer's feet jittering and twitching for a few moments before they went limp. He gathered himself as the sounds of men screaming and chanting began to build into a delirium from somewhere. He blinked away the semi-darkness and tried to make his mind bend back into shape. Something grabbed at him inside and pulled him to his feet. He looked down at the still body with a rock for a head, then over at the open door while the contents of the spilled bucket soaked into the rubble and dirt floor.

Another tremor shook the cave and he could only sense that possibly a welcomed end was near. Hearing the screams and realizing they were not his, his mind resumed a limited functionality that began to speak to him in a long forgotten insinuation that he was a master at survival under any and all circumstances. The volume of men screaming and chanting began to increase. He stumbled to the door frame and studied it, then touched and moved the door a little. It squeaked softly when he moved it. He *moved it*! Again, he pushed, and it edged forward and squeaked with a sound he had heard a thousand times before when that steel door slammed him back into hell. His red, bleary eyes tried to focus. He peaked out into the empty chamber he knew led to a long passage way that seemed to connect everything else in the cave.

Smaller rocks began to fall around him, one striking him on his face that strangely angered him into a cursing flurry that awoke every old friend in his psyche right down to his toes. Quickly, Parker moved back to the body of his jailer and began switching out his rags for the jailer's shoddy khaki uniform while the chaos came in echoes muffled in rock. A bombing, an earthquake, it made no difference at the time.

As he was removing the shirt and pulling the collar from beneath the rock that had fallen across the jailer's face, he noticed a pouch of sorts strapped around the jailer just beneath one arm pit. Parker had little curiosity for it at first, feverishly getting into the layers of clothing that were ripe with stale body odor. The pouch had some weight to it, though, so he grabbed it, hoping for a small gun or weapon of some kind. At that moment the lights went out completely and there was the darkest of dark. The sounds of men wailing poured from around him through the stone walls and he restrapped the pouch around his own body and hurriedly got into the rest of the clothes. The American-like chukka boots were an amazingly good fit, bringing an unfamiliar smile to his face. He felt his way and moved to the door, and as he opened it fully, the glow of a single wall torch in the outer chamber gave off enough light to make out the walls. Parker's mind began to churn out instructions and told him to turn back to the jailer. He pulled off the man's bloodied turban and fashioned it on his own head, then reached down beneath the rock and grabbed a handful of dirt, blood, and crushed tissue and began to smear in across his own face and down the front of his slightly undersized shirt to simulate wounds. It was likely the only time he was grateful he had lost forty pounds or the shirt would have never fit across his chest. Rocks continued to fall, some larger than the one that killed the jailer. Parker moved quickly, feeling the floor for his old clothes and grabbing them to use as a possible bandage wrap disguise. He gave them a quick dip in the jailer's mixture and covered his face except for his eyes.

He found the door that led into the main passage way and slowly eased himself out into the flow of men ranting and running back and forth and climbing over scattered piles of rock and boulders. There were some torches on, some out, no lights, an enormous amount of dust had kicked up and voices cried out in a reverberating frenzy of echoes.

Parker tried to sense a flow to get out, yet men seemed to be moving in both directions. Trying to blend into the chaos, he made sure the bloody wrap still covered most of his face and began following the larger group of men moving to his right.

"He's dead!" one man wailed.

"We're all dead!" another shot back, beginning to run faster as the rocks and dust continued to fall.

Strength began to pour into Parker, his thinner legs and arm muscles eagerly chugging down the blood being sent their way. He could feel his wits prodding him with each step. They stepped over bodies and limbs and ignored the pleading voices as they moved ahead, seemingly uphill, Parker thought. The men he followed were chanting in Arabic and moving as quickly as they could while he kept them in sight without getting too close.

When an evening twilight sky suddenly appeared above them, the men began to scatter in all directions. Parker found a direction of his own, and didn't stop until he was completely out of breath and dropped down under cover of some heavy brush. He could no longer hear their voices, no longer feel the vibrations of the earth moving. But the last words he heard his captors utter as he disappeared from them would always be clear. "Bin Laden is dead! Bin Laden is dead!"

His mission, it would seem, accomplished after all.

CHAPTER ONE

SHE HAD SAID MANY times all of this would kill her, and she was right. This thought, and little else went through the invented version of Sam Castle's mind as he watched the light rain hitting the casket.

"Ashes to ashes, dust to dust...."

There were few gathered; a couple of the neighbors, others with gray, vaguely familiar sad faces. But there was one guy he had never seen before; the one with the wraparound sun glasses and reddish hair slicked back. Pony tail. Looked like a pimp. Had it come to that, he wondered? Another pointless moment, just another pointless, random thought that drifted in and out like the others.

Then there was Dragon, in the olive-colored trench coat, representing a grateful government. The real message was that they felt Parker had lost his touch, he was more of a liability at this point, and he was probably too old for another mission, but they were grateful nonetheless. After all, the world was full of young, energetic thrill seekers that would love to have a license to kill.

It seemed God was insistent on a steady rain from a thick Iowa sky hovering over the landscape like an old patched up circus tent. Two years is all it took. Two years of so little said and nothing resolved. Cold and flat realities came too late. Not that it mattered. Nothing much mattered when a life was taken away. He would give her that. She said it often enough. When she talked, when she wept, and screamed, and wept some more, she would tell him how little it mattered. How little his brilliant career mattered, how all of it led to nothing. She finally said it would have been better if he had never escaped, never made it back. In the middle of another blasting, drunken episode just the week before she had again told him about her reoccurring dream of opening the front door of their house in Iowa and finding his head laying on the front step. There was a final look of terror stretched across his face, while bearded men in turbans stood there, hands behind there backs, laughing.

"Fuck you, you bastard...."

Those were her last words before a second series of strokes and a final heart attack took her and stopped her acid-tongued, anguished existence. He remembered nurses pushing him out of the way as they raced to her bed. There was a jumble of shouting and loud conversation. He slumped against the wall, a droning ring in his ears, tears stuck in the corners of his eyes.

"Mr. Castle. I'm sorry. She has passed," somebody important said.

It was three-something. Someone must have handed him a coffee. He used a fingernail to make criss-cross marks on the side of the Styrofoam cup. Everything he had or could say seemed stuck inside. Another criss-cross. Another. He vaguely remembered walking over to the hospital bed, leaning over her, reaching down to touch her cold face and brush back a fallen wisp of hair. He kissed her forehead and thanked his God for giving her what he could not.

By the time he reached the hospital chapel and hit his knees, he broke down and barely kept his balance. It lasted awhile, taking what little he had left in him. By the time he got back to his feet, he began hating himself for feeling a little lift. It was if someone had finally turned off the valve that was pumping the poison through his veins and he could breathe without hearing it whistle in his throat.

In the few days that passed, he cleaned up after her for the last time. Puke-stained bathroom walls, bed sheets smelling of urine and scat, a drawer full of unused syringes and the used ones he found in nearly every predictable hiding place. The cartons of Salem Lights, and the Skye Vodka bottles, some empty, some full. All of it went into double thick black plastic bags and out. He locked the door and checked into a Holiday Inn Express out near the Interstate, not sure if he would ever go back. If that was what was left of home, they could have it. The pimp, or whatever. It belonged to the government anyway. Let them deal with it.

A neighbor from across the street, Dorothy Steenbaum, was there, appearing to have borrowed her husband's trench coat for the occasion, a look on her face that said she was there just to make sure Gina was really dead this time.

"And so we commit the body and soul of Gina Castle to God's earth...."

Should have been enough for Dot Steenbaum. She could go back home and tell her kids what happens to crazy people that take drugs, park the car on their front lawn and sleep half naked on the driveway.

The old man with a sunken, crooked face from three doors down wiped at his huge nose, and another in a wheel chair with large bony hands grabbed and poked at his kneecaps. A young black female caretaker stood at the handles, panning the small gathering for a care.

His mind flipped things over and back. She was right, too, about his being there at all. She had him dead, rightfully, captured, sure to die or at least rot to death over time in some dark shit hole. How had she said it so many times? "On a noble mission to save humanity and the whole fucking world, and somehow moved his wife from first place to last place on the list of those worth saving."

And then she would really get into it. Fueled by the vodka, she would rant into the night, unleashing an incoherent haze of anger at him for not dying a noble death. Waiting faithfully, trembling in bed alone for almost three years, what did he expect? She was reeling into a life she would have never thought possible. The few friends she had made in their short time in Iowa had gone away. Damn the smug tolerance and pity! She found new friends. Friends that could take her pain away.

"Give me the life insurance any day," she would say before passing out.

Sam would leave the room at some point, head for the living room couch and lay there wondering which was worse, a dirt floor bed in Pakistan, or this.

❧

"Call me in a few days," Dragon whispered to Castle as he passed by and grasped his forearm. "Terribly sorry about all of this."

Maybe he was, maybe he wasn't, thought Sam. No matter. But he found himself wishing Dragon wasn't there and being grateful he was at the same time. Then his mind jumped back into the frazzle, the mad spin of thoughts back, sorting feverishly, filing, tossing, intent on keeping nothing, but afraid to throw anything out.

One evening a few weeks before he was in the backyard fooling around with something, when she stumbled out through the sliding glass doors. She was in a full length white night gown, balancing the tall glass of vodka until she could lean up against the back side of the house. She said nothing, but watched him for perhaps twenty minutes. He moved a pile of wood from one side of the metal shed to the other. He occasionally stopped to gaze back at her. Her eyes looked past his, mouth open, head bobbing slightly. She turned and felt her way along the siding to the sliding glass door, and disappeared. Hours later the paramedics were taking her out through the living room. The front door chimed open, chimed closed, and she was gone. Difference this time was he knew where she was headed.

If he counted Dragon, there were a total of fourteen. That was about a dozen more friends than he could count on his side. He hadn't planned it this way, but he made a point of keeping to himself over the past two years while Gina went out and continued her demise. She had never wanted to leave Boston, never asked for anything but to be Mrs. Jake Parker, or Karen Parker, to her closest of friends.

The silver-handled gray casket, the Platitudes model, with extra padding and soft lace edges at $6,995, began its descent. Sam took a deep breath, rumbled up another and watched as the casket suddenly jerked violently to the side and upended to an organ monkey screech that pierced the air. Crack! In less than the ten seconds that followed, the casket hit bottom, the lid fell against the side of the freshly dug hole and all was again still. Onlookers froze while the funeral director moved quickly to the casket and tried to maneuver it back into drop position. He struggled and leaned a shoulder in, but instead the latch on the lid gave way. Gina reappeared. For all he could do, the director stopped Gina from falling out by grabbing a dead breast and hanging on until help arrived by way of the minister and a helpful mourner. "Shit…" he said, with a bit of echo against the low sky rain.

Sam Castle instinctively moved towards his dead wife, but the slick soles of his best shoes were no match for the wet shiny tarp and down he went, stumbling through a cartwheel that left him face down in the bottom of the hole. A keen sense of the damp smell of busy earthworms filled his nostrils in one breath. The smell immediately reminded him of the cave in Pakistan. The clearance in that crevice was less than a layer of skin. He couldn't move. For a few moments, he thought this was how it would end, but by a fractional twitch at a time, he managed to slide back out with his head still attached at the neck.

Sam pulled himself away from the wet earthworm smell, stood up in the hole, got a foot grip on a handle off the side of the casket and eased himself up and out unceremoniously, noting from a corner of one eye the feverish work to get Gina pushed back inside the casket and the lid closed. No easy task. He tried to brush off his best suit. Big mistake. The drizzle had turned the dirt particles to mud, and his best suit was a mess.

Click! The lid closed tight, Gina tucked back inside, and a gathered group of cemetery workers that had been waiting to fill the hole repositioned the casket and fashioned two heavy nylon straps underneath before sliding it down inside.

"And so…," the minister continued, in a voice that feared something else horrible would occur at any moment.

Sam felt as though the remains of his own life were being buried as well.

It was late April, the garden soil needed to be turned, the grass was ready for a first cutting, and the basement remodel he began over the winter would sit until next winter. He took a hard look at Dragon, who was giving a hard look back, and decided right then it was time to make a move of his own. Fuck Dragon, and this whole damn thing. Dragon's hard look was a perfect design, the one that cautioned against getting any ideas no matter what the circumstances.

It was only the week before when Boone Chavez, Dragon's underling and insufferable mouthpiece had called. "Get your wife under control. We think she could become an embarrassment."

Dragon shifted and waited and watched Sam standing at attention as the circus around him finally died down. The cemetery workers were covered with mud but the coffin was finally at rest. As others scurried away for the dry sanctuary of their SUV's, Sam picked a yellow rose from one of the few bouquets piled alongside the hole and gently tossed it in with a final look. He could see a fold of the material of her dress had caught on the outside of the lid, but the jumbled options flipped through his mind for just a moment before he turned to leave.

He drove straight back to the house and went inside, cracked a blind in the den and waited. No Dragon. Nobody. He moved quickly to the kitchen, poured a scotch and went back to the blinds. He wasn't sure just why he no longer trusted Dragon, or anybody at the State Department for that matter, but as badly as this had all turned out, it was easy to have doubts. Doubts? People that peek through their own blinds at an empty street have more than doubts.

He gulped down the rest of the scotch and stepped out into the back yard. The rain was still light, but steady, as he walked slowly towards the shed along the fence at the back property line. He slid the door open and reached inside for the shovel.

"Yeah. Know how it is," he said to the weather beaten stuffed scarecrow as he tossed it down into the vegetable garden and began digging into the mud. Unless the earth had moved as well, this was the spot. It wasn't long before the shovel tip hit its mark. There was one sigh left in him as he dropped to one knee and reached down to get it. He pried open the top of the coffee can and looked inside, just to be sure, snapped the lid back on and carried it back to the house. "Do over," said Sam.

CHAPTER TWO

Sam Castle was heading west on Interstate 80 somewhere in the flattest flat middle of Nebraska, hands ten o'clock-two o'clock, with a numbness and nothingness above a vague sense of movement trying to work into full blown grief or avoid it altogether. He had prepared for his own death many times over, as if the inevitable result of a bad day at the office, but he could not recall any training in this grief process.

Almost forty, knowing somebody most of your life, loving her, then having it end badly and tragically. No training video, nothing on the curriculum at MIT for that.

Long before Sam Castle needed to be invented, long before Dr. Jake Parker put on Navy Seal gear and Colonel Jake Parker took various assignments with the State Department: there was Jake Parker, star quarterback of Glenbard West High School, reaching down from his perch on the shoulders of his teammates to hand the football he had thrown for the winning touchdown at Homecoming to a beautiful cheerleader. The look in his future wife's eyes at that moment was what carried him through those years wasting away imprisoned in Pakistan. But in this moment between memory search and grief, he could not shut out the more recent image of those same eyes, colorless, above sallow cheeks and a weak smile that fell short in welcoming him back from his ordeal.

As he readjusted his hands on the wheel, he soaked up the irony of having been all over the world, and here he was plotting his escape in the middle of Nebraska with no destination in mind. He was doing something unplanned and borderline irresponsible for perhaps the first time in his adult life. This act of driving somewhere without a destination, picking up Cheetos and Miller High Life along the way; just driving, drinking and driving at times, and reading billboards.

No one that knew him would think it possible, no matter what the circumstances. In his MIT days, thoughts, calculations, visions, and diabolical aberrations spilled from head to paper to computer with the breath of each day, leaving a smaller part of the world to be conquered the next.

As the ribbon of highway straightened into an endless line, he hit cruise control and began an exercise he had used nearly every day in his prison cell. First, he would bring as many as six voices into his head for a conversation; an unrehearsed dialogue that usually took on a life of its own after a bit. Then just when that process felt like it might consume him, he would kick them all out of his head and force his mind into complete emptiness, a Seinfeld-like nothing that would usually bring on the only restful sleep he found.

Maybe it was the beer in the morning, but nonetheless there was the beginning of some giddy release going on he was not going to fight. A pronounced freedom begat from a few beers and the open highway began to throw heavy thoughts about like balloons losing their helium. He began to chase the horizon with purpose and reached for the knob on the radio. Music, something jazzy, piano, sax, bass, drums. Softly at first, then he cranked up the volume and let the noise crowd out that mess in his skull. This was better. This feeling of driving forever was deliriousness, simply better than anything he could remember, going back to skipping a final exam back when he was a freshman in college. The opportunity to swim naked with Karen in broad daylight at a swimming pool owned by an out-of-town neighbor was just too much of a match for his eighteen-year-old hormones.

He would need to pee soon.

Reloaded with beer and Cheetos, he was turning the Explorer back onto the westbound ramp when he spotted a man maybe in his late twenties, sitting on a backpack, slump shouldered, staring at the ground and tossing a handful of small stones one by one. He didn't have a thumb out, but for any number of reasons or none at all, Sam stopped the car along side. He rolled the passenger window down. "Need a lift somewhere?"

"Been tryin' to figure that out." Up closer, maybe he was a man in his early thirties with pocked facial skin and hair beginning to gray at the temples pulled back into a short pony tail. A sadness held his deep eyes still like they waited to behold a cataclysmic event of some kind.

"Get in if you like."

The man's large face flattened, as though he was settling for less. "Okay."

"Sam."

"Lomis."

"Lomis. Where you headed? Or where you been? Your choice." As Lomis settled in, Sam realized a much longer, larger man had uncurled from atop the backpack.

Lomis eyed Sam and caught a glimpse of the open can of beer in the cup holder.

"Want a beer?" Sam asked.

Lomis scanned the horizon and his face lightened with approval. "Livin' dangerously?"

"Right on the edge. Join me." Sam handed him the plastic rings of cans. "No cooler. I haven't got around to that yet. Take one and throw the rest in the back for now."

Lomis popped the can open and took another look around before he brought the can up for a quick and heavy, and then tucked it back down between his legs.

The miles rolled off in silence.

"You got that look like you don't trust anybody," Sam finally said.

"There a reason I should?"

"No. Not really."

Nobody picked up hitchhikers anymore, did they? Almost a delicious thought for Sam, going well with beer and Cheetos. A poor slug having just another shit day, or a serial killer rattling the dice for a quick escape. It didn't much matter to Sam. He had known bad days and he had known killers of the worst kind.

They cracked two more beers.

Sam threw some chum in the water. "So my guess is you just got out of prison, maybe escaped, or at the very least, some woman threw you out on your ear."

Lomis looked away and scanned the perfect greening stripes of sun drenched farm land. Spring. A great day to be alive in most books. "And I could be good with a knife, too."

Sam sat up a bit straighter and readjusted his hands on the wheel. Ten o'clock, two o'clock. "Well, let's see now...." He mumbled it just loud enough.

Lomis checked up with some laughter. "Hell, man, what I just escaped was Daltry and the half-way house I been living in for the past three months. I've been fixing cars and drinking for the past ten years, man. That's it. My water mark was Homecoming King back in 1996."

"Quarterback?"

"Oh yeah."

"Any good?"

"Good enough."

"And then... ."

"And then it didn't work out the way I planned. I got a ride at Nebraska State but I couldn't make grades, or show up for the most part. Flunked out after a year and returned to Daltry with my tail between my legs and hid out for ten years at Ron's Garage, fixing Buicks and old pick-ups."

"Love?"

"Susan McBee," Lomis said without hesitation. He took a long pull on the beer.

Silence returned to the car for many miles. Most might consider Lomis Walls a bit odd looking; his head a bit large for the rest of him, a pair of darting, deep-end-of-the-pool eyes that seemed to hang on a precarious balance above sunken cheeks of pale skin and acne scars that ran along his jaw line on either side. To some, maybe most, he would look and sound like an eminent threat to the civilized world. Sam always went with the idea that everybody was dangerous and watched the dial on the scale from there.

"I'm just sayin'...," Lomis said softly. "About a mile off Exit 78 is one of the sweetest little titty bars in the universe."

Sam laughed back. "This is the middle of nowhere and it's two in the afternoon."

"Means you get a good table," Lomis said with a wide grin that twitched slightly as it eased back.

Sam and Lomis exchanged a few glances as the car flew by Exit 77. As Lomis ripped another beer from the plastic ring, Sam's mind followed a slow drift backwards from the funeral to that last time he saw his wife at the hospital. Then, with an unplanned change of gears, he was back in Pakistan, in the dark, huddled in a damp corner, insects crawling up his filthy pant legs, shivering and waiting anxiously for death. He would wait for the gears to change again. Sometimes he summoned up a haunting, hysterical laughter that echoed and deadened into the rock. And yet in other, rare moments of peace, he recalled his Transcendental Meditation Mantra from his college days. Managing to settle back and distance himself with eyes closed, he timed his breathing to twelve second intervals, and began to count in his head while the chant moved his lips. "Shea rem. Shea rem. Shea rem," he repeated rhythmically, finding the air beneath him rise, and a smaller, impossible world begin to brighten. Even when he slept, he was certain he had taught himself to keep counting. But after he had ticked off six days, something suddenly bit savagely into his inner thigh. He screamed and feverishly dug his fingers into the open wound to pull it out. When the warm blood stopped spurting, he realized he had lost his count, slumped to the dirt floor, and quietly wept.

"Probably over a hundred miles from Daltry," Sam said.

"I didn't say I hung there. I just know the place."

The car seemed to find its way onto the Exit 78 ramp and follow the directions Lomis gave it from there.

Too good to be true, Lomis was thinking. The beer was unexpected, and this extraordinary opportunity to mix and match pleasures of the soul, a blessing, a sign of only better things to come. This was Friday, the day they changed the women out. It would mean new eye candy. Maybe this time he would find a suitable bitch. It had been months since the last, but even if that didn't work out, he would dispose of this Sam guy, have a car and move on to, perhaps, Montana this time, or Wyoming, maybe Jackson Hole. Maybe slice up some fucking rich bitch and make it real bad. Set those smug bastards back a decade or two. But don't get too far ahead, he reminded himself. When he remembered to keep himself in the moment and allow his Gods to do the rest of the work, things generally turned out well.

CHAPTER THREE

THERE WAS THE YOUNG naked black woman on the table grinding her perfectly hairless vagina to the music a foot from his face, but Sam was wondering just why he had allowed the interruption. Hard to beat Cheetos and beer in the car, or even the Dairy Queen they had passed about a mile back.

Lomis was sitting erect, a longneck beer cradled between his legs, arms folded, fingers strumming on the sleeves of his windbreaker. A twitch worked and reworked through his left cheek while he studied.

"Miss Nebraska, I presume," said Sam.

The music was loud, bumpy and tracked right down to each vibration that shook the flesh of her inner thighs. She dangled large, engineered, chocolate-nippled breasts at him at the end of the song before jumping down and back to a small stage.

"Damn," Sam said, one eye watching Lomis react as well. He waved her off as if she was still on the table and looked around in the semi-darkness. A few shadows moved in corners and at the tables that lined the back wall. Hand jobs, Sam figured.

"Gotta piss," Lomis said, getting up.

Sam gave a thought to just getting up and leaving. He felt like the unneeded extra chaperone at the prom.

"Buy a girl a drink?" came a light Southern voice at the back of Sam's left ear.

He turned and took her in. Cute, a blonde head full of wiggling curls and a big smile. "Sure. Why not," Sam said.

"Buying the lady a drink?" The waitress chimed in within moments.

"Champagne?" The curly blonde asked.

"Of course," Sam said, smiling, amused that this drill had not changed much since that time long ago at a chummy bachelor party for a fellow Navy Seal.

"Where you from?" She drawled as the waitress quickly moved away with the order.

"Same place as you today," Sam said.

"You don't sound like you come from Beloxi to me," she said.

Sam shrugged and put up his hands. He had been to Beloxi on a training mission a while back. It was a pretty good imitation.

Lomis came out of the men's room and looked down a dark hallway illuminated only by the red-lettered exit sign above a door at the end. He walked to the door and checked to see that it still opened without an alarm going off and fiddled with the buttons in the side of the door until he was sure he had dismantled the automatic lock mechanism. The bright shock of the afternoon drilled him in the eyes before he stepped back inside, lit a cigarette and decided to give it a fifty count. "Fifty, forty-nine, forty-eight...," he whispered to himself as he leaned against the wall just inside the door. Stay in the moment, he reminded himself. It was never better than staying in the moment. "Sixteen, fifteen... ." He snuffed out the cigarette under his shoe. Shit. No luck. Then, suddenly a rustling shadow came down the hall. His eyes bulged and his jaw tightened as he pressed up closer to the wall. It was the black girl. She opened the door to the ladies room and went inside. Lomis pictured it, considered it quickly, and took two steps before stopping and looking upwards. He could do better, he thought. She wasn't worth it.

When he got back to the table he was enraged he would have to put up with the drivel of conversation going on between Sam and the curly blonde whore. He tried to shut it out, chugged back half of his beer and pretended to be interested in the lithe young thing circling and sliding playfully on the fire pole on stage. A series of black lights began to blink in sequence as she pretended to fall to the floor only to spring back up with legs impossibly spread and the g-string removed.

Lomis was pretty sure that was against the law, and turned away.

"Another for the lady?" The waitress asked Sam, leaning over him and trying to give him an eyeful of her own cleavage.

"Sure. Why not," Sam said with a little smile.

Lomis was in a zone, leaning back in his chair, looking around at a few scattered customers barely visible in the smoky darkness. Business was slow, even for mid day. He wondered if they even had the usual rotation of six girls.

"I do hand jobs for a hundred," the curly blonde said through her grape juice not so cleverly disguised as champagne.

Sam laughed a little and took another sip of beer. A hand job? It had been awhile. Too long. Way too long.

"What else is on the menu?"

"Blow job is two-fifty. Five hundred to cum in my mouth. I don't fuck." Her southern drawl seemed to leave her.

"Okay, then." Sam's mind flopped around like a sea lion trying to find a good spot in the rocks.

"I'm ready any time you are," Lomis yelled above the noise.

That was the cue Sam needed. He smiled up at her. "Going to sit this one out. Sorry."

"Where you headed so quick?" The blonde asked, touching Sam's forearm.

He pulled back and instinctively wiped his arm with his other hand. "It was fun, sweetheart, but not today."

"No, I mean...," she said, looking to see if the waitress vulture was lurking. "I mean, my man, Wyatt and I are looking for a ride to Jackson Hole, Wyoming. We both got jobs waiting there, but no wheels. We got money. We'd pay the gas."

Her southern accent had left her and the voice had become the third trailer home down on the left. "Or, we could work out a trade." The drawl returned. She was pretty good at it.

Sam finished his beer and looked around at nothing in particular. "Black Ford Explorer."

Lomis couldn't hear what Sam said but followed him out to the parking lot.

The sun was still shining brightly as they walked back to the car. The blonde fell in stride to his left and introduced him to Wyatt on his right. A young girl hooking, a boyfriend probably hanging on for drug money and a deranged killer. Sam smiled at his good fortune.

"What's in the little cooler?" Sam asked the blonde, noting she carrying a small handled plastic Igloo.

"Weight Watchers," she said.

"Go ahead and jump in back."

Sam gloried in the facial reaction from Lomis as he slid in behind the wheel. That twitch was working through his cheek again and was affecting his eye as well. In the rear view mirror, Sam could see the couple in back fixing their eyes on Lomis, then back on each other.

"Jackson Hole, it is," Sam announced, tuning the radio to a station giving the weather.

"Maybe…," Wyatt started before the blonde jabbed him in the side.

Lomis looked out his window as Sam began to pull out. "What the fuck, man," he muttered, wondering, as he often did, at the moments when doing nothing changed everything. He pictured, for the moment, the black girl, a lump on the floor in the stall in the bathroom, the blood flow starting to subside from her mouth and ass while he found his way down the road another way. Guts empty and shaking, but he had made the right decision on this one. But what was this, now? A smile began to pull at the corners of his mouth as they passed the dark green sign at the westbound I-80 entrance ramp.

"Clear sailing," Sam announced, switching the stations until he found an oldies format. "There's a few beers left on the floor back there. Help yourself, and give Lomis here one."

Sam eased back against the leather seat. Setting no boundaries; creating a new world from the ashes of the old. He had almost forgotten how. He glanced at the gray car hustling by him on the left. No hubcaps, black on black tires. Government plates. Could be anybody or nobody, but trying to guess what they might do at this point gave him an unwelcome rush. He pushed back at the reality and gave the pedal another ten miles an hour.

CHAPTER FOUR

"LET THE HONEYMOON BEGIN," the young man named Wyatt said as he wrapped the curly blonde up in his arms in the back seat and rocked her back and forth. She giggled, Southern style, and nuzzled back at him.

Sam caught the look Lomis had waiting for him.

Lomis hated times like this when he had to try to sort his thoughts while things he didn't understand happened too quickly. Yet, he had learned this about himself: if he acted too quickly, if he sprung out of his first impulse, the results were always more difficult to deal with, and just the clean up alone was always more complicated and time consuming. He took a deep, rattling breath and brushed at the denim shirt pocket for the phantom pack of Marlboro's. He pursed his lips and let the air out slowly. It had been almost two years since he quit; right after the night he feel asleep while smoking in bed in the motel outside of Little Rock. A flame licking at his arm woke him and saved his life. The motel burned to the ground, but he was long gone when it did and grateful to the devil himself that he wasn't any drunker than he was. The cigarettes just didn't seem so important after that. A smile twitched its way into his upper lip as he stopped rubbing the pocket. He was damn proud of quitting. The thought passed. He sat back with the beer Wyatt handed him and eased back into the seat, satisfied, proud, and patient.

"Okay," Sam said, "Now that everybody knows one another we should get along just fine. Let the highway do the talking." Sam hated small talk. There was enough of that in his head and he had grown weary of all those people as well. That's what this was all about. Same shooter, new dice.

"So, Lomis," Sam began, after about ten miles of static silence, except the giggling coming from the back seat. In the rearview mirror he could see Wyatt had his hand under blondie's blouse and she had a few deft fingers circling just to the left of his zipper. "Where did you do time?"

"Didn't say I did as I recall," he said.

"Maybe you didn't."

"Never done no time except rehab," Lomis said.

"How'd you get that look then," Sam asked.

"What look would that be?"

"That one." Sam nodded and pointed to his cheek for a moment. "The one that tightens your cheek like a winch."

This guy was a ride, alright, Lomis thought. Thinking he is real cute trying to read me and talking in riddles. Like it was some kind of game. Well, so be it. Two can play as long as it is only to kill time and nothing else. Even the thought of how he was going to kill Sam Castle brought a juicy rush inside that twitching cheek. New ground. Usually he didn't get this worked up if it was just some fucking guy. It was the smell of a woman that really got him going. And come to think of it, there was something beginning to hang in the air in the car that had that familiar scent to it. He listened closely as a belt buckle rattled, a zipper unzipped, then another. He turned his face just enough to get a glimpse. Wyatt's hand had snaked down the front of Blondie's jeans while her cocked wrist worked into his boxers. Their tongues dueled and drooled and they went about their business.

Sam turned the radio up a notch. Springsteen. "Young love," Sam said. "Let them be."

"Shit," Lomis muttered, shaking his head.

"Been awhile for you?" Sam asked.

"Hey man. Sometimes ten minutes ago is too long, you know what I mean?"

"Believe I do."

"Shit." Lomis put his head back into the head rest and chugged down his beer. He tossed the can over his shoulder, knowing he would hit something, maybe something good. But before he could get any satisfaction from it, there was a rustling, and quickly another beer rolled over the seat top onto his lap. A moment later, the empty plastic rings came along as well. "Shit." He opened the beer, glared at a smiling Sam Castle, and threw a hefty swig back. He assumed the little whimpering sounds meant the hands were back at work. Should turn around and look. Really should. But he didn't.

They crossed the state line into Wyoming to a series of lip-biting testimonials from the two in the back seat. Lomis fidgeted with his cigarette lighter and it occurred to him he had never set anybody on fire before. If only the scent of sex filling his air space was flammable it would have been a perfect moment to set them all ablaze and leap from the car.

Sam's mind traveled and logged miles on miles trying to remember the last time, or maybe the only time he had sex in the back seat of a car. As for Lomis, he was thinking about that butch-haired skinny bitch in Baltimore not long ago. A dark parking garage was always a good bit of luck, and she deserved what she got more than most. She was a wise-ass bitch. He had watched her waitress at Denny's for over a week, never smiling at a customer, never showing any emotion. A drone. Somebody's baggage. He felt nothing as he bashed her head in with the tire iron in the back seat of her Chevy Malibu. He left her bleeding to death, a puddle of his cum soaking into the cloth seat between her legs.

"Here's twenty bucks for gas," came the southern voice over Sam's right shoulder.

"Keep it," he said. "No need."

"Are you sure?" she cooed.

Sam eyed the wagging slender fingers holding the folded bill next to his face. He guessed they weren't packing hand sanitizer. "My treat."

He looked over at Lomis and noticed a bead of sweat had worked down and glistened on the skin rising on the blood beat at his temple.

"So Lomis," Sam said, darting another long look his way. "Seems to me this whole thing is making you nervous as hell. Now why is that?"

Lomis finished the last beer and tossed the can back.

"Hey, watch it, cocksucker!" Blondie shouted at Lomis, throwing the can back and ditching the southern accent once more. The can glanced off his cheek bringing a little smile to his face.

"He smiles," Sam noted. And the eyes? Sam had seen those eyes before, more piercing maybe, setting back above dark, thick beards and longer, broader noses. Death cold and liquid turned gel, never blinking, never sleeping, never aching to close. The eyes of a man that only came alive with the excitement of the kill. He knew the eyes of evil well. That didn't mean he was right about Lomis, but he liked the thought he might be; and for whatever reason, an excitement of his own was working through his veins. He eased back off the accelerator when he realized he had hit ninety.

"Yeah man," Wyatt added, "Like, dude, what the fuck is your problem, anyway?"

Lomis turned his head to look at the two and gave them a full smile that widened his big face. "I am truly sorry," he said. "Guess I forgot you were back there." He cocked his head and considered Wyatt. He figured he would gut him from underneath and let him bleed out through his shredded scrotum. He hadn't decided on how to do Blondie yet, but they had a ways to go yet, so there was no rush. In the mean time, he could have fun with the thought of Wyatt's eyes bulging out while the tip of his hunting knife tickled his spleen. "And Sam," Lomis nodded at Blondie. "Maybe you could hit one of those rest stops so the bitch can douche, and we can get that skank smell out of here."

Young Wyatt lurched for Lomis, but caught Sam's suddenly outstretched stiff-arm before he could get to the smile.

"Easy now," said Sam. "Small car, four people, all going to Jackson Hole. Give yourself some room, now. Just relax. Enjoy the ride."

Lomis shot him a look. His best. Nothing going on except that twitch in his cheek giving him dead away. Wyatt seemed more perturbed with the bruising his lower lip took from Sam's arm than anything else as he retreated to the open-mouthed sleeping beauty on the seat.

Sam chewed on the irony, bobbed his head slightly during the instrumental part of the long version of *Light My Fire* by the Doors, and continued to sort through an unending presentation of thoughts being offered up from that place inside of him in charge of putting out information for consideration. But there could be no question he felt an ease about things, specifically about the random order of things, and the fact he cared so little about having everything make sense. He sort of hoped the kids would screw all the way to Jackson Hole. And watching Lomis lose it was nearly as interesting.

His mind darkened for a moment as he got stuck in a visual of the place where people like Jim Morrison and Karen Parker rehabbed for eternity. Then he saw the sign. "Fine Food," Sam said, reading the small, but bright blue neons set back from the interstate in a corn field. "Exit Haunted Lake Road. Interesting enough. Anybody hungry?"

CHAPTER FIVE

"You folks ready to order?" Betty Purdy asked, breathing just as quickly and deeply as her Mexican papaya shaped body would allow. She readied a pencil with an eraser the glowed deep pink.

"We need to wait for Marbles," Wyatt said, scanning the menu for the tenth time.

Sam looked around. Gus and Betty Purdy's Steakhouse. Just right.

"Who the fuck is Marbles?" Lomis asked.

"Marbles," Wyatt said, "is my lady, dude. Margareth Lathum-Brown. You need to start being cool, man."

"Where the hell are you from?" Lomis asked.

"Wherever she says, dude."

As Lomis considered lengthening the suffering time Wyatt would need to endure, a little plastic container skipped down onto his plate from somewhere. He picked it up. Weight Watchers Applesauce.

Marbles took her seat. "It's Lomis, right? Well, Lomis, it's empty. I used it to douche. You can have it as a souvenir."

Lomis smiled across at her, opened the container, gave it a lick and flipped it back at her.

As each considered and judged the move, Betty's hot pink eraser flipped off the top of her pencil and fell to the floor.

"Marbles?" Sam motioned for her to begin.

"Can I get the crab legs?"

"Sure," said Sam.

Marbles smiled widely and completed her order.

"I'll have the Porterhouse. Rare," Sam said. "Baked. Ranch dressing on the salad."

Wyatt was next. "Meat loaf, dude. I can't believe you have meat loaf and mashed potatoes. I'll have that. And a bottle of Tobasco."

Lomis considered each of them, wondered if any of them would have changed their order if they knew it was their last meal. Wyatt would go first, for sure. *This dude's on death row and he orders fucking meat loaf for his last meal.* He gave Betty a look she wouldn't soon forget. "Give me the New York. Well done. I mean, cremate it. I want to see ash on the edges. And broccoli instead of the potato. Broccoli instead of salad." The Sam guy was a wild card, though. It was like he knew something- sensed something. Those eyes, the looks he gave him, coolness, alright, but something more. Like he knew the end of the story and was working it backwards. Then again, how could he? *Fucking dude would die just like all the rest.* But for now, imagine the luck once again. This time a ride and a meal ticket, and he didn't talk much, which was good.

"Some woman you are," Wyatt said as he leaned over and kissed Marbles.

"Ok then," Sam said. "Just four people gathered, no issues, no agenda. Just dinner," he said.

Lomis nearly jumped off his seat. As it was, he felt like he was already levitating. "Crab legs. Jesus," he muttered under his breath. "She orders crab legs. The whore wants crab legs and he gives them to her. Jesus."

"The lady knows what she wants," Sam said.

Lomis stood up suddenly and stiffly, put his hands out as if to preface a speech, then decided against it and began walking towards the front door. "I need some air," he said over his shoulder.

His lungs got their fill of the cool Wyoming night before he lit a cigarette. He could hear a female voice softly floating from somewhere, and instinctively began to shuffle his feet forward and around the corner of the building towards the sound. A girl in her early twenties was twirling the ends of some of her long, black hair while talking on a cell phone and puffing on a cigarette just outside a side door to the restaurant. A sense of the otherwise quiet and deserted nature around the free standing building began to play out for him. The lights of a gas station a few hundred yards down the road twinkled in silence. His eyes quickly covered every possibility while his heart rate took off with excitement. He loved the flood of surging warmth at moments like these. The anticipation always began with a rush that took his breath away and brought a vibrating pulse into his temples. He reached down and pulled up a long bladed stiletto from along his calf inside his sock. The blade was razor sharp, cleaned, ready, and he began curling it in his hand and running it up behind his forearm. He pressed the tip in against his flesh until the delicious moment came when he knew any more pressure would puncture the skin. She was pacing in easy circles. They all paced with those damn phones in their ears. Odd, but predictable habit afflicting them all. He inched forward and back, keeping himself in a shadow. He could see to the rear of the building, and other than a mercury yard light that spotted down on the dumpster, a wall of darkness was close behind. It would be easy to drag her back into it before she had any idea… Closer, now, don't give it away. Not just yet. Wait. Wait.

"Fuck!" She dropped the phone and the battery went spilling out to the pavement. "Fuck, fuck, fuck!" She yelled in a rage, quickly reaching down and stabbing at the pieces.

The side door burst open. "Cindy! Come on, dammit. Order's up," snarled an older barrel-chested man in a stained white apron and t-shirt.

Lomis ducked behind a wide prickly evergreen and froze, the stiletto still, twenty feet short of his prey. "Some kind of bullshit," he muttered. The girl gathered her parts and darted back inside as his pulse began to kick back. The hot rush flamed out. These incomplete missions, and there were too many to count, were near the lowest for him. But then he would always give himself props, like right then, for always giving them a better than even chance. He seldom used a gun. Boom! Splat! A circle darkening of blood, maybe some bits of flesh hitting the wall and maybe, at most, a second shot to the head to be sure. The metallic sour smell and it was over. So big deal. Knives afforded the opportunity of high adventure, shiny smooth hard blades like the stiletto, like the folded Swiss Army is his windbreaker, another in his back pocket, three different sized hunting knives, one serrated in his duffle bag, and the stiletto inside his sock. Rarely could the usually violent sex compare to the sensory explosion he felt as he pushed a steel blade into giving warm flesh or the muted crunch of a longer blade passing through its mark inside an orifice. The sudden scream of inflicted, unimaginable pain from beneath a duct taped mouth, the bulging eyes, the blood pumping, sometimes bubbling out as he began the sequence, as if conducting a symphony, building slowly, steadily to a bludgeoning crescendo and a spectacular soaking exhaustion.

"Just in time," Sam observed as Lomis sat back down to the plate Betty set down in front of him.

"Take it back," Lomis said flatly.

Betty set down a plate of meat loaf and mashed potatoes to a smiling Wyatt Kelso while she looked over at Lomis with suspicion.

"Not done enough. I can see it. No ash. No ash on the edges, it's not done enough. See that fat there? That fat should be a cinder if this was done enough. Take it back. Please."

The "please" ending gave Betty a reason to steady up with her hands on her big wide hips. Without a word, or a smile, she picked up his plate and retreated in a slow waddle to the kitchen.

"You are a righteous sort of asshole, aren't you?" Marbles chirped as she cracked her first crab leg open.

Lomis looked at her, steadied a gaze over at Wyatt who was all in putting tobasco on the meat loaf. "That's about right, bitch. You remember that."

"Dude. Chill out," Wyatt said quietly, shaking his head.

Sam divided his time devouring the great steak in front of him and quietly observing the others raise the dysfunction level. A hilarious waste, he thought.

By the time Marbles was working the last bit of crab meat from an ornery knuckled shell, Betty returned with and set a stainless steel plate crackling with heat and steam in front of Lomis. Atop alone was a knurled black powdery glob of char roughly the size of a partially shredded baseball.

"Enjoy," Betty said and waddled away.

Sam eyed Lomis curiously, as he had from the start, anxious to see how he would go about eating that steak.

Lomis picked it up with one hand, put the other on it to get a good grip and went after it like it was jerky. He liked all the eyes on him, watching him like he was some freak. They hadn't seen anything yet.

CHAPTER SIX

Betty kept her distance from Lomis, but managed to warm enough to Sam to recommend the Pine Bluff Lodge down the road for a place to spend the night. Sam figured anybody serving a steak that good likely had everything else right. Lomis voted they drive straight through to Jackson Hole, offering to drive while Sam caught a couple of hours of sleep.

"Not a chance," Sam said with a smile.

Free ride to nowhere or not, the only thing that kept Lomis from going after Sam was the God voice in his head telling him this guy might be more dangerous than he was. He just wasn't as confident Sam Castle would go down like so many others. At times, it was almost like the guy might have been a killer himself who sensed what was going down and was orchestrating the whole thing for his own entertainment. And though there was no question he would prevail no matter the circumstances, the God voice in Lomis' head was telling him to be patient with this one. It would never end. Someone had to be the first person to remain alive and free and forever. Someone who could also do this work of random selection and elimination.

"This looks like it," Sam said, easing the Ford Explorer down a dark, tree-lined dirt drive covered in pine needles. After a couple of s-turns the drive came out in front of a large two-story log cabin with a sagging front porch, a scattering of amber lights hanging on its posts and a pink neon sign burning a steady "VACANCY" in a picture window. They opened doors to the barking of dogs nearby. The wind had picked up a howl and the air felt like a cold rain was on its way.

"The fuck are we doing here, man?" Lomis asked.

"Has potential," Sam said. "Add some good behavior to your arsenal, Lomis. Try it on for size. It doesn't necessarily have to fit all the time."

Lomis wasn't one for throw-away laughter, deciding right then to ignore most of what came out of Sam's mouth.

"Cool," Wyatt said, stretching. The last of winter's dead leaves were hustling about. They all peered around in the darkness until they caught the lights coming from smaller cabins set in the trees a short distance away.

"Wait here, I'll check it out," Sam said. He walked up the creaking stairs of the porch and opened the front door. A set of jingle bells set at the door jam announced his entry. There were stuffed squirrels, rabbits, various elk and moose racks on the wall and an angry bear head, mouth open, blood-stained teeth bared, above the mantle of the stone fireplace across the room. A mellow track of soft piano music floated in the air as he walked to the small counter where a large woman appeared.

"Betty?" Sam's mind went into the math.

"My twin sister. No doubt she sent you up this way. Happens all the time. What did you have?" She sounded and looked exactly like Betty the waitress, right to the massive high hips.

"One of the best steaks ever," Sam added, smiling.

"Sure enough. I'm Darla."

"Sam."

"Needing a room. How many people?"

"Four of us."

"Wife, two kids?"

"No. Actually, a friend and another couple."

"Okay, then. How many nights?"

"Just one."

"I can put you all in the Bison Cabin. Three bedrooms, two up, one down. Queen beds in all."

"Perfect."

"That'll be one-forty."

Sam peeled off the cash and took the two sets of keys. "Is there a liquor store close by?"

"What ya looking for?"

Sam smiled. "Actually, a nice bottle of brandy or cognac or something."

Darla put up a finger and held it there as she turned and disappeared through a door frame hung with a dingy flower-print drapery. She reappeared moments later. "Martel or Courvoisier?"

"Martel. Perfect."

Darla grabbed a Kleenex from the box on the counter and wiped the dust off the bottle before handing it to him. "How about ten bucks."

"More like twenty." He handed her a twenty. "Thanks, Darla."

"Ice machine is around back of this building. You can drive right up to your cabin if you go back out the way you came in and take the first little opening in the trees to your left. Your headlights will lead you right up to it. Have a good one."

When Sam got back to the car, Marbles and Lomis were barking at each other pretty good. "Hey, come on folks, listen up," Sam said in a firmly raised voice. They both stopped instantly and looked at Sam. "Where's Wyatt?"

"Exploring, likely," said Marbles. "Even in the dark, I can tell this is the kind of place Wyatt could stay the rest of his life."

Lomis laughed and sat back down in the car. "The rest of his life...," he muttered, mocking her. "Just you watch, bitch," he added to himself.

"Wyatt!" Sam called out.

Some tree limbs crackled and split as Wyatt emerged from somewhere in the dark. "I'm cool." They all got in the car and Sam drove back up to the cabin.

A heavy wooden door creaked open to a great room perched on huge lodge pole pine logs and suspended beams. Scents of natural wood and old incense competed for the air and a clock on the fireplace mantel clanged ten times.

Sam nodded at Wyatt. "Yeah, man. I'll make the fire."

"I'm going to take a shower," said Marbles.

Lomis followed her up the open staircase with his eyes. "Good thing, too. Nobody going to stick it up your ass until you do."

"Just not cool, dude," Wyatt said, while he crumpled newspaper he found by the fireplace.

"Lame fuck," Lomis said just loud enough as threw himself back into a leather recliner.

Sam walked into the kitchen area and began opening cabinets to find glasses for the cognac. "Wyatt's right, Lomis. You need to loosen the strings on your guitar a little bit."

Lomis turned his head and his fiery eyeballs on Sam. "And how the fuck is it you think you know so much about me, huh?"

"Let's just say I'm known for my instincts," said Sam. "At times they have kept me alive while others around me perished."

"I swear," Lomis said, his teeth gritted as he humped up out of the chair and began to stroll around pretending he was interested in the place. "One more of your fucking riddles and...."

"And what?" Sam stood in front of him and handed him a drink.

His cheek beginning to twitch, his eyes bore a hole through the bridge of Sam's nose as he took the drink.

"Enjoy," said Sam. He walked away and watched Wyatt set the fire. "The way I see it, Lomis, you can pretend to be civil a while longer and sit around this nice fire that Wyatt's making and enjoy a quiet cognac, or maybe you can take a hike and see if you can find somebody else to play with. Assuming you still want to get to Jackson Hole with the rest of us, I see your options very clearly and they do not include the rest of us tolerating your being such an asshole." Sam's mind was in free fall with the ease of letting the moments enter and stay. Something he did not quite comprehend continued to move him across some imaginary line of reality on the fly. He didn't know who or what this Lomis guy was, but he was placed into the path of his life, literally along the road for the picking, then leading the way to Marbles Brown and Wyatt Kelso. There, for the record, was a car full of people looking for new beginnings. Poetic as all of that seemed, Lomis had the look of a man with issues rushing at him faster than he could either deal with or push them away. Above all there was coldness in his eyes and a reoccurring urgency in his behavior that Sam recognized from his past. But in the balance of things, maybe he was likely just another guy in his twenties trying to figure it out in a world gone crazy with speed and mixed message.

"How's that?" Wyatt asked, expecting some love for getting the newspaper to light up under a few logs in the fireplace.

The three sat quietly in old leather chairs facing the fire, sipping the cognac from the short, fat glasses Sam found.

"Dude. How cool is this?" Wyatt summarized, reaching into his pocket. He produced a fat boy joint from a cellophane snack bag. He held it on display in front of him.

"Why not?" Sam asked. He eased back into the soft, giving leather. "Perfect." His mind tried but fell short of remembering the last time he smoked weed. Bosnia, maybe.

"Maybe I will cut you some slack, jerk off. Maybe," Lomis said, sitting forward and watching Wyatt light up.

Marbles made her way back down the staircase, a white towel wrapped around her head like a turban and another much larger wrapped around her and tucked tight between her breasts. She eased across the arm of the chair and into Wyatt's lap as Lomis sucked the joint back. Heady stuff indeed, Lomis thought, holding the smoke in his lungs and cocking his face to take it all in. Marbles jostled around on Wyatt's lap trying to get comfortable while affording Lomis a few glimpses up between her legs. Comfortable and still and caressing the top of Wyatt's head with her fingers, and moving her legs just enough, she had Lomis on a swivel. She watched his eyes dart down on cue as she moved.

Cognac, weed, a fire, a big soft leather chair, a fine looking woman, maybe he should cut them all some slack. Be civilized, as the Riddler would say. All of this and a ride to nowhere. Cut them some slack, indeed. He passed the joint to Sam and leaned back into the smell of the leather, taking a deep breath, sipping, all the while keeping one eye riveted on her, awaiting the forbidden. She would adjust and move ever so slightly, knowing exactly what she was doing. The bitch.

The joint and the cognac finished, the quiet grew to the size of the room as chests barely elevated over lungs. Then Marbles whispered something into Wyatt's ear that made him smile and they got up and padded quickly up the open staircase.

Sam was either asleep with his eyes half open, or awake with his eyes half closed. Lomis watched through eye slits as the young couple tip-toed their way up the stairs and listened to the short bursts of laughter as they disappeared into the hallway at the top. He jumped a little when he heard a door shut, sipped at his empty glass, then got up and began pacing the room. When that fell short, he walked outside.

Those seeking it would appreciate the calm that was being offered up, yet Lomis fidgeted and pushed his finger nails through the paint peeling up from a porch railing. If it weren't for the lights coming from a few cabins, there could not have been a darker place on earth. Lomis began to walk slowly and aimlessly about, his mind in its usual unsettled state, beginning to remind him of the hunger, daring him, charging him with the responsibility to feed the beast. He walked past a few smaller unoccupied cabins until he approached another with a few lights coming from the small windows. He picked up on muted voices and soft laughter as he drew closer. Crouching down, he eased up against the side of the cabin and moved along the wall until he got an eye into the corner of a window. He focused into the narrow cracks between the slats of the blinds. From what he could see, a man, maybe in his forties, and a much younger woman appeared to be cleaning up a small table where they might have just finished eating dinner. He couldn't make out exactly what they were saying, but she seemed to be talking about a bag of garbage.

Lomis lingered motionless, then the man disappeared from view and Lomis heard a door open. He crouched down and spun around in the direction of the front of the cabin. A flashlight beam appeared, stuttered, pointed at the ground, and began bobbing to the rhythm of footsteps. Lomis stood up and fell in line about twenty feet behind, reached into a jacket pocket and slipped on his favorite black leather gloves. He followed the man until he could see the light shine upward to a small angled structure that was open over a set of large rubber containers inside of iron cages.

There wasn't any time. There was never any time, it seemed. That was the beauty of it; blood surging through every vein, bursting inside his brain like towering fountains, forcing him to act. As the man lifted the device over the garbage cans designed to keep out the bears and raccoons, Lomis pulled the stiletto out of his sock and began his move. With an explosive lurch forward, Lomis grabbed the man around the neck with an arm and pulled him up and back. The man gagged and struggled until he felt the tip of the stiletto at his skin in the middle of his back, tensed once into it to make sure it was what he thought it was, and froze.

"Don't move! Don't fucking move," said Lomis.

The man choked and spit and brayed, but his quivering lips could not shape anything coherent. The flashlight had spilled to the ground and gone out. They stood motionless in the dark, feeling the heat of each other's breath coming fast. Lomis pushed the stiletto into the flannel material of his shirt until the tip rested tightly into the stretching skin beneath.

"What do you want!" finally came the man's frantic words.

"I'm not sure, yet... ," Lomis said, happily, twisting the tip of the knife until the man flinched. "Is your wife a good fuck? I'm horny as hell."

The man flinched again and let out a sorrowful moan. "It's not my wife. Please…"

"Time's a wasting. Let's carry on this great conversation back at… let's say, your place?"

"I have money. I can give you anything you want."

"No you can't," Lomis laughed, eying the stars and praising the evil in the dark as he turned the man around and began pushing him back towards the light of the cabin.

"Seriously. I have money. Here. In the cabin. Anything you want…, just don't go inside."

"Gee, if I was you, I would be more concerned about me killing you right now than me getting the pussy inside that cabin." Lomis knew just how hard he could push without breaking the skin. "Now let's go."

CHAPTER SEVEN

THEY MOVED BACK TO the cabin, the man opened the door and they walked inside. "Lock it," whispered Lomis. They could hear water running. "Shower." Lomis mused. "Perfect. Squeaky clean. I love a woman with good hygiene." He pushed the man ahead cautiously and into a small bedroom. He could see a narrow bar of light coming from beneath the bathroom door.

"Lay down on the floor. Now!" Lomis forced the man down and dug a heel roughly into the middle of his back where the knife had been. He swung his arm up and grabbed the sash rope from the blinds on the window. Moments later he sliced off enough to tie the man's hands behind his back. "If you make a sound, I'll just kill you and leave. That's your option," Lomis said flatly, proudly showing the man how shiny and sharp and long his knife was. "Then again, maybe I stay anyway. You know, I hate getting ahead of myself." It was right at that point that Lomis started to feel at home again, comfortable and in control, with so many options, all his, and all leading somehow, someway, to the best of all worlds. "I say, let's kill some of these lights."

"Please... please...."

"You know, on second thought, I don't think I can listen to your whining. You got one of those pathetic nasally whines." Lomis cut off the sash of the other window blind and tied the man's ankles together, pulled off his socks and shoved them tightly into his mouth until he gagged. Lomis gave another shove to make sure they were firmly at the back of his throat. "Breathe through your nose, faggot."

Tears began to roll out of his bulging eyes as Lomis began pulling him around on the floor to get him out of the sight line should she come out of the bathroom. The water was still running. "Wait!" Lomis said to the man, cupping an ear. "You hear? She's singing! Sounds like that Bon Jovi tune. Ah! What's the name of that?"

The man struggled, his face bursting red as he gazed up at Lomis.

"Well fuck you, then," Lomis said and kicked the man in the face hard enough to hear his nose crack. "That hurt, right? But not much sound for a scream. Which is good."

He reached down and grabbed a handful of the man's hair and pulled his face up at an impossible angle. "You try to spit those socks out and I'll cut off your cock and stuff it down your throat. Got it?"

The man couldn't have nodded in any way. Tears continued to streak down the crinkles around his eyes. People like this, pathetic, bombed out shells heading for little far away places like these to get away from it all. Lomis had unfortunate news for them- *It all* was everywhere. No chance. The getting away meant arriving at an empty warehouse, wondering how the others before them died, and how long their suffering might have been.

Lomis heard the water stop running and hurried back into the room after cutting the sashes from two other windows blinds in the sitting room. The singing continued as Lomis scanned the bedroom, picking up a lavender scarf from a dresser top. The blood pounding in his ears was deafening as he pushed the man tight against the side of the bed on the floor opposite the bathroom door. "One sound and I kill her. Understood?"

The man shook his head rapidly several times. Lomis smiled, hopped up into the bed and pulled the sheets up over him, bunching the pillows around his head so he could not be seen, yet still get one eye on the door. He could see a shadow dancing in the light coming out underneath the door. The insides of his mouth began to water and sour. He thumbed the blade of the knife in his hand. It was still cold and clean.

The door swung open slowly, two bare feet with painted toenails appeared and the light went off, leaving just the one bedroom light to softly illuminate the room.

"I was just thinking," came a light female voice, "Is he in the mood to play tonight or not?" Her sexy giggle gave her intentions away. "Dinner has restored thy powers, master?" Lomis watched a foot move forward. He could see the bottom edge of a white terrycloth towel just above her kneecaps moving slowly towards the bed. "Then again, maybe my master is sound asleep?" With that, the feet left the floor and Lomis felt the full force of her body landing atop his and fingers attempting to find tickle spots that did not exist. He whirled up and out from beneath the sheets and spun out above her. She began to shriek hysterically as Lomis struggled to get a gloved hand over her mouth, then drew the knife into the view of her terror stricken eyes. She arched and flattened and twisted underneath of him, but he got a firm hand over her mouth and stuck the knife point at the bridge of her nose. "Don't move, cunt!" That mournful noise from the man on the floor took on a new low through the socks. The woman's chest heaved, the towel now open, Lomis could see she had average-sized coned breasts and smooth, white skin. He stared down at her and moved a hand to one of them. "A little too firm, eh? Did he pay for these?" He flicked the nipple and looked down at the narrow incision line. He loved making it up as he went along. It was amazing how accurate he was most of the time, or at least he thought so. Lomis flicked the tip of her nose with his knife, smiled brightly in the mirrors of denial and terror in her eyes and moved his hand down between her legs. "Shaved. For him?" He brought his hand up and put two fingers in front of her mouth. "Spit on them!"

She tried to turn her head but the sharp tip of the knife grinding into her chin kept her still. She opened and closed her eyes a few times and pretended this was not happening. Lomis winced as another groan came out of the man on the floor. "Spit on them!"

She spit whatever she could, then again, gathering little strength, but wetting his fingers as best she could. Lomis then carried the saliva on his fingers down into the lips of her vagina and began to work them in. Lomis began to breath hard as the second finger got in next to the first and moved up to wedge himself between her legs, moving the knife down against the front of her throat. He got his jeans open with the other hand and released a massive erection. He watched her eyes and nearly came at her reaction. They all reacted that way when they saw it. He was blessed with little else it would seem, save a twelve-inch cock with a girth wider than any dildo on the shelf. It took a lot to get the thing up, and sometimes it was even painful, or caused him to become lightheaded. But when he got it up where it stood proud, he would just sort of smile and go with the moment, swooning a bit, finding a song on the golden horizon while he watched it wave in front of him. It was nearly as savory as the look in the eyes of the next recipient to be. Her eyes could not have been bigger, more transfixed, focused in a mixture

33

of terror and amazement. "You like?" He asked, laughing quietly. "Just wait." He nodded down towards the man. "Little one, eh?"

"My God, no!" She finally gasped.

"Oh. You can speak," said Lomis, leaning forward and easing the tip into her pink folds. He played there for awhile and could feel her getting wet around it. "You put in or I put in, your choice," he said. "Put you hand on it!"

"Fuck you, you bastard." Her eyes fixed and her mouth opened and she tried to look down at it, but he stopped her with a jab of the knife. "Do it."

It always amazed him why they would not simply cooperate and enjoy, and when he grew predictably impatient he had no choice but to bury it inside her with a single full thrust of his hips. Her scream brought another awful sound from the man on the floor which fueled the fire that began to fill Lomis. She spread her legs as widely as she could and her legs bounced wildly in the air as she grabbed and pounded at his back side.

It was never *rape* to Lomis. It was a logical sequence of events, a meeting of man and woman, a culmination of what they were designed to do together. He would look down at himself splitting a woman in two, and then back up into her eyes. Instead of the terror, he saw deception, as they tried to cover up their desire. He had convinced himself they all loved it, every last one of them, dead or alive.

The man on the floor had tried to gradually work the socks out of his mouth, but stopped altogether when they seemed to wedge further into his throat the more he tried. Instead, he listened now to the little moans, the nasty filth of words coming from Lomis as he pounded into her, and finally, the grunting from both of them that raced to an explosive scream and a chilling silence that followed. The tension in his body faded into a hollow, his breathing slowed, his mind printed picture after picture until they faded out to a dull yellow-white.

"Oh my God," she repeated in a mantra. "Oh my God." She craned her neck to look down as Lomis withdrew, fixated on the long glistening shaft that bounced at an angle down his thigh, grazing hers and leaving a shiny mark.

Lomis had laid the knife down along side so he could grab both cheeks of her ass for another go, but suddenly and awkwardly withdrew, reared back and cracked her across the face with his best back hand.

"Enough of a taste of the Gods for you, bitch. For now. "You'll be dreaming for awhile about when I'll be back in the middle of the night. If I can find you here, I can find you anywhere. You remember that when you close your eyes every night, no matter where you are. You hear?" He cupped her mouth in his hand for a moment and gave her a throw away slap on the cheek.

As was his custom, Lomis looked for the purse, the wallet, anything that would tell him afterwards who his lucky victim was. A little turquoise beaded handbag on the bureau dresser was a dead giveaway. He rummaged inside until he found her wallet. "Fifteen! Spectacular, Stephanie," said Lomis. A little smile appeared across his face as he thought it through and admired her lithe little body lying motionless on the bed, save a heart beat that bounced the tight skin between her breast creations. "Daddy?" he asked.

Her eyes found something on the ceiling and stayed there.

Feeling another bounce in his loins, Lomis walked over to the man and reached down to pull his wallet from the back pocket of his blue jeans. The man looked up and got a first hand glimpse of the hanging cockmeat that had stuffed the woman moments before, and sunk to a low he would have never thought possible.

"Holy shit!" Lomis beamed. "John Perkins, the second. Son of the infamous Iowa Governor John Perkins? Are you kidding me?" Excited, he pulled things out of the wallet and let them spill to the floor until he found an I.D. card he liked even better than the driver's license. "Yes, it would be the younger Senator Perkins. How the hell do you like that, senator. So, let's see," Lomis continued with enthusiasm. "It would seem the senator is here in Wyoming, transporting a minor for the purpose of having sex?" He walked over and turned the man over better so he could see his eyes, then pulled the socks from his mouth. The senator moved his jaw around and gagged on the air before laying his head back completely exhausted and beaten. "So… it would be no big deal to me, senator," Lomis went on, "seeing as I got nailed for that rap when I was only twenty-three. But we do have an interesting situation here, don't we? Better than anything I could have come up with. Just when I thought I was going to have to kill the both of you, which seems only logical, right? Yet, you sad, pathetic, son of a bitch; you could be my meal ticket for awhile. Just for awhile. I would let you off the hook at some point. When it no longer feels like fun. But," Lomis walked over and pressed his flattened hand across Stephanie's stomach. "I might want to fuck your bitch again. What do you think?"

"I think you are a sick fuck," he answered. "That's blackmail."

"A fucking genius, Stephanie. The man's a fucking genius." He put the I.D. card in his jacket pocket and finally pulled up his jeans, watching her watch him as he stuffed his unit back inside and zipped. "Well, I gotta go. "It's been an unexpected pleasure. You two enjoy the rest of your evening. Ciao."

Lomis went out the door and disappeared into the woods where he set up to look back at the cabin to watch what they would do next. Twenty minutes later the lights went out and all that was beating up against him was the quiet and cooling damp of the night. He walked up a hill to a clearing, admired the full moon above and howled with laughter. While listening to the coyotes howl back, he considered whether he should just keep walking. He was positively electrified with life and his good fortune. But after further consideration, he slowly walked back to his cabin, humming a ColdPlay song from the "As We See The World" concert he saw in Minneapolis a few months before.

Lomis cracked the unlocked door, walked inside and made his way over to the last bouncing tiny flame of fire. Sam Castle was slumped back in the big leather chair, head tilted to one side, mouth open, snoring like a walrus with asthma. Clutched in his hand about to spill was a glass holding a remaining finger of cognac. Lomis gently pried the glass from his hand while the snoring did not miss a beat. He glanced down at the empty bottle of Martel on the end table, saluted Sam, and threw back the last of it.

CHAPTER EIGHT

MORNING BROKE BRIGHT AND full of happy blue sky. "An unbelievable day," Sam Castle pronounced as they pulled out down the gravel drive and headed back out to the highway.

Lomis spotted a teenage girl throwing a light travel bag into the trunk of a silver Mercedes parked in front of a familiar cabin. He smiled over at Sam. It was okay. Left undisturbed, he probably would have slept in until after noon, but with the early morning racket coming through the walls from Marbles and Wyatt, sleep was over. He double checked that he still had the Iowa senator's I.D. card in his pocket and settled back in for a well deserved nap. Instead, his mind rolled out scene after scene, possibility after possibility. Half asleep, he saw himself slitting Sam Castle's throat by some trout stream near Jackson Hole. In the end, a stupid, speechless fuck was all Sam Castle was. He wasn't quite sure what he would do with the fuck buddies in the back seat, but it would come to him. It always did.

"Way cool," said Wyatt. "Thanks, man."

Sam had pulled a morning beer from a plastic ring, glanced at the snoozing Lomis Walls and tossed the rest back over the seat. He followed that over with some beef jerky and tore into one himself, washing it down with the beer, laughing to himself and looking at his watch. Seven-twenty in the morning. Hilarious. Not funny at all if he was, say, nineteen and attempting his first serious search-for-yourself road trip; but at almost forty something, and knowing a road trip from great directions to nowhere, he was having a quiet time of it, intent on just stringing it out to see where all this would lead.

He took another big swig and smiled with a little nod of thanks for his unlikely passengers. "We should be in Jackson Hole in time for another huge steak for lunch."

"Hey, boss." Marbles had leaned forward within whispering distance of Sam's ear. The precocious, plausibly real version of her voice had begun to earn Sam's appreciation. The smell of her perfume had him recalling a time when he wished he was getting more than just a whiff. "Would it bother you if we mess around back here. I mean, you know, with the monster asleep and all…."

Sam looked over at Lomis slumped into the passenger side door. "He must have had a long night." He reached back and pulled her chin up a little with a couple of fingers so he could kiss her cheek lightly. "Throw me another beer, sweet thing. No need to ask."

With that said, Wyatt flipped the back seat down, pushed the travel bags to the side and down they went. Sam had twenty miles or so of Lomis snoring through an open mouth, but it was the pumping naked ass of Wyatt in his rear view mirror that took the moment. Sam adjusted the mirror just past it until he got an ass-free clear view through a section of the hatch window.

He strained to remember when sex was a contest and he was one of the contestants. These two grinding machines in the back seemed to stop only long enough to get their breath and a slug of beer before they pounced on each other again.

Lomis suddenly shot up rigid in his seat, screamed at the top of his lungs and stared straight ahead out the windshield. Marbles screamed back, shot her legs around Wyatt, and locked her ankles in at the small of his back.

Lomis turned around for a moment, got an eyeful of a variety of body parts and turned his gaze back to the road. "Frickin' circus," he said, shaking his head and eyeing the beer can cradled in Sam's lap, not knowing it was empty.

Sam turned the radio on. Female, Soulful, pretty nice, but he couldn't place the artist or the song.

"We could use some beers up here," Lomis shouted with more than a hint of sarcasm.

Exactly two beers left in the rings came flying by and bounced off the dashboard, followed by a sawed off hunk of rewrapped beef jerky.

Jackson Hole seemed to be waiting quietly as they drove into the town. Spring snow still capped most of the mountains above the western and want-to-be western one and two story buildings that gathered below. Sam's eyes tightened with memories of other mountains, those in Chile, those in Pakistan, and wondered what is was exactly about mountains that altered moods and made people reconsider their lives as incomplete. Perhaps it was their permanence and patience and immortality. For starters.

Lomis toyed with the tiny Swiss Army knife inside of his jacket pocket. He was fond of using the small ever-sharp blade to slit the younger throats. The skin would snap back against it immediately as if attempting to begin a healing process. As good as the night before had been for a non-kill, he felt exhilarated with the prospects of again being somewhere he had never been before with a whole new world at the edge of a blade. His blade. He had to figure out a vicious end to the two in back rubbing his nose in it, but it would come to him. He needed to first get his bearings, wait for the green light, and, as always, the way would come to him, even if that meant better options in the mean time. He was always impressed with his own patience, his tolerance for the insanity around him to die down as he waited. Growing up with two violent alcoholic parents who took turns trying to kill each other, he had learned to wait for most things. He waited for them to come home, to fix dinner, to fix breakfast, to fix anything. Finally, one early evening, his father killed his mother in a rage, then turned the gun on himself. The back of his head exploded on the dining room wall as Lomis watched the end of the new Power Rangers episode on the television, waiting for someone to fix his dinner.

He was three days into age eighteen when he raped his first woman, only to find plunging a knife into her repeatedly was nearly as much fun. Though Lomis didn't really count it, he had really killed first in a dormitory in Columbus, Ohio when he was twelve. He had smothered a fat kid with a pillow in the middle of the night because he could no longer put up with the way he kept grinding his teeth in his sleep. No one had seen it, no one suspected him, or so he thought. When kids looked at him, they quickly looked the other way. Lomis figured this was a gift; an ability to spook people before they got a good look at his oversized head and evil eyes. He spread enough fear to go around. Nobody would take a chance at ratting him out less they chance a similar fate.

Lomis moved in and out of foster homes, dormitories and social service agencies getting as much attention and interest as the paperwork it took to get him along to his next bed. In between times, he lived on the street in places like Hoboken, Baltimore, Raleigh, Coral Gables, Dayton, Chicago and Des Moines. This whole idea of opening up the West for him was intriguing, and, in his mind, Sam Castle was partly an honest stroke of luck, but mostly divine providence. Maybe he wouldn't have to die, at least miserably, but then that damn talking in riddles thing was enough in itself to justify it.

"I'm thinking this is a shot-and-a-beer joint under all the nifty rough sawn cedar crust," Sam mused. He smiled over at Lomis in a most forgiving way. "What do you think, hot shot?"

"Hot shot?"

"It's a little tag I give to people that have it all figured out. All kindness intended, really. Not many do."

"Says you."

Sam nodded and shrugged. "Looky there, Talbot's Whiskey Hole. Looks like a perfect place to say our good-byes, don't you think?" Sam's voice had taken on a little black-and-white western tone. He rubbed at the stubble on his face and gave serious consideration to letting it grow out, picturing a cooler version of his already very cool self.

"What's goin' down," came Wyatt's voice, waking from a well-earned nap. Marbles stirred and stretched, hooking a leg over Wyatt's as they pulled each other back up in a sitting position- two kids, criss-crossed-applesauce, folding their hands in front of them and waiting for lunch to be served. "Jackson fucking Hole, babe," he muttered to her. "We made it."

Marbles giggled a little bit and checked down in there to make sure Wyatt didn't have an erection left to deal with. It seemed he did, so she began to work it with her hand while taking in the majestic scenery.

Had Lomis looked back and caught a glimpse, God only knows what might have happened; but he was caught up in a new canvas of a world taking on color and filling the space in his head. His eyes closed, an odd smile moved across his face, and his head began to bob side-to-side as Sam pulled the Explorer into a space in front of the Whiskey Hole. Marbles moved it up a notch and coaxed Wyatt into firing a nearly empty shot.

In the side view mirror, Sam could see it clearly- a white, windowless van pulling into a space across the street. He wondered how many white, windowless vans there were in world these days. His eyes narrowed over a jaw that tightened and retreated over a long whistle in his windpipe.

"Everybody out. I'll buy the first round, then you're all on your own. God bless America," chuckled Sam.

An attractive woman in a nicely pressed blue denim western shirt emerged from the white van and placed an infant into a stroller she rolled out of the back.

Lomis moved around the streets of Jackson Hole like he had been there a hundred times before, keeping one eye on the potential; the rich looking women in their snug fitting, European made Western jeans and hot pink embroidered blouses, and the other on the meanderings of Wyatt and Marbles. He was curious to see where they would end up by dark, filtering and blending a plan B should it not work out just exactly right. Either way, he was sure he was in for a big time in a new place and the anticipation began to burn inside of him. He ducked into a little gift shop and examined some beaded sun glass holders as he peered back out the front windows. Wyatt was sitting at a small table across the street eating away at something as Marbles walked up to him sporting a lottery winning smile.

"We start work tonight," said Marbles. "Can you believe it? My mother's uncle does actually own the place. Five-thirty."

"So, we're set."

"Sorta. I think my uncle's a perv, but I can deal with it."

"Awesome." Wyatt grabbed at the mozzarella drizzling from his sandwich.

Sam had checked in at the Los Quisos Hotel, took a suite with a third floor balcony looking towards the mountain range to the North. Sitting back, feet up on the railing, a Corona in one hand and a fresh croissant from the bakery next store in his other. "Welcome to Sam Castle's life," he said to the highest peak, a frosting of snow above its purple grays. "To you, Karen," he said, saluting with the Corona. A belch came up and reverbed the last syllable.

Meanwhile, Lomis had followed Wyatt and Marbles until he determined they were staying at a small motel at the south end of town. He watched them go to room nine. That was good enough for him. He continued on and found a nice spot near a clearing on a tree covered hill a few minutes outside of town and set up a quick camp, laying down the wool blanket from his back pack and settling into another nap. Days were for sleeping, nights were for the glory of the constant chase and the occasional kill. With one eye flittering open, he could see a rabbit munching some grass a dozen yards away. He smiled, pulled out a six-inch hunting knife, balanced it between his thumb and index finger, and gave it a quick flip. It found the belly of the rabbit and he began to laugh as the rabbit fell to the side and its legs began to kick at the air. When it stopped kicking, he stopped laughing and lay on his back looking up, staring at the pine needles and bits of blue sky and clouds moving above them.

Wyatt would be first, and she would watch, he figured.

Lomis grabbed a dinner of eggs over easy and rye toast at Katy's Corner and napped afterwards on a park bench near a statue of some obscure Civil War general. A little after one-thirty, Wyatt and Marbles held hands as they walked back to the motel after finishing their first night on the job. Lomis watched them approach and put the optional ski mask on this time, just in case. After all, he might want to stay around for awhile, maybe reprise his handyman role, maybe find some rich widow client for cover and make a few bucks while figuring the rest out. He waited patiently in a narrow alley between two buildings that sat nicely in a dark shadow.

"Don't move!" He slid in behind them and froze them on the walk.

"My God! What?" Marbles shrieked.

"Shut the fuck up!" Lomis quickly moved in front of them and brandished the favored stiletto.

"What the hell man, it's that Lomis dude," Wyatt observed wearily. By his own standards, he hadn't worked this long or this hard for quite some time. Maybe never. "What do you want, man?"

"I'll figure that out when the time comes. Turn around and take a detour back down through that alley."

"You're not serious." Wyatt was too tired for all of this.

Lomis moved the tip of his knife into the middle of Wyatt's back to turn him around a little more quickly.

"Dude! We're poor. You should have figured that out by now. You can have our tips from tonight. That's all we got, dude."

"Hey, fuck you, Wyatt, I'm not giving this asshole my tips," Marbles added quickly, then turned slowly as she went into an expletive-deleted run at the male species.

"Keep walking," Lomis said quietly, moving the knife over to the middle of Marbles' back. Either of you makes a move or a sound above this wonderful conversation we are having, I run the knife straight through. Get it?"

"Jesus…," Marbles continued. "You shit excuse of a man. Fuck you. You weren't born with the balls to fuck around with me."

"Hey, cool it, babe," said Wyatt.

"Cool it, babe?" she mocked as they ducked into the alley. "What. Are you joking? And you said you were a bartender. You couldn't pour a draft without foaming the profits over the side. What the fuck was that? You were a fucking embarrassment."

"It's not my expertise, babe."

"Really. And what is?"

"Are you kidding?" Wyatt nervously eyed Lomis in the darkness.

"Dude? Are you kidding me? It wasn't that good, big boy, unless you like your pencils thin and short."

"I said, keep it down," Lomis cautioned, jabbing the knife hard enough to draw a muddled scream from Marbles. "I'll bet I'm bleeding, you fucker!"

"You'll bleed, alright. Just keep it up."

"This is insane, dude," added Wyatt.

Lomis led them out of town to his newly established home, greeting them by securing their hands behind their backs with plastic cable loop fasteners he had picked up at the new True Value hardware store in town.

Marbles had not stopped jawing for a moment. "All men are pigs," she went on. "Pigs, pigs, pigs." She spat for emphasis.

The moon was giving off just enough glow on this beautiful night. Lomis turned off the small flashlight he had been using and walked a slow tight circle around them as he fashioned them standing back to back. "Not after any damn money," he kept whispering over and over until Marbles shut up long enough to hear him and recognize the fear that had been welling in the base of her throat all along.

Everything went silent, save a coyote in the distance. "Well, for starters, we know he is useless," Lomis said, walking up to Wyatt.

"Dude." Whatever words were to come out of Wyatt's mouth after dude were hacked up into gurgling liquid as Lomis jammed the knife into his sternum, giving it a jerk upward to make sure he had severed everything going to the heart. "No fun at all," Lomis said as the blood choked off Wyatt's last scream while he crumbled forward to the ground.

"No! No, no, fuck, no!" Marbles screamed. "No, no…,"

"Shut the fuck up!" Lomis grabbed her viscously around the neck and pointed her face down in the direction of Wyatt's flailing body. "*You* said he was useless," Lomis whispered in her ear. "You killed him. You killed a useless, poor son of a bitch and rid the earth of him. You should be proud of yourself, bitch."

It was everything she could do to try to get her next breath. She trembled as a heavy back pack of fear began pulling at her; in one moment sure she would die, in the next calculating what she might do to try to stay alive.

"I won't fight you if you want to fuck me," She blurted.

"Christ, I already figured that," Lomis laughed as the last sounds gurgled and weezed from Wyatt's body.

She stood like a pillar as Lomis turned his small flashlight back on and began to roll Wyatt's body sideways until it disappeared over an edge in the dark. It seemed the True Value had a nice selection of short handled shovels as well, and the one he bought earlier in the day made short work of digging a shallow grave in a shaded area beneath a snuggle of branches and bramble. He was surprised he found a spot with the earth so soft and rock free. So he kept digging until the grave was big enough to hold at least a few Jackson Hole folks. Life was sweet, sometimes, with its little subtleties and simple surprises. As he dug, he hummed some old hymns his mother used to sing, until she passed out in the middle of the day on that old beat-up gray couch.

"Marbles, let me say I'm thankful you're here with me tonight," said Lomis, as though the first date was just beginning. He could never predict what would get to him and demand he act. He was as hard as rock, an erection so big and uncomfortable he unzipped his pants and eased them down as his dick sprang out like an ironing board falling out of a closet. He pointed the flashlight down its full length and waited. Marbles could have been looking about anywhere in the dark, but if she looked in the direction of the only light around, she would know she had arrived at the freak show.

"No man alive has a cock that big," she said.

He walked towards her slowly, keeping the beam trained on the prize, until he was inches from her. Her soul empty, clever jibe missing,

Marbles simply dropped to her knees, remembered her hands were still tied behind her, and opened her mouth as widely as she could. He caught her rhythm quickly with the light and watched her cheeks billow. Tears were coming from the corners of her eyes, but she was working it pretty good. Or so she thought. Lomis got his hips into the action and used one of his hands to cradle the back of her head while he jammed another couple of inches into her until she gagged and spit.

"Don't you dare, bitch," he cautioned her. "Take it or die right now."

Marbles struggled for breath and could feel the flesh at the corners of her mouth ripping open as Lomis tightened his grip on the back of her head. A low laugh filtered through his heavy breath as he got her slobbering all over him. He smiled down at her, held his breath and shot his cum into the back of her throat, While crushing her head down to his scrotum with one hand, he used the other to sink the knife into the hollow at the base of her neck until it rested in the brain stem.

There was always a chance some bitch would bite off his dick if she didn't die fast enough, but it was always a chance he enjoyed taking. Maybe five or six times he had done this, he wasn't sure, but each time, right after, it was an opened-eyed, glazed face with no bite left in it staring up at him. To Lomis, he was proud of his feel for the timing of it, the glorious synchronization of it. He was sure they all were grateful to have gone out that way if they had to go.

CHAPTER NINE

SAM WAS IN THE midst of yet another unwanted nightmare full of dark holes and stinking damp when he felt the first hit. His body lurched up awkwardly from its sleeping contortions across the chair on the balcony when another hit him on the side of the head. "Ow! You mothe...." As he stood up, his feet knocked over a collection of empty Corona bottles assembled on the timbered deck beneath him. His bleary eyes took on the dark of the night. "What the... ."

"Hey, Riddler, you awake up there?"

"Lomis? Jesus, man. What the hell?" Empty bottles clanked around Sam's feet and echoed in the stillness.

"I am a creature of the night," Lomis advised from two stories down. "You going to invite me up for a beer or what?"

Sam drew open an eye to the illuminated dial on his watch. "It's almost four a.m."

"So, like, what is your point?" Lomis sounded almost joyful.

Dull and weary, Sam coughed and wiped at his face. "Come on up." Sam shook out and began to figure he had been asleep for several hours at this point. "Wait. I have a better idea...," Sam said, his voice gaining a little volume as he got up and leaned over the railing. "I'm going to hit the road, I think. You can come along if you like."

Lomis stopped in his tracks. This was a big decision, it seemed, but one he would need to make quickly. Then he brightened. "Sure. Why the hell not?"

"I'm going to grab my things and I'll meet you down in the parking lot."

"I'll be waiting."

Sam fished the last Corona out of the lukewarm water in the ice bucket and cracked it open.

Lomis found a tree trunk to his liking a few yards from where Sam's black Explorer was parked and sat down. He took a knife out of his sock and ran his finger down the edge, put it back, then took out another from his jacket and did the same. Sometimes, he figured it helped him sharpen his thoughts, taking a moment, making sure he was seeing the bigger picture. He was certain he hadn't left anything behind where he buried Marbles and Wyatt. He never left anything behind, ever, no matter if he intended to go back or not. They were buried, the earth and brush returned to an original state. He was careful about these things. Always. It was why he would never be caught. His ego did not demand he leave some feint trail to tantalize would-be captors. No. Not at all. Nor did he think of himself as a normal among all the crazy people. He was smarter than that. He simply had a gift for taking his cause to action instead of living it inside a shell, an unfulfilled, incomplete soul. No malcontent prophesier of doom and gloom was he. The ideas would come from anywhere. Like now, another unexpected idea to twist and play with, and although it would extend the life of his next intended victim, there was usually a reason for these things when they happened. Keep the knives sharp, clean, travel light, pick up after, and move on.

❦

They crossed into Idaho and Sam seemed content to drive where the road took them. West, mostly, towards Sun Valley, Idaho, another touristy Mecca with plenty of money and sequined denim. He cradled a cold beer, a fresh bag of Cheetos and listened to some early Bob Dylan greet the early morning sun.

"Lay, lady, lay...," he sang along softly.

"I need to use the phone," Lomis said, his first words in over four hours. If the guy had been a chatterbox, Sam would have dumped him early on. Quiet was good. Always good.

"Here," Sam tossed him his cell phone. "A man traveling without a cell phone these days...."

Lomis picked it up off his lap and laughed.

Pure evil, Sam thought. That was an evil laugh that came from somewhere nobody goes.

"I don't use no cell phones. I need a phone booth."

"Earth to Lomis. You looked around lately? Phone booths are about as common as an honest politician."

"Maybe."

Sam studied Lomis. The twitch had started in his cheek. "Alright. You spot one, I'll stop."

Lomis laughed again and tossed the cell phone back at Sam. Being careful came natural to him. Always.

"There!" Lomis pointed. It wasn't more than five minutes when a phone booth looking worse for wear appeared along the roadside in front of a wobbly corrugated metal building nearly obscured by rusting junked machinery and old cars. Lomis held up his hands. Vindicated. Always.

"Five bucks there's no phone in it," said Sam as he eased the car onto the gravel shoulder. He had already figured Lomis for a nut job. No news there.

Lomis moved quickly towards the booth. No phone. Taped to the broken glass door was a torn piece of cardboard with the inscription "Fone Inside". He figured inside meant the only building within a sight line so he waved at Sam and began to weave through the metal grave yard. As Sam followed with his eyes, it occurred to him Lomis was extremely broad across the shoulders and narrowed to a small waist; an athletic build that did not jump out with a first look at him.

A small bell rang at the door jam as the door creaked open into a small room of clutter under a grid of water stained ceilings tiles. A loud, low-pitched rumble vibrated the filthy linoleum tile floor beneath his steps and seemed to be coming from behind another door at the back of the room. "Keep Out" was hand painted in red on the door.

"Anybody here?" Lomis yelled. He walked slowly through the second door and saw a short, chubby, middle-aged man wearing dark green overalls leaning over a bubbling vat of liquid.

"Shouldn't be in here, partner. That's the reason for the sign," he yelled back over his shoulder. He appeared to be setting a rack of something inside a large steel open tank. That settled up, he turned around and approached his visitor. "Help you with something?"

"Sign outside says there's a phone in here?"

The man looked at Lomis with an Irish grin that split his round face. "Crimanee, that phone has been out forever. And... a sign? I don't know about any sign. Hell, nobody comes around looking to use a phone these days. I got one of them new Razor things myself."

"You got a land line?"

The man shot Lomis a puzzled look. "You mean…."

"A regular telephone."

"Why would…,"

"Jesus H, man. I'm just asking to use the fucking phone!"

The Irish grin disappeared. "No need for that tone, son."

Lomis tried to ease it back. "Sorry. Sorry. It's just that my cell phone's battery is dead and it's sort of an emergency." As usual, whenever he attempted to force the calm and gentle, his cheek began to act up.

"What kind of emergency?"

"Kind of… ?" His eyes ablaze, Lomis spit his next words into the man's face as he reached out and grabbed his overall straps with both hands and began shoving him back with mock laughter coming from deep in his throat. "This emergency!"

The man stumbled awkwardly but Lomis pulled him back up and sized up the round face and broad nose for a perfect landing as he reeled back and buried a fist into the middle of it, sending him back pedaling and stumbling until he flopped into the dark brew in the tank, screaming as a fierce uprise of foam ate away his clothes in moments. Lomis knew the smell of sulfuric acid, and while he wasn't exactly sure what solution the man had fallen into, it appeared to be a pretty good bet it would be something to watch. The screams came again, but the acid began dissolving his throat flesh and silenced his cries for help. Lomis watched, then reached for a steel rod angled up near the tank and extended it to what was left of the old man, letting his mostly bone fingers get a good last hold before pushing him back down and under with it. "Hah! You stupid fuck," Lomis bellowed. The one booted foot remaining above the churning gave one last fitful kick before sinking.

A newly re-chromed bumper on the rack next to what was left of his clothes was ready.

Lomis talked with himself while he calmly walked around to a smaller office in the back and found a grey metal desk covered with letters, empty snack bags, Sunday ad supplements and an old paint-spattered telephone. He pulled the I.D. card out of his pocket and picked up the phone, smiling when he heard the dial tone in his ear.

"Senator Perkins' office," came a pleasant enough mature female voice.

"Got me the private line, eh?" asked Lomis.

"Excuse me, sir?"

"Yes. Well, is the good senator in?"

"Yes he is, but he is not available at this time. Can I ask who is calling?"

"Oh sure. Alright. You just tell John the good buddy he met up with a couple of nights ago will be back in touch shortly. You tell him, ma'm, if you will, that he should leave instructions with you that when L.W. calls, he should most certainly be informed, even if he is to be interrupted from a very important meeting, as L.W. is most difficult to call back but really, really needs to speak with the good senator very, very soon." Lomis waited for an acknowledgement that did not come. "You got all that, ma'm?"

"I did. Yes, sir."

"Then unless you can raise the senator up in the next few moments, we'll just leave it at that."

"Well, then I suppose this will have to do. Mr. L.W.?"

Lomis laughed into the phone suddenly. "Oh geez. Aren't you nice. Thank you ma'm and you have a nice day."

CHAPTER TEN

Sam softly strummed the curl of the steering wheel as the reunited Eagle's definable harmony poured from the speakers. He watched the old building for any sign of Lomis. He could just leave him. Leave him like he found him. Waiting for the next thing to happen or not happen in his life. But Sam's cold steel side seemed a proper back drop for the rest of him to play along to the tune of this new adventure he was on, which now seemed to include this sad, desperately angry soul with no apparent link to either a past or future. He bobbed along like some distorted mirror image of this Sam Castle, reminding him of other prisoners he encountered in Pakistan, the ones that died because they were perceived to be of no real use to the cause. It would figure Lomis Walls would have had his head sliced off early on.

Sam jerked forward as Lomis flopped back into the front seat.

He gave Sam a nod and settled in easily, the lift of a kill like an injection of helium in the soles of his feet. "Thanks," said Lomis.

Silence resumed its proper place as neither would give in to the beginnings of a conversation that would neither acknowledge nor confirm the underpinnings and snippets of weirdness each took pride in delivering to the other. It had become a game neither would admit to playing; a game neither could visualize losing.

Sun Valley. Sixty-eight miles, the sign said.

"Miss the lovely couple?" Sam asked from the silence.

Lomis gauged and whistled a breath. "No matter. He was an idiot. She was a slut, and a fucking bitch. Their world will swallow them up."

Sam considered the words. "Your way of expressing fondness, no doubt. Rest in peace."

Lomis nodded and turned to the side to force a nap. He needed the time alone with his thoughts. Lots of it. Lots of thoughts that constantly needed sorting, restacking, prioritizing. When was the last time he had killed without a knife? Where did that belong in the order of things? Highly random in the shuffling order of his things. Unusual that he didn't know the guy's name. He always knew their names by the time he killed. Senseless, it occurred to him. It was senseless not to know the name. He had been impatient, acted hastily. Next would be sloppiness. And after that? These thoughts quickly knocked him off the high. His restlessness returned, he could feel his cheek twitching, eyes fluttering open and shut.

The matter of killing Sam was at a strange distance for Lomis. Out of one half-opened eye, he watched the mountains in the distance gain horizon. No. Sam was more of a silent accomplice at this point. Maybe a sidekick. That was worth a twitching smile. Lomis Walls aka Cloyd Archibald aka John Bell aka Thomas Kingman; all loners, all worked alone, until now. Lomis wasn't quite sure how many names he had used over the years. The only one he remembered well was Thomas Kingman, the one he was sure would hit the F.B.I. Most Wanted List a decade before. But it never happened. That victim fell into a coma before she could give a good description of the man that had raped her and left her for dead with the thick blade of a hand axe in the side of her head. Lomis Walls was still as lucky and elusive as they came.

"What exactly is it you do?" Lomis asked, suddenly and unexpectedly feeling playful.

Sam's mind had been in random/repeat on the visual of the coffin breaking open. "Real Estate."

"Like what? An investor, that sort of thing?" Lomis slid up and took in the beauty of the mountains rising on both sides.

"Sure."

"So then, what's this ride to nowhere all about?"

Sam laughed and sipped his beer. "Maybe I own some land out here somewhere I haven't seen yet."

"Maybe. Or maybe you're some weird fuck on the run." Lomis leaned over to grab another beer when suddenly there was a burst of air and shattered beads of glass flying everywhere. Sam struggled to keep the car on the road, but lost it to a narrow soft shoulder of loose gravel as he jammed his foot into the brake pedal. "Oh shit!" Lomis yelled as he looked out his side. The car was sliding along an abrupt edge that went down a steep drop of rock and tangled trees. They lurched and tipped towards the edge while Sam held the wheel firm, braked hard and tried to coax the front wheels left. "Come on, come on," he said softly as the car skidded and wobbled to a halt. They sat still in the smoke and dust, oddly peering out through the opening where the windshield used to be, not sure if they were momentarily going over or not. "Don't move!" Sam said. He ignored the glass dust clinging to the hairs on his forearms and slowly opened his door. "Okay. Now, easy, move across your seat into mine as I get out. Real easy now."

Lomis picked it up and smoothly shadowed Sam's moves to keep the weight shifting to the driver's side of the car. Below to the passenger side was a ravine steep and deep enough to keep the Explorer flipping over a hundred times. He had no intention of being in it when it did. As Lomis carefully slid across the gear shift box the car began to sway and hover and lean. Lomis froze in position but the car picked up momentum and carried over the side, throwing him back into the passenger seat as he tumbled and screamed along. Sam made a futile grab but was left watching in disbelief as Lomis and the car flipped over once, then again before lodging up against a jutting clump of tangled pines growing sideways out of the sheer rock. He peered down through the cloud of dust and rubble. "Lomis?"

There was nothing except the sound of smaller rocks and boulders careening down further past the car to the unseen bottom. "Fuck! I think my arm is broke! Get me the fuck outta here!"

"Hold on!" Sam yelled down, the echo of his voice against the stone walls following those of Lomis.

A loud gasp shot out. "The fucking Riddler. Hold on, he says!"

"Don't move!" Sam quickly began to assess the possibilities of getting down to where the car was wedged. Then what to do, and the chances of the car staying in its position, and for how long. The driver's side door had ripped off in the tumble and as he eased himself over the edge onto a small outcrop he could see into the car where Lomis was lumped into a ball against the closed door on the other side.

Sam didn't know if he could trust the boughs of some smaller pine trees to hold him, but he thought he might be able to use them to ease himself down towards the car. That was all the time he had for a plan as he moved down to the first tree, pulled on its sappy thin limbs and needles, then down to the next.

"Shit!" Lomis yelled to the birds. "I'm gonna fucking die like this?"

Sam ignored everything else and concentrated on wedging his Nikes into little rock crevices while he descended and closed in on the car. Only once did he let himself look down. The bottom, if there was one, was heavily obscured and beyond what he could see. Suddenly his left foot gave way leaving him hanging by one hand attached to a young Ponderosa pine.

"Don't you fall, you motherfucker!" Lomis screamed.

Sam struggled and tried to get his body to swing back and forth. His arm felt as though it would tear off at the joint, but whatever he summoned up inside got him swinging until his feet could touch the rocks again, only to bounce off and weaken his grip with each swing. Finally, one foot caught and wedged in tight, giving him enough leverage to pull his body closer and get a second hand on another tree limb. Something cracked and he quickly moved the second hand to another limb just before another crack sent the limb he had been holding onto down into the canyon. Both hands grabbing and regripping the second limb, he drew his other foot up against the rock and tried putting some weight on it. For the moment he was motionless and safe.

"Don't give up, man!" Lomis called out.

"Just shut the fuck up!" Sam yelled back. "Can you reach the glove box between the seats?"

"Jesus… ," Lomis stuttered as he moved a reluctant hand out and shifted ever so slightly to reach the box cover. "Okay."

"Open it." Sam began to move again, this time more carefully, slowly, figuring if he died first, it wasn't going to make any difference to anybody. He could clearly see the scattered tree limbs might get him close enough to the car if he took his time, assuming there was time.

"Okay. It's open."

"Reach inside, carefully, slowly, and see if you can find my cell phone." He lost visual with the car as he darted beneath some heavier brush, pushing out against it with his feet as he slowly inched down while hugging the rock.

"Got it!"

"Okay. Put it in a pocket or somewhere safe on you for now. Can you do that?"

"Fuck the FOR NOW shit, man! Just hurry, whatever your fucking plan is."

"Let's go back to shut the fuck up."

"Okay, okay. But hurry, man, I can't feel my one arm and my ankle... . Shit! The car is moving again. Fuck me!"

Sam kept inching down. He peered down through the limbs and could see the front end of the car on its back. He got close enough to reach out and touch it, but didn't take the chance. He began to move laterally with the rubber edges of his shoes searching and gripping while his fingers did the same until he got even just above the driver's side where the door had been ripped clean. He maneuvered himself out and over a pair of soft but thick pine limbs he could bend together and got his arms to hang over the opening where Lomis could see them.

"I can see your arms, Kimosabe. Now what?" The car began to shift, dropping an inch, then two more.

Sam could not see down into the car. He sensed the pine boughs he was balancing on were near the max before they would give way. "You have to somehow find a way to get a hold of one of my hands. We go from there." The sweat began to pour out of him and ran down the tip of his nose as he hovered over the door opening and got his arms down a fraction lower.

"So here's the thing...," Lomis began. The only sound was a haunting echo of a light breeze knocking around in the stone. Then the birds began to squawk above. A call to all. The party was about to begin. "As I see it- I miss, I die." His musing voice annoyed Sam more than he cared to acknowledge at that moment.

The car dropped and bounced.

"You decide, fuck stick. I'm down as far as I can get these tree limbs to hold me. And just so you know, I can't guarantee they'll hold you and me."

"Fucking swell."

"You're call."

"On three. Be ready."

"I'm on it."

"One, two... threeeeeee!" Lomis lurched upward with a quick move and screamed as he shot his arms out for Sam's. Sam got one arm and grabbed on at the wrist. He was sure the tendons were ripping and shredding everywhere but he grabbed tighter as Lomis tried to get his broken arm to move upward. Lomis screeched again as his forearm slammed back down against his body at a ninety-degree angle. "Fucking hell!" he shouted in anger.

"Come on!" Sam yelled back. Try it again!" Suddenly the car shifted down a foot, then began another roll. Lomis spun on Sam's one arm while the door opening moved down around him, the jagged edge of the door hinge ripping through his pant leg and gouging deep into his thigh. In another moment, limbs cracking and a thousand birds squawking, the Explorer heaved into a slow roll that gathered steam and Sam watched it tumble down into oblivion past his grip on Lomis. "You've got to give me your other arm, asshole!"

Lomis screamed something incoherent but somehow flipped his arm up where Sam could grab it. When he did, the sounds that gurgled and shot out of Lomis' throat echoed in that ravine and for miles beyond. The birds picked up on it and began circling lower.

Sam's adrenalin seemed to pour into his ankles, which held both their lives in suspense by the unknown strength of a crook in a pine bough. Lomis continued to scream, but when he looked up, Sam was certain the screaming was pouring out through a wide smile.

Sam inched Lomis upward with whatever he had left to give, trying to press him closer to the rocky ledges. He wasn't sure if he was slipping or what was actually holding or giving way, but it didn't matter at that point. He grunted in anger at his own Gods and he could feel the burn in his chest as his lungs and heart tried to keep up. "Can you get a foot hold!" he yelled down at Lomis. Try to get a foot up against the rock!"

The good arm came loose, leaving Lomis dangling in excruciating pain by his broken arm, but the swing of being on just one arm brought his feet closer to the rocks and he was able to get one down against a rock edge. Sam's summoned up the strength to hang on as Lomis got the other arm back up and Sam began to ease him up the side, an inch at a time.

When Sam pulled himself and then Lomis back up over the side to welcome flat ground, the echoes of the larger birds calling each other bounced off the mountains and down into the rocks below them. They were calling off the party.

"What the fuck just happened?" Lomis ventured, his contorted face studying what was left of his arm. "And you?" He studied Sam's face.

"You some kind of super hero in another life or something? That was some unbelievable shit you just pulled off."

They both looked back down over the edge when they heard the big explosion.

"Might have been a rock coming off the slope back there," Sam said, glancing up and around, seeing if there was anybody buying that theory. He looked down at Lomis. "Still got the phone?"

Lomis reached inside his shirt pocket and handed Sam the phone with a proud smile of sorts, his cheeks twitching rapidly.

Sam stared it down, dialed "911", but his finger wouldn't hit the "send" button. He waited for his thoughts to clear, but nothing was happening. "Some kind of bullshit, Parker... "

"Say what?"

"Nothing. Relax. You're alive, I'm alive. Just chill out for awhile." Sam got up and walked a short distance away, then hit the speed dial. "Give me Dragon, please. Tell him it's Sam Castle."

CHAPTER ELEVEN

Lᴏᴍɪs sᴀᴛ ᴏɴ ᴛʜᴇ edge of the examining table looking across the room at the flare of shapely hips that belonged to the nurse that had been finishing up the trim on his arm cast. She was slightly bent over, washing her hands at a sink. He locked an eye along a side view of her jaw line, imagining it taut and bulging out. A shiver shook down all the way through to his heels when she turned to him, smiled and grabbed a paper towel to dry her hands. He filed that away.

"That should just about do it. How are you feeling?" she asked.

Lomis nodded and smiled back. "You're the best." He wanted to embellish, not to waste the opportunity. He imagined her swooning, nearly unconscious from the fucking and beating she had just taken. "I almost hate to leave."

When Lomis came out the front door he was sporting a casted arm in a black sling, a butterfly bandage on his forehead and limping noticeably from the stitched up gash in his leg.

"You going to live after all?" Sam asked.

"Thing is… you don't get a scratch, and you get to be the hero," Lomis said. "How the hell does that happen?"

"That doesn't sound much like a thank you."

They sat down on a bench just outside the front door. "Still… some weird shit with you," Lomis said. "You are some scary dude."

"Coming from you… ." Sam left it there.

"Yeah. Well, maybe we are both like that. Stick your chin up at death and dare it."

Sam's mind wanted to go back in time, but he fought it off. "Interesting theory."

"Theory, hell. I mean, don't think I don't appreciate what you did and all. I just figure it was more what you had to do because of who you are. Most wouldn't have even thought about trying that kind of stunt. I figure you're just one of them natural hero types. You can't help yourself. You're that guy. But, thanks, anyway, Riddler. You covered the clinic, too. My hero."

"No hero, Lomis. Just doing what people do."

"My ass. Not the people I know, Riddler."

Sam's cell phone buzzed. He looked at the screen, wondering again why he would be getting a "restricted" message instead of a number way out here in the middle of the Sawtooth Mountains. He flipped it closed without answering and put it back into his pocket.

"What now?" Lomis mused. He figured taking a hike down the road in these parts was not the best option. Sam Castle was still the best option.

"You figure I'm stuck with you now, is that it?"

Lomis laughed with an evil flourish. "Where's that old man that gave us the lift?"

"I believe that's his Jeep over there in front of the saloon."

"That sounds about right at this point." Lomis looked around, then stopped. "You got a call into your insurance company?"

"Nope."

"Police?"

"Nope." Sam shook his head and cracked a half grin. "Nobody. Other than the car sitting at the bottom of the canyon and whatever tales that old man is telling in the saloon right now, it didn't happen. Makes you wonder why, right?"

"Doesn't make me wonder anything. You're the damn Riddler. I was just trying to figure my next ride." He nudged Sam with his good arm and pointed across the road. A store bought "For Sale" sign was taped into the rear side window of an older dark green Dodge pickup truck.

"Wait here," said Sam.

"Why?"

"You kinda scare people."

Lomis smiled tightly at the compliment.

"And you enjoy that a little too much. So sit tight," Sam added quickly.

Sam slowly walked across the road and looked up at the mountains rising on either side. Mountains were mountains. Pakistan, Idaho, all of them majestic and bigger than life, all potentially honeycombed with terrorists and crazed world-enders. Always known for his uncanny insight and gifted powers of logic, Sam's bolts were, at best, all a bit loose, his walk breezy and affected.

"Good afternoon," said a stunningly beautiful young woman who looked completely out of place. She wore a black and red checked flannel shirt, blue jeans and high top hiking boots that looked like they had been busy. Long dark hair covered her shoulders and ran a third way down her back. He guessed maybe mid to late twenties, large green twinkling eyes on a golden face of undisguised natural beauty.

Sam nodded, smiled and tried to be less obvious. "Would the owner of that truck out front be around?"

"That would be me."

"Okay." Sam was fresh out of poise as he considered how complicated an answer that was. "Okay, then, how much you asking?"

She meandered from behind a cluttered desk of maps, blue prints and worn manila files, in no apparent need of speed to close the deal. What an extraordinary smile, Sam thought. "Two thousand," she said. "Runs great. No rust. I've put a hundred- sixty-thousand miles on her. And most of them with a smile."

"Like that one?" Sam studied her another few moments. Maybe longer than that.

She offered an even better example. "Are you flirting or buying?"

Sam Castle? Jake Parker? Flirting? What was that, exactly? he wondered. "Sold, I guess." The words fell from his mouth as if they belonged to somebody else. They stared at each other until it got uncomfortable. For Sam.

She laughed. "Would you like to take it for a drive first? Check the back for dead bodies?"

"Uh."

"Actually, on face value, the clothes and all, you look kind of homeless."

"A little accident down the road. Car went over. I had to do a little climbing. No big deal, really."

"Come on. I'm feeling dangerous today. I'll let you take me for a ride."

"Okay then. But my guess is killer green eyes like yours could sell used cars or recruit souls for the devil. I'd buy and I'd go peacefully. I don't suppose you take American Express?"

They both laughed as Sam pulled a rubber banded wad of hundreds from his back pocket.

A blush rose up on her as she magically pulled the title out of the clutter on the desk and it was done. "I caved in and just bought a new Subaru."

"Alright. Now listen. A beautiful young woman dressed up like a surveyor or a falconer. I have to ask." There were racks of thick rolled-up documents and papers with official-looking stamps scattered about.

She handed him two sets of keys. "Today is Tuesday. I do outsource work for the EPA. Tomorrow I am the Mayor of Kershaw, and on Thursday I freelance a little surveying and engineering work, and then I'm the mayor again. So if it was Wednesday or Friday, tall stranger, I would be officially welcoming you to our fine city. As it is, we are engaging in American commerce."

"You're the mayor?" He wasn't exactly sure why he was amused, but he could tell she was used to the reaction.

"Liv."

"... Sam," he said, using the keys for a prop.

"Just re-elected for another two-year term, matter-of-fact."

"What kind of shape did you leave your opponent in?"

Liv smiled and planted a hand on her hip. "Unopposed. Again."

"Wow. Are you that good, or that scary?"

"Both. Absolutely. And, it helped to have a grandfather than had been the Mayor for twenty-six years." She walked over to gaze out the plate glass windows in front. "That's him across the road talking to that man with the brand new white cast on his arm."

"My... associate. Lomis."

"Gannon, my granddaddy, is easily the most amazing person on the planet. You're friend is getting an earful whether he wants to or not."

"So in your small world of small worlds here, it so happens your granddaddy gave us a lift into town when he drove by our little situation."

She turned and studied Sam long enough to make him shift his weight while he continued to twirl the car keys.

"Gannon was the oldest mayor in the State of Idaho, and I'm the youngest. Kind of a nice passing of the torch, we like to think, but actually I have my sights set a little higher."

They both watched the old man joshing with Lomis. Lomis was waving the new cast and casting a spell of his own.

"So you're the one that's going to save us all, I hope?" Sam asked.

"All I can. If I can put enough money together, I'll run for the House of Representatives in another two years. A senate run after that, then a wild rush up the steps of the White House."

"No ambition, huh?"

"I assume you aren't really laughing. Green will be reinvented and revitalized. It has to be. There will be no other choices left than to save ourselves from ourselves."

The conversation and laughter came easy as they poked at each other for over an hour. But one thing was very clear to Sam- this young woman was dead serious about her intentions to prove she could change the axis of the globe.

He wasn't at all certain it was by design or not, but Sam felt drawn into the unsettling aura that followed the lead of the aforementioned killer green eyes of hers. And she smelled like freshly cut flowers just set out on a sunny country kitchen table. "Is there a Mr. Savior of the Planet?"

"I'm currently taking applications. Come on," she said, patting his forearm to stop him from twirling the keys. "I'd feel better if you took it for a drive first. And I can give you the Kershaw tour. It's not to be missed." He would have followed the smile anywhere, but the glimpse of her from behind as he opened the front door for her was a bonus. Faded blue jeans painted on a tiny frame that flared into a snugging set of hips that moved her along smooth as silk.

Sam looked across at Lomis and the old man. It was, in fact, a small world, and a nice little world that seemed to be getting better by the moment, no matter how close death was but hours before. No matter who or what awaited him outside this little valley, it or they could wait. Indeed. He was thinking what a great option sex used to be, and still should be. The nightmare of the funeral was still there, etched up close under the skin, but beneath, deeply beneath, was an empty hole that used to be filled with something he craved that only a woman could provide in every way. He had to get that back into his life, someday, sooner than later.

He started by watching the boots on her little feet bringing her back to earth with each step, then his eyes moved up to celebrate the synchronization from hip to toe while all that gorgeous hair shimmered and bobbed around. His thoughts had been centered on disappearing over the horizon in a green pickup truck, a diminishing point, gone to the world. This shot of oxygen running into his bloodstream, while unexpected, felt warm and welcome. All at once, he regretted calling Dragon.

The truck gave a shudder and started up with a squeak that quickly dissipated. He revved it a few times then let the choke settle back into a smooth idle before he put it in gear. A mix of thoughts continued to pour in and out of his head as he looked over at her.

"Gently," she said with a little smile. He wasn't sure if it was regret in her voice, or just a moment lost getting ready to say goodbye to an old friend forever, but as the idle wheezed back, his eyes caught hers and locked with no further explanation needed. They eased into the squeaking bench seatback, their eyes following each other, not knowing what or why, but neither willing to take a guess.

"Do I know you?" She finally asked, blinking first. A blush quickly followed. She could feel it on her face and attempted to hide it with a quick swipe of a hand. She tried not to look at him but he was right there, now with just the slightest grin on his face.

"I think so," he said. "Somehow, I think you do." He pulled the gear shift into reverse and backed the truck around before pulling out onto the road. He could not be sure what kind of look he had on his face when he gave Lomis a glance as they passed by, but if he could have added words to it, it would have added nothing at all. Lomis, at that moment, was a distant, odd little memory.

"Take a left just over the top of the hill," Liv was saying, mostly to the windshield.

He looked over at her. Too long.

"The road, Sam. It's Sam, right?" She shook her head and looked out the side window to get away from his gaze and try to keep hers under wraps. A smile forced its way on her and held.

Right down to the two small scars across his right jaw line, and some fresh scratches she would need to ask about at the proper time, this almost seemed like what she would have ordered in the catalog. He looked like he could use a shower, but she liked him this way. She began apologizing to herself for picturing him in the shower, but she was stuck there awhile, glancing back over at him, up, then down while he was watching the road and making the left turn.

He didn't ask, she didn't say. He kept driving for a few miles on a hard-pack gravel road that was taking them through purple-gray mountain vistas beneath deep blue skies along a swift moving stream that looked like emeralds gleaming under the bright sun.

"Here. Turn right," She said.

"I thinking I would follow you anywhere," said Sam.

She looked over at him, puzzlement and a bit of the blush still there. She had him about drying off after his shower at this point.

"The truck sounds great, by the way." Sam smiled at her, locking back in, but not forgetting the quick unforgiving nature of a mountain road. "Good thing, since I already paid you, right?"

"Good thing," she said. "You can pull over there."

Sam did as he was told. They got out of the truck and he followed her around and over behind a clump of Aspens and rocks to a foot path that began to lead up a steep hill. The views were what the views were, but it was nearly impossible for him to take his eyes off the movements of her torso in front of him, falling into a deeper trance with each sway to the left, then right, then left. And so on. Heady stuff indeed for Sam Castle.

"I don't waste the words when I come here," Liv announced as they reached the top and stood overlooking a green valley flanked on either side by jagged mountains of purple rock and perfect stands of tall lush pines. A rushing stream at the lowest point calmly turned to disappear in the distance. "Listen closely," she said, hushing her voice.

Sam moved along side of her and looked out across the valley, listening.

"Hear it?"

"Hear what?"

She turned slightly and reached up to cup his ears gently with her hands. They were warm hands. He looked down at her and waited patiently.

"The ocean?"

Liv laughed and pulled her hands back, keenly aware Sam had not taken his eyes off of hers. "If you can't hear it, it's not your place. Not yet."

"Not yet... ?"

"Am I staring too?" She asked.

"I think so. Eyes like that... you could hide anything behind them. You could steal a man's soul and he wouldn't know what hit him."

"I get that sometimes. But that doesn't mean I don't like it."

"I could get lost in those eyes. I could." Sam had to repress the urge to just grab her and swallow her whole, instead settling for the hand she offered as they walked along the rim, needing few words to understand why they were there.

"So what do you think about when you come out here?" Sam asked.

"Just take a deep breath and look around."

"I get it…,but the first thing that comes to my frazzled brain is what I am *not* thinking about, just walking along this edge of certain death, just rolling along, following you like a child would a teacher."

"Hmm. Philosopher or master bullshitter?"

"How can you be one without the other?"

"Accepted." Liv gave that long main of black hair an obedient toss back.

Sam moved up closer to the edge of the rock. "I've been in places like this before… . Thing is, I never gave much pause to my thoughts at the time."

"Do it. See what happens."

He waved an imaginary wand across the valley, then looked up at her and smiled.

"Don't over-think it either."

They continued to walk along precariously close to the edge. Sam laughed at the idea there was any danger in it. Not in the same day. Not a chance.

She gave him a look that said she might be reconsidering. "Hmmmm. Very sure of yourself, eh? I could be a serial killer luring you here to push you off a cliff."

"So could I."

"What if we both were. Now that would be interesting."

She considered all of that for a moment and stored it for later. "I like you, Sam. Something about you sort of instantly there and honest. Are you?"

He immediately presented himself for consideration.

She rubbed at her chin and then they resumed walking. "Over six-foot, around two-hundred pounds, nice body, medium blonde hair, a full head of it, dark eyes and a playful smile."

Sam chewed at his gums in silence.

"Couple of scars under the jaw line from a time not worth recalling," she continued. "Scars are always intriguing."

"You play well," he mumbled, feeling a rush of heat building nicely about his chest and lower. "My turn?"

"I think I already know what you are thinking about me."

"I don't... ."

"Careful. I just talked about your apparent honesty. Don't mess it up with a big fat lie."

"Well, aren't you something else?"

"Mostly Basque, they have me believing. Some Irish got in there, too. Never knew my real parents."

"Me either. What are the odds?"

They both let that sit a few moments and took in another view of the valley.

"Odds? I don't believe in odds. Republicans believe in odds and polls. I believe in what needs to be believed, and I go from there."

"From what I can tell, it could be a great deal of fun getting to know you, Miss Mayor."

"What do you like best about me so far?"

Same mused with it. "Hard to choose just one thing."

They stopped, turned up a narrow path between two large boulders which led up to a larger flat rock surface in the sun where they sat down. "I occasionally play the bass guitar in a mountain rock band on the weekends. My worst fear is global extinction before I'm thirty. And my best quality is my ass, I think."

He motioned for her to stand up and she gave him a quick turn. "Can't disagree."

She sat down closer to him, brought her eyes within inches of his and they stared away.

"Hard not to make a case for the eyes though," Sam said finally.

She soaked in every bit of the attention she was getting. "Doesn't matter much what two people know about each other, really, does it? I mean, once they get beyond the presumption of innocence and figure out they aren't going to kill each other? At least not right off?"

"I'm there," Sam said. ""Actually. I just want to kiss those lips and close my eyes, and imagine yours are closed and drift off...."

Liv slid into him and planted her full lips onto his lips just hard enough to shut him off, then retreated and allowed him to kiss her tenderly and hotly, their lips parting, exploring while the birds above chattered and bellowed their appreciation, if not outright jealousy.

In time, they released, opened their eyes and resumed the staring thing they had begun earlier. His hand moved up to run through her jet black silky hair, smoothing it back, his fingers sending back a pulsing, delicious confusion that floated and ran every other thought out of his head. "Any idea what is going on here?" he asked.

"Truth is... ." She kissed him on the cheek, then the other. "I need a hot date for the election party this Saturday night. Interested?"

Sam looked up at the warm sun, scanned the valley and the mountains, sniffed the heady combination of her fragrance and the cool air, and suppressed his grin the best he could under the circumstances. "I need to check my schedule... ." Suddenly, Sam stiffened and quickly stood up as though he were stung by a bee.

"What! What is it?" She yelled at him, getting up as well and looking around for the culprit.

Sam grabbed at the sides of his head with his hands and shook himself back into reality. "Idiot! Dammit! I need to get down to the car."

"What car?"

"The one at the bottom of one of your canyons."

"Why?"

"Assuming there is anything left of it..., I can't believe it took me this long to remember. Christ!"

"Okay. Wow, I've never had that reaction when I asked a man out before."

Sam pulled her close and kissed her again, his arms wrapping her tightly and pulling her feet up just above the ground for a moment before setting her back down gently. "That's a 'wouldn't miss it for the world kiss', in case there was any doubt. Now, we, or I need to figure out how to get down to that wreck."

Liv eased back, savoring the kiss for another moment, then held his face to look at him again, running her fingers across the two scars at his jaw line. "If it is where I think it is, it happens to be easier than you think. I know a road that leads down to the bottom of the canyon and this truck you are buying has been there more than a few times."

"Great. We should get moving then."

"We should?" Her green eyes sparkled with fun.

"Trust me."

"Not on your life."

Liv was finding some humor in the pace Sam was forcing behind her as they made their way up the path back to the truck. "You get that close to me it's going to be hard for you to watch my ass work up this hill," she said.

Sam stood still for a moment, watched her climb briefly, then shook his head and resumed his push right behind her. "Thanks for the heads-up," he said.

"You're welcome."

"Where did you get all of that?" Sam asked, catching his breath and pulling out the keys as they neared the truck.

"All of what?"

"That... confidence, I think I would call it."

"Oh that. That would be Gannon, Josh Gannon, my grandfather. You would hear people around here just refer to him as Gannon."

They hopped in and Sam jammed the key in the ignition. "All in the family here in Kershaw." Behind the words, his head was a growing inferno of infighting thoughts and confusion. How could he have let this slip by in his mind? How could anything have been more pressing or important? Slip by? Nothing just slipped by him.

"Gannon is likely the greatest human being on the planet." Liv went on to list a few dozen reasons as to why she thought her grandfather walked on the water as they drove.

"How old are you again?"

"Screw you, Sam. Drive."

Sam floored it and spit gravel into the wind. "Some kind of day," he muttered mostly to himself.

"Turn left after that crooked pine tree on the right."

"I don't see a road."

"There isn't one. Put it in four-wheel drive and head down the hill. Trust me. There isn't enough traffic to knock the weeds and brush out of the way, but, trust me, it's a road."

Sam eyed her in between the anxious moments guiding the truck over the bumps and jolts. "I should trust you, right?"

Liv eyed him back with little concern for the rocking, descending truck. "I'm going to change the world, Sam. By the time I'm thirty, you'll be thinking about writing that tell-all book about what a beast I was in bed, but it won't matter. Nothing in the past will matter by then. The only thing that will matter will be the survival of the earth and the only thing that will matter to people is if you are part of the solution. Who you slept with along the way will be, at best, mildly amusing.

Sam kept both hands tightly on the wheel as the truck took on an impossible downward angle. "So let me see if I have that straight. I've known you for a few hours and you have already bedded me down, dumped me and left me longing for the incredible sex we once shared. But denied, I attempt to instead capitalize on my pain with a juicy book deal while you become the first woman, *and* the youngest President of the United States of America."

"There might be two books in there, Sam. And make a hard left where that run of boulders ends."

"So you're twenty-two... ?" He had to ask at some point.

"A pretty good guess."

Sam just shook his head. Fast forward, freeze frame, slow motion, she had him doing all of it. "I sense big mystery with you? Am I inventing it?"

"Mystery? Me? Where did you say you were from again?"

"Nicely played."

After another hour or more of bumping around and down, miraculously, the tangled, burned out apparent remains of his Explorer appeared on the landscape. He put the truck in park. "I believe, that is it. The fact that I'm not part of the char takes the edge off a bit."

"You go ahead. Have your final moments. I'm going to look around. It's been awhile since I've been down here."

Sam moved towards the car. As he got closer, the smell of spilled oil, sour hot steel and melted plastic filled his nostrils and reminded him of dangerous places far back in the dark spots of his past. There was only one thing of interest to him, and he went directly for the twisted back hatch, leaned down to peer inside and pulled up the floor panel that covered the car jack storage compartment. He had wedged and secured the coffee can there with enough duct tape to get it through to hell and back, but it was gone. The duct tape likely would have melted after the car exploded, but he figured the can should still have been there. And diamonds don't burn, or have legs.

Sam's heart skipped a few beats as he began scouring the remains of the car and the anxiety only grew as he filled with the growing realization his ticket to nowhere was nowhere to be found. He walked a tight circle around the car, increased the size of the circle until his path met up with the base of the cliff, then reversed until he was back up to the car. Nothing. Next he gauged the falling trajectory the car had likely taken and began climbing the rock face.

"Obviously you didn't find what you were looking for?" Liv's voice echoed up to him.

Sam looked down at her, back up at the sheer vertical ahead of him and decided it was hopeless to continue upward. He made his way back down and walked over to her, his anxiety vanishing, almost hysterically, as though nothing that important could mean less in the presence of this... this woman.

"You look like someone took the bat and ball and went home," she said, standing in front of him and reaching up to gently kiss him and give me an eye screwing to die for.

"Did I just dream you were going to do that?"

"Dreams come true, Sam."

"I'm going to take one more quick look and then... ."

She smiled up at him. He smiled back- a smile loaded up on preoccupation. Sam walked over to the car, walked completely around it and kneeled down at the rear to give a final consideration to the impossibility that the can had somehow come loose from its moorings. He shook his head and craned his neck before dropping his eyes dejectedly. Something in the dirt and siftings of crush and gravel caught his eye. Then again. A sparkle. He reached down and between two fingers lifted the tiny, sparkling object up close to his eye. It was one of his, alright. On the ground, not in the car. It could have been up on the side of the canyon somewhere, a search for tomorrow perhaps, but in his gut, he felt someone had been there before him; someone who walked away with millions in uncut South African diamonds.

CHAPTER TWELVE

"Here's to ya," Gannon said, tipping the shot glass back and giving it a swish and a rattle against his dentures as he always did before gulping it down. "Much appreciated."

"No problem. I appreciate all you done for me today."

"What you suppose happened to your friend?"

"I expect he found his own way. He's a smart son of a bitch."

Gannon gave just the slightest nod, which could have been at Lomis but more likely brought the bartender back to refill the shot glass. Gannon had logged more hours in Al's than most anywhere else over the past forty years. The Kershaw Village Hall was located in the back half of the funeral home at the end of Howard Street, but any real business at hand was done right there under the dim light from the pool table and the beer neons in Al's. Gannon called the meetings as long as anybody could remember and Big Al, a village board member, poured the drinks for as long as anybody could remember.

Gannon shot another one back while Lomis pointed to his cash laying on the bar. A shudder crawled up Gannon's aching spine as he pictured the new world of Kershaw with its young mayor, Livian Gannon. It would be interesting to watch, yet, probably better that he wouldn't be around for much of it. Six months at best, the doc said.

"Two rides. Two drinks. No need to buy anymore," Gannon crowed. Then he broke into a broad grin and a laugh that quickly succumbed to a vibrating cough that turned his face crimson and choked off the air.

Lomis leaned back and watched Gannon wretch and bend over on his barstool with great interest. Perhaps a delicious moment. Foaming at the mouth would make it all just about right.

Instead, Gannon recovered, pulled his thinning old frame back upright, re-cocked his Chicago Cubs baseball cap and got an elbow to the bar rail. He pulled a handkerchief out and wiped his nose and his face, which began returning to the color of heavily weathered flesh.

"You dying or something, old man?" Lomis' voice did little to hide his morbid curiosity.

"Yep." Gannon spit out with a heaving breath. "That's about it." Gannon drew a deep breath. "So you never said."

"What's that?"

"Drive you all the way down to that canyon floor and you come back with just that damn can. So what's in the can?"

Lomis looked down on the floor at his feet where the blackened, dented coffee can sat inside his back pack. "Can't tell you that, old man. If I told you, I'd have to kill you." Lomis laughed in mock courtesy.

"Don't matter none then," Gannon shot back. "Now does it."

"But what if…," Lomis looked around and took a swig off his long neck bottle. It was just the two of them and Big Al, who was in his usual CNN trance looking up at the old television up on a shelf in the corner. "What if I were to tell you the can is full of diamonds I just inherited from a rich uncle?"

"Well, I'd likely say you was full of shit."

Lomis shrugged. "Okay."

"On the other hand," Gannon began to cough again but it didn't take hold this time. "Let's just say I happen to be an old amateur gemologist. And, up in Seattle, a good friend of mine, well, Ike, see, is one of the best wholesale guys out West here. He buys most any rock he thinks he can sell to jewelers and gem shops out on the coast or back east for that matter. Palm Springs- all them rich bitch towns along the coast- they pay outrageous money for anything a little exotic looking. It's a damn crazy truth."

"Yeah." Lomis barely smiled, a twitch beginning to set up in his left cheek as his mind began to unravel trying to keep up with the dimensions that were cutting through the blood thirst. Money. What would he do with a lot of money? What the hell would he do first? Would it feel the same to be rich and kill as it did to be poor and kill? What if it didn't? What then? Maybe, it would be even better! Then again, hell, they were probably worth next to nothing or nothing at all.

"So what would that matter to you, anyway, old man. At your age? Just being nice?"

"Not exactly. If you knew my sweet little ambitious granddaughter, you'd get my drift pretty quick."

Lomis nodded, but figured none of whatever that meant counted for anything. "You ever set something up like this before?"

"Set up what?"

"Whatever you want to call it is fine by me."

Gannon shook his head and called Al down for another shot. "If it's hot, forget it," he murmured.

"If they were stolen, old man, why would I be carrying them around in a fucking coffee can? Listen, my uncle was an eccentric old bird and he buried everything he had in his backyard. When he died, he had no family of his own except us nieces and nephews- five of us. His will was a little treasure map of his yard with instructions for each of us to dig up our inheritance."

"Yeah? Not a bad story line, but I'm just saying I got no reason to trust you as far as I could throw you." Gannon sipped and studied.

"Let's say... it would be better for everybody concerned if I just disposed of the diamonds kind of quiet like. You know, it's just that I got the lion's share and the others don't need to know. Fact of the matter is I was heading on out to Palm Springs myself."

Gannon eyed him over a sip of beer. "You don't seem much like the Palm Springs type to me, unless you're going to be a cab driver or something."

Lomis tightened his grip on the beer bottle. "If I told you I've killed men for throwing that kind of shit at me, do you think I'd be lying? You're one brave old coot, I'll give you that."

"Whatever. So what are we talking about here? Let's see what you got, Mr. Big Time."

Lomis tugged at his beer and considered the old man's craggy look. He would, or could kill him later anyway. Maybe play this one out. They could be useless hunks of quartz or crystal for all he knew, but the can had looked so odd wedged into the exposed tire jack compartment. The fire from the explosion had gutted and blackened everything. He was only after his back pack, which he would later find forty feet away hanging from the scraggly branch of a tree at the base of the cliff, but as he thumbed at the rubble and the odd looking can, it tipped over and the tiny sparkles began to take aim at the rays of the sun.

"Oh, hell. You want a look?" Lomis reached down and pulled the can up out of his back pack, prying open the tin lid with a quarter. "My uncle could have set me up for all I know."

Gannon drew his reading glasses out of a front chest pocket and set the can in his lap. He looked inside, picked up one, then another and looked up at Al who had resumed watching CNN. He drew one of the tiny gems closer to his eye and put it up against the light coming from over the pool table. He got up and walked closer to the light, eyeing it closer yet, rubbing and angling it between his fingers. Gannon looked back at Lomis and walked back to get a few more from the can and repeated his examination, then put them back and sat down.

"Can of quartz worth about fifty bucks at best if you found a sucker to buy them. A better idea would be to line the bottom of your fish aquarium with 'em."

Lomis studied the old man and thought about running the knife he had in his sock through Gannon's left eye, the one he used to make his analysis. Al wouldn't even notice.

Gannon studied back, waited and sipped his beer. "Then again, putting all the bullshit aside, let's say they was worth some real money. Then what?"

"Well I got no reason to trust you much either way, old man."

"You wouldn't trust a dying man?'

"We're all dying."

They jabbed back and forth about some nonsense while Gannon felt the fluid in his lungs getting heavy against his chest wall. He had recently come to know it as the signal to cut the booze off or he risked a choking attack that could be his last. Booze, cigarettes, even a fading thought of sex were all out the window at this point. It seemed most anything at all could activate his body's reaction to the growing cancer inside of him and send him into a reeling coughing fit or simply steal his ability to breathe.

"I could just continue on my way and figure it out when I get to wherever I'm going, you know," Lomis continued.

"And where's that exactly? How was that? Palm Springs? Your cab awaits you?"

"Ain't really none of your business, but let's just say I won't be staying here."

"Yeah, well, we're kind of hard on strangers around here anyways."

Lomis threw back the rest of his beer and looked down at his casted arm in its sling. That would have to come off. Soon. "So who's telling the bigger lie, old man? I mean, one of us is lying pretty good."

"Oh?"

"I'm just saying... ."

"You think you are a pretty smart son of a bitch, eh stranger?"

"I get by."

They ordered another round. "Put it on my tab, Al," Gannon mumbled. Al waved over his shoulder and got back to CNN. "It's Lomis, right?"

Lomis nodded.

"Lomis, the way I see it, we could sit here and feed each other this horse shit all night. No sweat off my balls."

I hear that."

"Thing is, if they were worth something, and I can't be sure how much without Ike Rosenfield getting a look..., but let's say I could get it done for you without... raising any fuss... . We go fifty-fifty."

"Whoa! Listen to you!" Lomis let his evil laugh out. "That sounds like some bullshit deal to me. You're out of your mind. Fifty-Fifty. Jesus."

"Oh, I don't know," Gannon pushed at the skin just under his chin. "Underneath all that shit of yours, I expect I see a man more desperate than that."

"Your ass. I'll give you desperate. Okay, you old coot. Twenty percent, but not a dime more."

"Twenty-five."

"Fuck!" Lomis screamed loud enough to force Al to turn just slightly from the television. But only briefly. "Okay. Okay. What are we talking about anyway here? I mean, how long will this little deal of yours take?"

"We can get a plane up to Seattle out of Hailey tomorrow. Be back day after; cash in hand, assuming we can find that damn rascal Ike."

"Plane? I ain't getting on any goddam plane. I don't fly, old man."

"Chicken shit under all that other, eh?" Gannon scratched at the stubble on his chin. "Then I guess you'll have to trust me."

"Fuck that, too."

"Look, son. Where the hell do you think I would go? I lived here my entire life. They say I got maybe six months. Some days, like today,

75

feels like the last and so be it if it is. My only family, my granddaughter is here. The money, if there is any, is for her." Gannon coughed and laughed at the fantasy that took a quick pop through his head. "A beach hut in Tahiti sounds pretty tempting, sucking on firm little titties and Mai Tai's and all, but look at what you got here, boy. I'm not going anywhere and by this time next week this could well be just another empty barstool for Big Al to refill and you'll still be walking around wondering what to do with that fucking can."

"I don't think so." Lomis cradled the can like it was his first born.

"Okay. So be it, then. You change your mind, I live up the street. White, two-story clapboard house, Four-Sixteen." Gannon picked up his money, left the usual five spot for Al and struggled to his feet, steadying himself with one hand on the bar stool.

Lomis took another real good look at Gannon. Tall, a bag of bones, no ass hanging under drooping denims, the shadows of the dim lights ghosting into the deep crevices on his face. Killing him was not an option. Better ideas came to him, one, then another.

"Who's Ike?"

"He's the man."

Lomis twisted and fooled with the label on his beer bottle. "Okay, old man. You win." He handed him the can. "I would kill you in a heartbeat; you do understand that, right?"

Gannon took the can and grimaced in pain while trying to suppress the laughter. The pressure inside his chest was growing. "Meet you right here, day after tomorrow, seven o'clock."

Lomis watched as Gannon threw up a wave at Al and slowly made his way out the front door. Through the big plate glass windows on either side of the door, the orange glow of sunset bathed the small gathering of buildings known as Kershaw, Idaho. Gannon tried to suppress the smile on his face but there had been damn little to smile about lately, so he let it go and let it stay on for awhile.

Lomis Walls waited a few moments, then stepped outside and leaned back into the building as he watched old man Gannon slowly make his way up the hill with the coffee can tucked under one arm. A swirl of thoughts and second thoughts played through his head but he soon had a smile of his own to suppress as he watched the nurse across the way locking up the front door of the clinic.

CHAPTER THIRTEEN

IF SHE GOT INTO a car the idea would go away as quickly as it had appeared. Purse under her arm, she walked across the small parking lot and began ascending a hill along a dirt and grass walkway.

Hold steady, Lomis told himself. This could be too good. Too good. He craned his neck as he watched her dart into a building that looked like a small market or general store of some kind. He began to walk towards the building and as he did, the idea took on dimension, purpose, and every hair on his back flew out rigid from his body. To even have the ability to think like this, to plot quickly, to build the scene, to picture the act, all of it; the only thing missing was the actual feeling itself. That never came. He could never create that sensation of all sensations. That still required a man of action. But he was every bit that.

Lomis straightened his rumpled clothes as best he could and made sure the casted arm was setting as it should in the sling. He mustered up some expression designed to exact pity from an easy mark and walked into the store. He moved up to an aisle end cap near the door and pretended to ogle half price items from deodorant to toothpaste, checking the expiration dates like always, then setting them back down. He got one eye into watching her from behind as she stood at a display of lipsticks and small bottles of make-up and removers. That was indeed the fine ass he remembered from earlier in the day. He waited, fidgeted, and when she turned and caught a glimpse of him, he put on his best grimace as he tried to retrieve a plastic bottle of mouthwash he dropped perfectly to the floor.

"Oh my, what have we here?" She cooed, watching him pick it back up and fumble to put in back on the shelf. "Looks like you have decided to stay in our little town for awhile?"

"Yeah, it kind of grows on you when you start looking around with them mountains and all." Lomis was shooting for the sound of a shy country boy with just a touch of education.

"How's the arm?"

"Oh gosh, it's all right. The rest of me hurts more like I got hit by a train or something."

"Get yourself some Witch Hazel. I'm a big fan of Witch Hazel for about anything and everything." She walked to the other aisle and pulled up a bottle of the greenish yellow liquid from the bottom shelf. "Here you go."

"What exactly do you do with that?"

"You rub it on what hurts. You know, massage it in."

"Thanks." Lomis offered his best version of puppy dog eyes.

"You have the wildest eyes," she said. "I noticed that at the clinic."

"Yeah?"

"Yeah. I mean... just, I don't know, really."

"I lead an interesting life, yes. Like, in my line of work, I need to have eyes in the back of my head."

"Doing what?"

"I'm a ... consultant," Lomis said, almost taking it back. Then a smile tried to force its way onto his lips. "But right now... I'm just traveling around. I wanted to do the back roads travel thing right after I graduated, but never got around to it before the work poured in." He shook his head. And so he once again welcomed back that ability to adjust his voice and tone to fit the man in the story he was beginning to tell. Being educated, sounding educated, took some work, considering he only had two years of high school, but he was pretty good at it if he thought it fit the situation. He had pretended to be many people and things from different places in pursuit of his life's work and more often than not found himself pleasantly surprised at how well he pulled it off.

They spun through some small talk while Lomis threw in an occasional grimace to try to make her think he was still in some degree of pain in need of soothing. The truth of it was he enjoyed his own physical pain when he encountered it. Whether it was a head slam by a competing street drunk or some victim trying to dig her fingernails into his flesh while he bludgeoned her to death, there was redemption in pain, a cleansing moment that seemed to invigorate his nervous system;

awakening those passive nerve endings that never saw the light of day in most people.

"Any decent place for dinner around here?" Lomis asked.

"That's easy. The Crow's Nest up on the bluff."

"Is it walking distance? Last time I checked, my car was still at the bottom of a canyon."

She laughed. "Probably not in your condition."

"Oh. Right."

"I suppose I could give you a lift, though."

He brightened noticeably. "I have a better idea. Why don't you join me for dinner at… The Crow's Nest?"

She shot a quick smile back his way. "I would, if I could, but I can't. My roommate is cooking dinner tonight."

"Roommate?"

"I live with somebody. We have a place up in the foothills."

"I see. Well, thanks, I'll take you up on the ride though."

"No problem. Give me a few minutes to get my things here. My car is parked just around the corner."

"Take your time. I'm going nowhere fast. I'll just wait outside for you."

She shrugged. "Did you forget what you came in here for?"

"No," said Lomis, flustered for a moment. "I… was just going to ask for directions, and there you were. And I got my directions, I guess."

"Those are some eyes," she said, and turned to finish her shopping as Lomis drifted back out the front door. He pressed back up against the outside wall and caught his breath, fighting off the beginning pressure of an erection. He closed his eyes and tried to get his breathing under control, suppressing, pushing everything back into a holding pattern. He reached down and felt the knife still there inside his sock. The feel of it steadied him. He pulled his back pack up to his chest and let himself free fall in one of those moments of visualizing; the sensual preludes coming in a dizzy progression of color graphics whirling around him. Touching, tearing, slashing, penetrating, all urgings that wrapped him up like cellophane, demanding he act or die.

The attractive nurse walked out with a flip cell phone on her ear. She spotted Lomis and walked slowly towards him. "Would you like to join us up at the house for dinner?" She put the phone back in her purse. "I warn you I never know for sure what we are eating until it's on the plate, and then sometimes, well anyway, not exactly the Crow's Nest."

Lomis shrugged and grinned widely. "Your roommate. He's okay with that?"

"He is a she. And she loves it when I bring home company. Trust me on that."

Lomis took a deep breath as if this was worthy of the moment, when in fact he was just thanking his Gods for the kindness shown. "Then, sure. Why not?" They began to walk together towards her car. "Hey," Lomis said, "How do I know you're not some crazy lady luring me up into your lair?"

She did her best to give him a menacing glare.

"I mean, I don't recall you had on one those name tags they usually wear in hospitals."

"The clinic is hardly a hospital."

"I guess what I am saying is I don't even know your name."

"Is that a fact?" She smiled. "Odessa."

"Odessa?"

"You seem surprised? I get that a lot."

"And as for you, Mister From Nowhere. As I recall, you had no insurance card, no ID, no credit cards."

"Somewhere down the side of a mountain... ." Lomis interrupted, pointing to his arm. The only card he had on him was the Senator's ID card tucked nicely into the front pocket of his denim shirt.

The house was a one-story clap board cottage that had been sitting under towering trees and the shadows of a cliff above for maybe a century or two. Lomis followed Odessa along a narrow path between tangled brush on either side that led to a front door nearly hidden from view. A small bare yellow bulb covered in cob webs and unlucky insects burned just above the door opening. As they walked inside, a syrupy sweet perfume hit Lomis with a flash of nausea.

"Welcome to Michaelen's house of pain," Odessa announced with a mocking tone. "Follow me into the kitchen my good man and we shall likely find the sinister sister stirring up a nasty brew."

Lomis followed, his eyes taking in the huge black tiki doll head and odd wood carvings that appeared oversized for the size of the front room.

Blue hippie beads in the door opening to the kitchen clicked on each other as they walked through. Standing at an old cast iron stove was a woman of deep black color with braided hair that ran down her back and draped across an ample chest. Greens and blues ran in streaks down the hair braids and each tip appeared to be nearly glowing in bright orange.

"Uh huh. Second patient you dragged home this week, Dessie," the black woman said in a tone deep enough to rattle the hippie beads.

Lomis smiled nervously, unable to distinguish between his confusion, fascination and the intermittent static of anticipation. "Walking wounded," his voice limped out.

"We take all comers, honey, so sit yourself down at the table and pour yourself a Chianti." The words fell from between her large lips in a straight line. Something she was probably very used to, Lomis surmised. It had been a long time since the word intimidating crossed his mind, but it only took moments in her presence and the overwhelming sweet incense to step him down a notch. She was worth the watching, wielding a sizable knife as she cut up something and tossed a handful into the large pot on the stove. "I'm Michaelen," she offered. "Dessie's pretty bad on the intros."

"Lomis."

Odessa was fetching glasses from an overhead cabinet and set them on the kitchen table next to the open bottle of Chianti. She motioned for Lomis to sit down and did likewise, then poured the wine. "Don't get too caught up in Michaelen's idea of herself." She winked.

"First we eat, then we fuck!" Michaelen bellowed. "That's how we roll here, honey. Alright with you, Lomis?" She made sure she got the reaction she was looking for and exploded with a laugh that came from the purple painted toenails on her large bare feet.

Lomis drank the wine eagerly while his mind swirled in a frenzy, his eyes darting, cheek twitching, visions of blood spattering everywhere as he looked around and tried to focus on Michaelen for the moment. The way she said the word "fuck" had him nearly flopping out of the chair.

"You alright, Lomis?" Odessa asked.

"I'm fine. Just a little twinge of pain here and there. Then it passes."

Odessa sipped. "This is the part where I'm supposed to say she is really harmless. But she's not!" Odessa had quite a hearty laugh herself.

"Thing is," Michaelen interrupted, "most men anymore are either wimps or pimps. Here we are just two women alone up in the mountains doing what we need to do to get by. And it ain't easy unless you break it down. So we break it down. We eat. We fuck. Sleep. Work. Eat and fuck. What else is there worth anything at all? Anything more than that starts with a dishonest moment because we are fooling ourselves to think we need more that. You get it, Lomis?"

"I do. I ...do."

"Gotta know right now if you're gay. If you are, no big deal, it just changes things."

"Do I look gay to you?"

"Yeah, sort of."

"Well, I'm not. Let's just leave it there."

"Whew!" said Michaelen. "Dodged another bullet. Seems we keep running into twinks everywhere. Not that it's wrong," she said, laughing deeply. "In this house, when we want dick, we get us man-dick, not fag-dick." She made sure Lomis could see how big and round her eyes were.

Lomis thought of pinching himself to see if this was all some kind of weird dream. "Sure."

"Go ahead," said Odessa.

"What?" Lomis asked.

"Tell her to go fuck herself."

Lomis laughed nervously and shook his head, which felt like it was filling with sand.

"Oh sweetheart, you have no idea, but it's okay to pretend you do," Michaelen said, stirring through some steam from the boil she was waiting for.

Lomis fidgeted and adjusted in his chair, again trying to lay a finger on the source of the strong perfume that continued to permeate the breathing space, overpowering whatever it was Michaelen was cooking up.

"I assume you like squirrel, rabbit and pack rat stew?" Michaelen asked Lomis.

Lomis flinched and twitched, trying to come up with the right answer.

Odessa and Michaelen shared the laughter. "He's going to be fun," Michaelen offered.

Odessa reached over and touched the casted arm. "She's kidding. At least about the stew. But God only knows what mood will strike her after dinner. Here, have some more wine." She poured as Lomis presented his empty glass. Odessa looked into his wild eyes and smiled playfully. "I guess we'll just have to wait and see." She winked and filled her glass as well.

"All this great fun you two are having at my expense," Lomis began. "You've put all this on before, right?"

"Of course," said Odessa.

They continued to play the parts they had chosen and tried to raise the ante with each dart in the conversation, but by the time Odessa opened a second bottle of Chianti, Lomis was losing patience and interest in the game.

"Bathroom?" He asked.

"Back down the hall on your left," Odessa said.

Lomis opened the medicine cabinet above the bathroom sink and gazed over its contents while he took a step over to take a piss. The tiny bathroom was layered in pastel gauze and white lace and the ever present sweetness that held everything hostage. Lomis grabbed a prescription bottle of Vicodin, popped three down, tossed another handful into his pocket, put it back and shut the cabinet door. Then he shut his eyes and began to stroke.

A few minutes later Lomis emerged through the beads into the kitchen. "I thought I would change the tempo of this conversation, ladies."

Odessa froze at the kitchen table and Michaelen dropped her wooden stirring spoon into the large soup pot. Their eyes were glued to the half-hard dick snaking out of the zipper of his jeans and bouncing its tip against his inner thigh well down towards his kneecap. He sat down at the kitchen table, jeans pulled down around his ankles.

No one said a word, or moved for a few moments.

Michaelen cocked her head as a deep breath whistled back out her mouth and and turned the burner off on the stove. "Dinner can wait." She dropped to a crawl across the kitchen floor, arrived at the table, got a grip on the base of his cock and winked up at him. Christmas time, a new toy in hand, the biggest and the best. "Lookie what I got here," she said, looking back over her shoulder for Odessa.

His head began to rock with an uneasiness. Unwelcome thoughts stabbed around inside of his skull. He pictured the old man holding the can, walking away, maybe walking away just that easy with the closest thing to a fortune Lomis would ever sniff. And where in the hell was that fucking Riddler…, Castle? What the hell was he up to? He would turn up again in this. He was too smart. Too quiet and craftly. All the while, first Odessa, then Michaelen, then both, stroking it, sucking it, licking it up one side and down the other, trying everything they knew how to raise it to full mast.

"What is the story, darlin'?" Michaelen asked, signs of exhaustion in her voice. "You can't tell me you walk around with that massive thing in your pants and it doesn't work."

"Maybe he's another watcher," said Odessa, laying down on the kitchen floor and beckoning Michaelen with a curling forefinger.

Michaelen crawled over to Odessa and drooped a large breast over her face. Odessa got after the nipple while they both looked back over at Lomis to make sure he was taking it all in.

Lomis gazed at the two of them; his head bobbing a little in deference to the symphony chamber music coming from the ceiling, then looked down. It wasn't happening. The voices inside his head were laughing at him. They knew. He knew. He needed to start smacking them around, tie somebody up, hear the screams, maybe carve away at a face, plunge the blade into organs, listen for the bloody gurgling success, penetrate, again, and again. He knew. As these thoughts took over, he could feel the warmth return, rising, lengthening. Sweat broke out on his forehead and he began to hear his breath coming quicker.

"Oh God, it's working!" Odessa yelled out loud enough for Michaelen to acknowledge with a nod and a quick feasting eye. "Keep doing it, Mik."

The wheels in Lomis' head kept grinding away. And what if he were rich? Lomis Walls basking in wealth and luxury without a care in the world? This was an overwhelming thought, above all others, that brought a smile to his lips, but as he looked down, he found his cock retreating to half mast.

Odessa knocked softly at the side of Michaelen's head. "Forget it, Mik."

Michaelen sighed, stood back up and returned to the stove, her grand black breasts jutting out as proud as they could be. "Anybody still hungry?"

Lomis was at full battle with keeping himself under control. His better sense, the one that brought him the reason and purpose and kept all things in their proper order until each event came and went, argued against the raping or killing or anything that came with the natural order of things. Instead, it was telling him to hold back, to keep a low profile, play this out. The town was too small, his deeds too difficult to hide, his escape route uncertain, and add the unknown sides of the Riddler into all of this, he could not afford to take any uncalculated chances at this point. He pulled his pants up with little ceremony, gave the kitchen table a finger tap and chugged his wine down.

"Maybe later," Odessa said, sitting down to join him. "We're not going anywhere." Then she leaned over with a whisper. "We'll figure it out, don't you worry."

The awkwardness of the moment continued to attack him from all sides. The twitching in his face was traveling around and down his arms and legs. There was only one thing left to do.

"I don't think you ladies would mind terribly if I skipped out on dinner and made my way back to town."

"Don't be silly," Odessa said flatly as she fluffed her hair back into place.

The beads were already clinking behind Michaelen as she huffed off into another room. "That boils over, you scream, child," she threw back at Odessa.

"Actually, it's not that far," Lomis said. "The walk would do me good. I think I probably overdid it on the pain meds."

"Are you sure?"

Lomis could tell by the tone of her voice she was as anxious to get him out of there as he was to go. He nodded with a twitching smile and made his way back out the front door, skipping the goodbyes with Michaelen.

The moon was full, a bright glow bouncing off everything except the shadows. He stood at the edge where the short gravel drive met the street and turned slowly to look in every direction, finally stopping to fix on the small, leaning building at the other end of the driveway behind the house. It was a one-car garage with a closed panel door that was too cockeyed to quite make it to the bottom. His mind began to clear of the anxiety forced on him by the pair of conspirators and he began to walk back towards the garage. There were no exterior lights but he could see well enough to find a side service door. One firm turn on the old wobbly knob and the door opened easily. His eyes always had an amazing ability to adjust quickly to the dark and seemed to provide an additional source of light he never fully understood. With the additional glow peeking from below the crooked garage door he began feeling his way along the walls until he found what he wanted. He smiled. He fully expected to find a shovel in just about any garage, but the favor that only the best of the Gods could give him was one made of the lighter weight alloys with a good grip. After all, digging graves with one arm would be one helluva challenge and may take him all night. Because once again, he would be digging deep enough for two.

Then again, first things first. Time to make camp, settle in, embrace the night. There would be the light of a million stars to dig by.

CHAPTER FOURTEEN

SAM HAD ALMOST FORGOTTEN how great it felt to put on a new flannel shirt, new jeans, new everything. He found a bottle of Ralph Lauren men's cologne sitting in her medicine cabinet. A delicious jealousy consumed him as he did the math and splashed some on. This was what Liv said getting dressed up meant in this part of the country. Fresh jeans, pressed flannels, clean boots and a shave. In fact, Sam could not remember the last time he carried his thoughts so lightly.

"Are you just going to stare at me all night or are you going to tell me how I look?" Liv asked, trying to finish with something in the kitchen while Sam leaned up against a wall, watching her every move.

"You know how you look."

"Maybe. But how do I look to you?"

"Hmm."

"You have to think about it, or are you trying to come up with something snappy that will impress me?" She finished, shut a cabinet and slowly walked over to him and stood a few inches from his face, allowing him to add her fragrance to the mix. "Well?"

Sam's head began to swoon and it was as though a thousand different parts of an assembly line inside of him began to crank up into full production after a long layoff. He nearly fell over but caught himself. "You take my breath away."

"A dog fart can do that, Sam. More. More originality, too."

"Please, don't kill the moment for me." Sam closed his eyes and held her close.

She felt as comfortable in his arms as anything she could remember. "Maybe not original, but I like it," she said, then pulled back out of his embrace and looked up into his liquid eyes. "And how long have we known each other?"

"Three days. And a few hours, give or take," he said.

"And this is our first date. Just so you know, I don't put out on the first date. Never have."

Sam tightened his arms around her waist and pulled her back a little closer so he could try to suffocate in the warming sweet air that came with her. "Technically, our first date was up on your point a few days ago."

"Not a date."

"The coffee afterwards."

"Not a date."

"Okay. Lunch at your office the next day then. That was a date."

"You didn't ask and you weren't invited. You just showed up with a bag of croissants. That hardly qualified as lunch even, let alone a date. But I loved it. Which doesn't count either, by the way."

"Drinks after your meeting last night? What was that, then?"

"Drinks. After my meeting. It was wonderful. But it wasn't a real date."

Sam relaxed a bit and looked down, pretending to be hurt or rejected, a child still in there, anxiously awaiting and readjusting to an old trusted tactic.

Liv pulled his chin up, watched the big smile cross his face and gave him a long, deep kiss that sent him on up into unfamiliar air space. Any thought of anything else but this moment was impossible. Any thought of remaining and acting like a reasonably grown adult was impossible. Any thought of how and why this was happening now officially didn't matter in the least.

"That worked," Liv whispered in his ear, gently pushing her pelvis up against a growing firmness at the front of his jeans.

"It was working when you opened the door."

She gave him another short kiss, bit the lobe of one his ears and drew back. "The new mayor can't be late to her own party."

"It wouldn't take very long...."

"I'm sure of that. In the mean time, put that thing away before you hurt somebody, and let's get going."

Sam reluctantly followed her out the door, laughing, angling and adjusting his jeans.

Liv caught his act and gave a laugh as well. "Why don't we take *your* new truck, just for new times' sake," she said, giggling.

Sam's gait had returned to normal by the time they reached the truck. Liv lived a few miles west of town in a cozy double A-frame cedar house Gannon had built for her twenty-first birthday. The house sat just so on a flat parcel of twelve acres he owned near the base of the mountains to the east and great sunsets to the west. She had a few horses and chickens and an evolving assortment of dogs and cats that stood sentry as they drove out along the long dirt drive back to the main road.

The official Kershaw Town Hall was in the back room of Barkman's Funeral Home, and had been for going on sixty-five years. Old man Barkman had long since passed, and not all that many of Kershaw's population of 906 were croaking off at a rate to warrant the business being full time. Barkman also printed the Kershaw Gazette, a semi-weekly four-page newspaper, and ran a mail order clothing business long before the days of the internet. With no apparent heirs to his estate, the Kershaw City Council anchored by then Mayor Gannon voted to buy the building, make it a municipal gathering place of sorts, and keep the funeral business going for reasons that seemed obvious. The only catch was when somebody died they needed to rent the mortician that lived in Sun Valley for a couple of days to prepare the body and get it properly buried. Rumor also had it some middle-aged, crazy woman named Doris had a key to the place and charged men twenty bucks to screw in an open pine box coffin in the basement.

"More people than I thought," Liv said as they arrived. Some thirty or so cars were parked and angled along the road or wherever they could find space.

Sam grabbed her not all that gently for one more kiss before they walked in.

"Jesus, Sam," Liv said, breaking away gently and resisting the temptation to just give it a grip. "Thank you for the love, but you cannot go inside that way."

"How 'bout I'll just stand out here all night and wait for you."

"Just… think about something else. My God, are you on Viagra or something?"

"Don't sell yourself so short," Sam said.

She gave him a playful lingering glare.

"Okay." Sam stood back a few feet and wondered if he had ever felt more childish since the innocence left for the very last time. "Okay.

We'll be fine. Just give me another moment. And by the way. You look way beyond mayoral. Beyond this world, actually." He considered her shimmering silk, dark pink blouse with a proper but suggestive scoop neck, tight-fitting jeans, the modest, single diamond necklace and matching earrings and the sterling ring bracelet with a tiny PEACE charm. "You are something out of a storybook I never got to read when I was a kid. The one I always wanted to read. The one about the beautiful princess that made everything right just by touching it with her magic wand."

"Oh my...." She reached for his hand. "I dare not get too close, I fear. And, whatever you are on, I want some of that. Later."

As they drew close to the door, she looked down to make sure he was neutralized. "I'm going to have to explain to Sarah Johansen just exactly who this strange man is along side the new mayor of Kershaw."

"Who is Sarah Johansen?"

"Nobody special, like the rest of us here in Kershaw, but she is generally the source for the beginning of any rumor worth listening to. She provides us all here with a public dialogue whether we need it or not. She'll get one look at you and she'll be off. But just a forewarning-she has the mouth of a trucker that's just been cut off by a young punk driving daddy's Mercedes and would have you believing you and whatever army could never keep up with her libido."

"Danger's my game," Sam said, giving her a smile.

When they walked in, the small room erupted in cheers and applause, and while Sam could feel the overload of eyes on him, he managed to slink to the side and allow Liv her own moment free of having to introduce her new stranger-friend-lover. He quickly found the small stand up bar in the far corner and got a beer in front of him to cradle. He guessed Chardonnay for Liv and had the glass filled and waiting for her.

Liv's brilliant smile seemed to take on proportion as she worked her way through the room shaking hands, hugging and kissing. More hugging and kissing than hand shakes, to be sure. He pictured her gliding through larger state rooms and warming everyone she touched or even those who just got a glimpse of her. The relaxed confidence beneath an even, unforced smile, eyes that could not, would not betray, and just enough movement and angle to her face and head to make it real while she carried her shoulders square. There was no hurry in Liv. She squared up and looked people straight in the eyes, and she listened to a person as though their voice and message was the only thing that mattered. It just wasn't possible someone that young- that young and beautiful- could work it that well. Mesmerized, excited, laughably jealous and possessive, Sam leaned back to get a better look at himself as this played out.

"And who might you be?" asked a deep voice over his left shoulder. Sam turned quickly expecting to look up, but his eyes traveled downward to the clever smile of a diminutive old woman in a long, flowing, fire red dress fit to take her back to the prom.

"Sam Castle, ma'm."

"Sam Castle." Her head bobbed as she sorted it out. "Don't know any Castles from around here."

"Iowa." He tried to match the crowd noise.

"Say again?"

"Iowa. I'm from Iowa."

"Whereabouts? Potato farmer?" The smile had given way to purpose. Sam considered it. "No, not Idaho. Iowa."

"Oh." She seemed okay with that and stopped searching his face to survey the room.

"Can I get you something to drink?" he asked.

The lady looked back up at him curiously, her lips quivering and pursing unconsciously. "Scotch rocks. One ice cube."

The drink was already laid out in front of him as Sam's eye caught the knowing glance of the bartender. He shrugged, shook his head and moved on to the next order being shouted in his direction.

Sam handed the lady her drink and she grabbed it with a playful wink. Her wrinkled face made a guess of her age mandatory, but she also had a glow of energy about her that was obvious while she stood there, a half smile, little eyes darting everywhere, as if looking for someone important. "She's a fine mayor alright- just watch that little gunny slut go all the way to the White House before it's all written up. I'll be dead and gone, but you stand a fair chance, Mr. Castle."

Sam nodded in polite agreement while her terminology bounced an echo through his head.

"Look at her move through that crowd. Graceful, smiling, and eyes like that.... And she's got the words right. She can speak her peace with those nimrods, and while they're all still stuck in gear figuring out how to get in her knickers, she's got them right where she wants them. She's gonna be something, I tell you."

"Ah! So that's it," Sam added.

"Say again?"

"She's got me doing the same thing."

The old lady's half smile took on a deeper set. "You come in with her. I saw that. You already dining at the table, stranger?"

"What is it around here? Everybody is so nice to strangers."

"Not many of us here, I suppose. Your odds are better. The men here mostly drink. The women mostly fuck, if you ask them nice. It's an easy place to be. We don't get all defensive about our little piece of the world being invaded because nobody stays all that long before they move on. So we figure they have a right to be treated just like one of us while they are here. Kind of a creed-like."

"I see."

"So you set your sights on the highest mountain here, eh?"

"Say again?" The crowd noise in the small room was amping by the moment.

"I hear she's as good a boning as there is."

Sam considered his answer but lost the ability to form the words.

"And speaking of a good boning, here comes my honey," she said, setting her glass on the bar and opening her arms to hug the former Mayor, Joshua Gannon. "Where have you been, you old cunt hound? I've been sliding off seats for days waiting for you."

Gannon drew back from the hug and planted a good one right on her quivering wrinkled lips. He looked up at the red banner that read "Congratulations Liv" hanging up on the wall behind the bar and ordered a whiskey.

Sam drew back and got a double gulp down while still processing the kiss that lingered longer than he cared to see.

"I was up in Seattle for a couple of days. Still rains there like a son of a bitch," said Gannon.

"That's why we live here, sweetie. I was just telling Sam here all about our fair town." She turned Sam's way. "Sam, meet your intended's grandfather, Josh Gannon. Just call him Gannon. The men shook hands with Gannon's eyes drilling into Sam's.

"We have met," Gannon said. "Still around, I see."

"Your granddaughter has been nice enough to show me around," Sam added quickly.

"Yeah. Well, take a look at her," Gannon craned his head and presented the room as evidence. "She don't much discriminate between friend or foe and she's been known to pick up a stray many a time. Usually it has four legs."

The old lady looped one arm around Gannon's and picked up her drink with the other hand. "Actually, you're damn lucky you showed up old timer cause I was just about to start working Sam here. You are a good looking man, alright. Most of the strangers lately been kind of gangly. Downright ugly. Like that boy you was helping out the other day, Gannon, the one with the broken arm. What was his name?"

"Lomis Walls," Gannon said without hesitation. "I believe Mr. Castle here knows Mr. Walls. They were the two that fell down the canyon south of town a few days ago."

"But then I already knew that, didn't I," she said with a high pitched laugh that lingered.

"I think I have that right, Sam? I had a few drinks with Lomis over at Al's. As things worked out, he's actually up at the house right now hopefully getting a good shower. God knows he needed one. Sort of a strange creature, isn't he?"

Creature was an interesting choice of words, thought Sam. His instincts told him a guy like Lomis should have been long gone from Kershaw by this time.

"We should mingle, dear," she said, squeezing his arm. "Now that I know you're here I can let Mr. Castle back out the bedroom door."

Gannon kissed the top of her head and allowed himself to be pulled into the crowd. "Horny old broad," he threw back at Sam.

Sam ordered up another beer and looked down at the untouched glass of chardonnay on the bar.

"That was pretty mild," the bartender said, handing Sam the beer. "Sarah cleans it up pretty good when Gannon is around."

"Sarah Johansen?"

"There is only one."

Sam finally managed to catch Liv's eye and watched her angle that graceful frame towards him between short conversations and hugs. He put the glass into her outstretched hand and watched her take two short sips while listening to a heavy set man finish his monologue. When he did, a one armed hug followed and she folded in next to Sam at the bar.

"You alright?" she asked.

"I met Sarah."

"What was that like?"

"She warned me you were a slut."

"A gunny slut, you mean. She's usually right about most things."

"I was actually thinking of you as protection from her at the time," Sam said.

"Good. Hold that thought." Liv set the drink down and was whisked off to meet another State Representative, one of the few she didn't already know. Her work over just a few years had brought her in touch with many sensitive, emotion-driven Idaho environmental issues that were constantly in the forefront of the news. It starts with being easy to look at, which she was, and for anyone who had met her, they also found a cool head with a fast and furious tongue to go with an intriguing talent-set that begged for a political future. She would have seemed easy pickings for the Democratic Party, but the Republicans were not exactly throwing in the towel. By any measure, tiny town notwithstanding, this little function for Liv seemed packed with state political whiz bangers setting up to make their claim. When the older, former mayor Gannon had limped through the front door, the crowd seemed to wheeze, a few claps could be heard, but like much of the past, it all succumbed to the moment, those in it, and the next agenda.

Sam was perfectly happy just watching her move around. All of her, from any view point. An unfamiliar ease was settling over him. To think this all started with pulling the tarp off the Explorer in the garage and telling the car aloud to head due west. Through the extraordinary journey and casual disorder of things he now found himself in a place called Kershaw, Idaho, once again in the mountains, this time captured by the likes of a young woman with untold weapons and battle savvy.

But the easiness crept away just as quietly as it had arrived. The situation surrounding the missing diamonds tore into him, sat front and center in his head, big enough for all to see, if only they knew. While Liv had been busy doing her thing, he had been over every inch of that canyon. Twice. The only clues were the two tiny diamonds he found on the ground by the car. There wasn't one to be found anywhere else, which suggested to him they fell to the ground as the coffee can was picked up from the car and taken away. It didn't take much for Sam to think that Lomis Walls had something to do with it. What wouldn't make sense then is why he was still around, unless he didn't really have any idea what he had. A guy could find out though, couldn't he? Then what?

Sam watched as Liv made her way with some urgency to the man that had just walked in the door. They kissed, embraced a little tighter than Sam would have liked, and talked with their lips only inches apart before throwing their heads back with laughter. Sam didn't like that either. Then she took his hand and led him back through a throng of people, introducing him as she went. Sam told himself the jealousy was only a mild case.

They finally made their way to the bar and Sam stood there, trying not to look like he was keeping count. Liv found time for a wink in Sam's direction, got the bartender to give her good looking man friend a drink and turned him around next to Sam.

"Sam, meet Senator John Perkins from Iowa."

They shook hands. "Senator. A pleasure." As good a specimen as Sam was, he observed quickly that Senator Perkins could jump right off the pages of GQ. He had seen him in pictures and on television back home in Iowa.

"I'm just 'John' to any friend of Liv's."

Sam looked over at Liv and nodded politely to the senator.

Liv was beaming up at both of them. "John and I fire from the same fox holes on environmental battles."

"Us against them. You would want her on your side," the senator added quickly, seemingly for Sam's benefit.

"If John plays his cards right, maybe we take a run at the White House sooner than later," Liv added.

The Senator poked Sam in the side. "Somebody needs to remind her you need to be thirty-five to run for President. God knows I've tried. She just says she will get the law changed."

Sam shrugged and smiled along.

Liv gave John a playful shot to the arm. "I do not believe you are here, John."

"Are you kidding? Anyway, I wanted to surprise you. More fun that way, right? He gave her a tight hug that sent a stinger down Sam's left arm. "I want to say I was here at your humble beginnings. Of course I would know nothing of humble beginnings myself, I regret." The attempt at wistfulness was wasted on her. "Mayor today. Madam

President tomorrow. Sam, If she kicks me off the ticket maybe I can get another job like Ambassador to Tahiti."

"Now here comes the brag about the little family compound in Tahiti. Not every true environmental fanatic is poor like me, Sam," Liv said.

"Hey, it's been in the family for almost 100 years. Not my fault it's there."

The conversation took on a predictable glib tone and went on until the insults and irony died down. Sam tried his best to hide the puzzled look he was sure he was wearing. Shifting his weight leg-to-leg, assuming his back-up singer role for the moment, he began scanning the room as though he were supposed to be doing that. His life had often depended on knowing exactly where he was and where everybody else was, so it was not a surprise he spotted a very cleaned up version of Lomis Walls the moment he came through the door.

CHAPTER FIFTEEN

It only took a moment for Lomis to consider he might have been guilty of a rare mistake in deciding to come in. Old man Gannon had told him it was just a little gathering of locals; that it might be "interesting". He liked the old man in a way; make that in *twenty-five-thousand* ways. It was more money than he had ever seen. He loved the touch of it, flipping and fanning the bills, and the smell of it; ink, blood, he wasn't sure what it reminded him of more.

He had always felt more comfortable at the frame of a window, peeking in from the cold and the dark, and now he knew why. The noise was deafening and made no sense and the scents in the air seemed to be fighting for space, what space there was. His eyes immediately began to dart and water and it was everything he could do to suppress the small twitch in his cheek from spreading and ripping his face into shreds. As he worked for his next breath he spotted Sam Castle staring at him from across the room. His feet were glued to the floor only three steps into the room and could move no further. His heart heaved up into his throat in pulsing waves of blood looking for somewhere to go and hide while the sweat beaded above his upper lip and at his temples. Bad mistake, Lomis, he repeated back to himself. Get out! They all know! Get out!

He got his feet to move back a step and turned quickly out the door and slipped off into the dark, looking back only after retreating to the safe place behind a clump of heavy brush where he had hidden his back pack and its now valuable contents. If his sanity was returning, he would expect to see Sam Castle outside the front door of the building. Looking. He was there, alright. Probably wondering just what the hell was going on with all of that. Probably wondering where in hell his diamonds went and suspecting somebody named Lomis Walls had something to do with it. Hah! "Motherfucker has no idea how to keep up with me," Lomis said quietly over his lips, a laugh coughing up and surprising him. "Shssssh," he hushed himself. When Sam turned back to go inside, Lomis relaxed and the twitch began to subside. "You see that?" He asked a tree as he leaned into it and kissed it. He ran his tongue up and down the roughness of the bark and spit out the pieces that came loose in his mouth. "No control. No control. Never. Never. They are all lunatics, talking in tongues, smelling like the stupid and rich. The only problem?" He asked the tree. "I can't kill them all. First, it would not be wise. Second, there is not enough time. But! But there is time tonight. So let's get on with it, shall we?"

He walked up and down the empty streets and paths of Kershaw, his jaw twitching and moving in a three-way conversation he replayed aloud as he kicked at small rocks and sticks. His mind kept rewinding to the moment earlier in Gannon's kitchen.

"Twenty-five thousand?" Lomis had gasped as he listened carefully to the words rolling out across his lips.

"Twenty-five thousand," Gannon had repeated. "And that's after my twenty-five percent."

"Whatever, whatever. Let me see the money. Let me see it!"

Gannon opened a door that led to the basement, and as Lomis listened to the heavy clop of boots going down wooden stairs from his seat at the tiny kitchen table, he imagined a familiar figure forming in the shadows of the dim light.

"No matter," came that annoying meek voice from the past, that of Father McCready, turning now, facing the wall, naked, shackled and cowering. Father McCready had long since died of a heart attack, but Lomis kept bringing him back from hell in hopes he would find a way to kill him anyway.

He was only nine, living in a ramshackle orphanage in Cincinnati, and had hoped to figure out a horrendous, tortuous end for the good Father who had a fondness for fondling and sucking nine-year-old penis.

"No matter," Father McCready had repeated. "You'll just kill him later anyway.

"Yes. Yes I will," Lomis had said aloud.

"Will what?" Gannon had asked, returning from the basement, tossing a twisty-tied, black plastic garbage bag onto the table.

Lomis laughed loudly, an echo bouncing off the boulders at the base of the nearby mountains. He knew Gannon couldn't hear or see the good father. But he was there, right in Gannon's kitchen, naked, shackled, and castrated, the blood continually running down the insides of his legs into the bucket that held his shriveled former man parts. He was great fun for Lomis to have around, giving sound and visuals to one of the many insistent voices in his huge head.

"Twenty-five thousand dollars," he repeated again, laughing and shaking his head. The Gods of Lomis Walls ran the universe. Even hell was showing its admiration for his work by once again sending him the good father for a few moments.

"That look about right to ya?" Gannon had asked, spreading the stacks of hundred dollars bills through his bony fingers.

Lomis possessed an internal compass that gave him an uncanny ability to find places and track back no matter what the circumstances. It was in full operation as he walked and closed in on the little house at the base of the mountains. The real question was whether they were home or possibly down at that pitiful mess of a gathering in town. He moved up the driveway next to Odessa's car and touched the hood. It was warm. If the Gods were still with him, they would both be home.

A switched flipped over inside him and heat began to pour out from his middle. He could feel himself stirring and knew it had been too long. There would be hell to pay for this, and he knew he was in the right place at the right time. His big head craned up and around as he leaned up against the car and looked at the house. Dull light came from the windows, possibly candle light, he thought. He breathed deeply and recalled that thick sweetness that permeated everything inside, though not pleasant, it had become part of the erotica as he reprocessed it to fit his scheme.

He walked softly and edged up to the kitchen window and peeked through a narrow opening between the bottom slat of the cheap blinds and the window sill. Hah! The luck! The Gods of fate! Michaelen stirring a pot at the stove, large, naked breasts jiggling! He could hear her faintly singing something. Joyously! Hah! He adjusted his angle to get a peek at the kitchen table. Odessa! A bottle of Chianti. He could not tell if she was naked as well, but it didn't really matter at this point. His blood was on full boil. An erection began to rise until it strained against the zipper of his pants. He told himself to calm down, to be patient, but a sudden feeling of being out of control washed over him, grabbing at his chest, sending shock waves up through the top of his huge skull. He flattened back against the side of the house, pressing tight, feeling the tremors inside his body, the twitching everywhere as he held on, waiting for all to pass. He had no calming technique, no happy place, nothing to lead him away from this. Nor did he want that in any way. He reveled in this edge; it was as though he played and cheated with death, his toy of choice. If it didn't kill him, if he did not explode into a million pieces, he won the game, and he moved on with emboldened confidence that he was yet stronger for it. And justified. With his head tilted back against the siding on the house he could hear Michaelen singing. He closed his eyes and waited. The calm as he knew it would come back to him. Maybe this was all too much for one day. It was an oddly tedious process at best trying to figure out what to do next. Go, quickly, get far way from Sam Castle in particular, find somewhere to blend in and carry out in style. But he liked it right here in Kershaw! That was the problem. And, he felt he would be cheating Odessa and Michaelen out of their destiny if he left them with such an incomplete history. He was a great believer in fulfilling his role in the continuum of the history of the world he knew.

The calm was returning. His heart eased back inside his chest cavity, the quivering subsided and his hands steadied. The moon was full, the air clear, windbreaker crisp, carrying scents of winter ending and late spring bloom.

"Good evening, Odessa," Lomis said as she opened the front door wearing a yellow satin robe. Lomis had drawn his casted arm across the front of him, lest Odessa forget his wound.

"Lomis?" She was most parts surprised and confused and one part polite.

"You know I was out here walking on this beautiful night and, well, I just got to thinking how we kind of got off track the other night and, well, I just thought I could make things right. I thought we could maybe take a nice walk and then make things right."

"It was no big thing, Lomis, really." She seemed nervous and looked over her shoulder to see if Michaelen was on her way to the rescue yet.

"Well, maybe not to you, but I just felt I shouldn't leave things that way."

"Mich?" Odessa's voice rose. When she turned to look for her again, Lomis stepped through the half open door and grabbed Odessa around the waist with his casted arm and twisted her around until she could feel the tip of the knife in his other hand at her cheekbone. "Yes, call her. Please, Odessa. This night belongs to all of us."

CHAPTER SIXTEEN

ODESSA LET OUT A series of gasps that choked the words off and she stood rigid, eyes popped, unblinking and terrified.

"I'm busy in here right now, Dessi," came the shouting firmness of Michaelen's voice from the kitchen. "If I overcook this sauce by thirty seconds, it's crap." She resumed humming some tune her head was making up as she went along, took another long pull at the joint hanging on the edge of the counter next to the stove, wiped away a little spot of red sauce she had dripped down on a breast, then licked the finger clean.

"Just say ok," Lomis whispered, shutting the door with his left foot. "Say it!" He dug the point of his knife in until he got a spot of blood.

"Okay!" She said a bit louder than Lomis would have liked, then whispered back at him. "Why are you doing this?"

"Because this is our destiny."

"I thought we already tried that."

"That was a joke. Now. Bend over!" He commanded. Odessa did as she was told, and began to flinch as Lomis ran a hand under her robe from behind her and put a finger inside. "Wet. You little slut. You're already wet." Lomis moved behind her and positioned her in front of the couch. "Get your hands down and brace up, bitch." Her hands trembled as they settled and gripped into the middle cushion, and when she heard his zipper, her heart skipped a full beat. "You make a sound and I swear I'll slice you up. You got that?"

As Odessa nodded in silence, Lomis got hold of his aching erection and positioned it at her entrance. He laid his cast down across her back, grabbed her shoulder tightly with his other hand and readied himself. "I dare you to make a sound. I fucking dare you." He jammed himself into her in one motion causing her whole body to flinch and recoil like she had been shot. A whimper that would have been a scream came from her open mouth while the rest of her face wrinkled tight in defense. Her legs began to give out beneath her but he held her up solidly back against him and began to piston into her with a vengeance. "Been too long, bitch!"

They both looked up at the sound of the hippie beads in the hall leading from the kitchen. Michaelen froze into a pillar as she tried to comprehend. Lomis was stroking so hard and deep Odessa's feet bounced up from the floor at the top of his thrusts. Her eyes circled and tried to focus on Michaelen in the same way her open mouth wriggled to form words that never came. Instead, she began a low, steady howl that punctuated on his thrusts and gathered courage on the reloads. In the soft yellow light of the room, Lomis wasn't sure if Michaelen could see the knife in his hand flattened out on Odessa's back with the tip at the base of her scull.

An evil smile set up on Michaelen's face as she crossed her arms on her naked breasts and leaned into the wall while she watched. "You go girl," she said, shaking her head and turning back for the kitchen. "Don't mind me, people."

"He's... raping....," Odessa's squeaking words weakened to a gasp as she felt the steel tip of the knife still set to kill at the back of her skull.

"Yes... he... is...," Lomis grunted, then, challenging himself, he pushed her face down into the couch and jerked and jammed into her violently until he came, shouting and swearing at the ceiling.

"Lord, almighty!" Michaelen sang from the kitchen. She shook her head again, stirred with one hand and used the other to a press a fat boy joint up to her lips.

Lomis staggered momentarily, ignoring the incoherent ramblings coming from the stillness of Odessa beneath him. He allowed her enough room to get her head back up from the couch cushion and began to move the tip of the knife slowly down her spine. Under any other circumstances, this would have been the time for Odessa to die, but instead he found himself angling and swaying, then prodding into the wet pressure that was still there for him and soon found another rhythm that brought a wide grin to his desperate face. This time, he decided, she would take a sustained, traditional, ritualistic fucking. But no sooner had he settled on it when the voice inside his head screamed out to him. "Turn over!" He screamed back.

"Why...."

"Why? Fuck, why not? Turn over, bitch!"

Odessa turned over and sat on the couch while he spread her legs. "You do it. Put in it in your ass, bitch," he growled. He loved this part, letting his victim get a hold of him, watching as they struggled mightily with the reality. The cunt bitch in Minneapolis had refused to touch it. He was sure she enjoyed it perhaps the most of any of them and afterwards, cut her hands off and let her scream and bleed to death naked, tied at the waist to a lone tree in a remote cemetery.

Odessa's face was coated with dried tears and she seemed in a permanent daze as she reached down and grabbed the huge angled cock with both hands and guided it into her.

"Now grind on it, you bitch!"

Odessa began to crank her hips slowly, but Lomis quickly forced the pace and she had to pick up with it. The strain pulled back on her face as he looked down on her and eagerly watched the roll of her eyes. Anguish, orgasm, was it not the same thing? Eyes twinkling, jaw firming, he committed to meeting hers with his. "Now you're raping me, bitch. Go ahead!"

Lomis reasoned that each of his women had fulfilled their life in those last moments. In most cases, a killing was appropriate, and even merciful. Next to the killing itself, he was mesmerized by those last looks unique to each woman. There was nothing more powerful on earth than being able to completely possess a woman before her death. Those that he let live, while few, such as the Senator's little tryst, would never be the same. He reasoned they would ultimately die thinking about him. That saddened him at times, thinking himself weak, and possibly unfair, but those thoughts would quickly pass and he would move on to continue his work.

Michaelen listened to the final roar from Lomis and could wait no longer. She turned off the stove and pushed through the beads into the living room. She took her snap shot. Odessa on her back, satin robe draped and hanging to the floor beneath her, legs spread to each side of Lomis, who stood there, shirt open, jeans crumpled at mid calf, chest heaving, dripping sweat onto Odessa's tiny breasts while he braced on one arm. Then she saw the knife in his hand.

"Tell me that's just part of the kinky," Michaelen said, feeling uncomfortable with the words.

Lomis looked over at her and down at Odessa, then realizing Michaelen had likely seen the knife, wagged it at her and beckoned her to come closer. Lomis used the long tip of the knife to circle one of Odessa's nipples. He picked up her limp hand and toyed with it while Odessa lay still beneath him, eyes down, dull, watching his ooze drip onto her belly.

As she slowly walked closer, Michaelen wrapped her arms around her breasts as though she was suddenly embarrassed by being exposed and stopped in her tracks a few feet away. She felt the spirits of hell in the room, stretching their way out through the body of Lomis Walls, seeing through his glassy, wide-angled eyes. She shuddered at the sudden notion she was vulnerable to this spirit. It was her custom to fend off the spirits that usually swept down off the mountains in the middle of the night and tried as they might to speak to her, sending her a message she could never quite understand. Maybe this was it. All along, it had been a warning. "So you are here," she said, gazing up at the ceiling.

Lomis shot her a satisfied look and pointed to his swaying cock, giving it a little entertaining pump. "All right here, waiting for the big black mama next."

Michaelen laughed. "Oh honey, you are the devil his self. Imagine that. You are the devil his self right in my living room."

Lomis was elated, almost unable to contain himself. "I am he that you seek, child." He eased himself back from Odessa and turned to present himself to Michaelen. "Where are your manners, child?" He walked towards Michaelen, waving the knife back at Odessa. "And don't you move, white bitch. I'll cut this black woman up so fast you won't know blood from skin." He stopped a foot in front of Michaelen and moved his hips upward to give her a better look at what he had in store for her. "You been wanting to suck on that your whole life, black mama, so get to it now." Lomis pulled her towards him, pointed the knife at her face and forced her down on him.

The moment she bit down he whipped her away. "Damn! fuck!" he screamed and cracked her cheekbone with a full fist, sending her head crashing into the wall. Odessa pulled up into a ball on the couch and closed her eyes, hands over her ears. "Fucking bitch!" Lomis screamed, going after Michaelen, slapping her face with his good hand then cranking his casted forearm across her nose. It was all he could do not to crush her face completely when he realized it was not a good place for her to bleed. "You... " he calmed himself and looked down at his cock to see if it was bleeding. Best he could tell he was alright, and still rock hard. "...Try that again, you will die a slow death, I assure you...."

"Why...?" Michaelen rasped. "Why are you doing this, you sick fuck? It doesn't have to be like this." She wiped at her lip and gathered herself into a sitting position on the floor.

Lomis lurched towards her and grabbed the back of her hair and forced her up against the wall. He adjusted his grip, shook her head side to side as hard as he could, then positioned himself at her mouth. This time she opened with a shrill cry and he sunk himself to the back of her throat. "You better breathe through your broken nose, black mama. I'm not done with you yet!"

When he was done with her, Lomis tied Michaelen up with an extension cord, then ripped a lamp cord loose to use on Odessa before turning back to Michaelen. "Car keys?" he asked, winking at her as they both listened to the Odessa whimper.

"In the kitchen, you fucking nut job," Michaelen said. She spit at him and caught his chin with a thin strand.

"Fucking... outstanding," Lomis said, turning and walking into the kitchen. He found a set of car keys hanging on a hook near the back door and quickly moved back into the living room. "Lovely night for a drive, don't you think, ladies?" he asked. He cut some of the extra cord from Michaelen's binding and used it to lash up Odessa's hands in front of her. "What the hell is with you, girl? Man, you are one boring fuck. No wonder you're a carpet muncher."

Odessa looked up him, her eyes pleading for sanity, for the nightmare to end, to wake up tomorrow and be grateful for the sun.

Michaelen's mouth was so swollen she could barely get words out. "fu... yu, yu cuksukr."

"Now that's funny," Lomis said. "Say, we'll just take a little ride so you two can't get a head start on getting me tracked down, ok? And of course, if you did, I'd have to come back and kill you, wouldn't I? And I wouldn't want to do that. I'll drive you to the other side of town, throw your keys somewhere and take off. No harm, no foul. Okay?"

They both looked up at him in a complete daze.

"Okay then, get up, both of you." He pulled Odessa up off the couch and straightened her robe, tying it, then gave a lingering look at the large nipples on Michaelen's jutting breasts. He cupped one firmly then tweaked the nipple between his thumb and index finger. "We need to get you a robe, too, don't we?" Se sunk his fingers into Odessa's arm. "Don't be going anywhere. We'll be right back."

Michaelen and Lomis moved off to a bedroom to fetch the silk robe hanging on a hook behind the door. Lomis gently draped it over her shoulders and moved it around her and her bound hands, his fingers stopping to retrace their paths as they felt her warmth underneath mix with the smooth fabric. "Odessa!" Lomis yelled. "Get in here. Now!"

Odessa stumbled into the room and leaned into a wall, each step reminding her of the searing pain still burning inside her middle. She imagined she was nothing but torn pieces of useless flesh inside and would never be the same.

Lomis bent Michaelen over the bed on her elbows. "I almost forgot how you black mamas got this hip thing that presents your pussy for fucking." He got in behind her and flipped her robed up. "Oh yeah," he said, hardening once again and circling her vaginal lips with the end of his cock. Then he looked down and joyfully watched her face contort against the bed sheets as he wedged himself in with a series of short penetrating jerks until he hit bottom. "Look at that damn pussy jump up to meet me. You gotta love a thing like that, Odessa. Watch now, we're gonna get this thing going real quick like." Lomis began moving his hips and spitting angry words and uttering sounds that seemed to be in another language, pounding into Michaelen until she started to cry out in pain against the sheets. Hearing her gain volume, Lomis stopped his ranting and a smile drew broadly across his face, his jaw tightened, a wild twitch worked through his temples, he grabbed her around the waist with one hand from the front side and drove his thrusts with violent force until he felt something give way inside of her. She screamed for him to stop, then again, but he was grunting like a wild animal and held her even tighter, buoyed by his success, trying to spear at whatever he had damaged or broken. "Black cunts are all the same in the end, mama. Can't take the white man's fucking." Lomis looked at Odessa to capture her eyes while he breathed noisily through his mouth and bucked and rocked his hips forward with a final burst. That feeling was always there for him right then. The immediate emptiness of being back at the unmerciful beginning of nothing. Saddened and suddenly knowing this moment of completely predictable insanity he would once again endure, he considered the hotter than usual flush around his cock as he pulled back out, looked down and saw a heavy splat of cum and blood puddle up on the floor between his Nikes. "Get up, cunt!" he yelled at Michaelen, pulling her back up by her hair, turning her around and slapping her twice before throwing her into Odessa. "And you make a fucking mess, yet!" He grabbed at the bloodied sheet and crumpled it, taking a few moments to wipe himself clean, then cleaned up the floor and moved to Michaelen and jammed the sheet up between her legs. "Get anymore on the floor and your dead. Understand? Get some bleach. You, Odessa, get some bleach, bitch. Now! Step to it!"

Neither woman could verbalize. The terror had sunk in and taken over. The only question that floated in and out was how to survive, if they would, or how and when they would die.

When he was satisfied they had bleached and cleaned up any possible trace of blood or fluids in their playground, Lomis straightened and tightened the robes around the women like a tailor admiring finished work, picked up the empty plastic bottle of Clorox, and grabbed the sheet he had stuck up between Michaelen's legs. He looked down on it. "Good chance you won't bleed to death. Let's get you some slippers and get in the car."

Lomis drove the car north of town a short ways, then turned on a gravel road and drove another couple of minutes before stopping. They moved out of the car and he urged them to walk just ahead of him down an apparent path. "I'll take you to a safe spot, you'll stay there until you see the tail lights from the car disappear, then you can walk back to town. I'll leave your car back in your driveway. I'll be long gone when you get back. You'll never see me again. I think we can rule out you having any goddam cell phones jammed up your cunts." He stopped a moment to enjoy. "Hey, that's funny, right there," he said, mimicking Larry the Cable Guy.

"You think you'll get away with this...." Michaelen rasped. "Never...."

"Mama, I wouldn't do it if I didn't think I would get away with it. What in hell is the matter with you? You should be enjoying this more. Especially you. This is your moment in history."

"You're one sick puke," she muttered, thinking she could not be in more pain. Odessa was unaware she was whimpering audibly with each breath.

Lomis heard her but was growing weary of all of it. Odessa was surprisingly the better fuck, but none of it was particularly good.

The emptiness continued to claw at him longer than usual and he committed to never doing the double thing ever again. No memories worth carrying. It was mostly like work.

Lomis pulled a tiny LED flashlight from his pocket and panned ahead. "Just over the next rise." As they continued to walk ahead. Lomis dropped back and turned the flashlight off. The two women stood still suddenly, looking up to the moonlight, then fumbling for each other in the dark. Lomis gathered speed and crashed into them from behind, hearing only the beginnings of screams as they fell into the hole he had dug days before. They struggled to try to gain footing while Lomis turned the flashlight back on to assist his aim of the carefully selected large rocks from the pile he had stacked just in case this option presented itself. He caught Odessa square in the forehead with one rock and she fell helplessly to the bottom of the hole. Michaelen was screaming filth and swearing vengeance as the earth gave way under her grip. Lomis held a large rock above his head and took aim at her head below him, but instead watched and listened with amusement as she struggled to climb out. He set the rock down and waited until she was nearly up and out before training the flashlight beam on her. With the little energy she had left she dragged herself on all fours until she collapsed on level ground.

Her breath was coming in uneven gasps as Lomis spun her over on her back and put a heavy knee down on her chest. "Never really thanked you properly for that little biting incident back at the house, did I," he said. With that he moved his knife into his good hand, steadied her head back with his arm cast across her forehead and forced her mouth open. He moved the blade in quickly against the vibration of her attempts to scream and worked it down far enough to get most of her tongue with a quick gouging slice, tossed the clump of ragged flesh into the hole and rolled her in after it. Then he listened. Under the pale blue chards of moonlight came the sounds of a mortally wounded animal gurgling blood, choking on itself, spitting the blood only to find it could not keep up with the flow.

"So long, black mama. Won't miss your sweet ass, unfortunately." He flashed the beam down on her face for a final look. He was most pleased. No need for the rock. He smiled, nodded up towards his Gods and grabbed the shovel instead.

CHAPTER SEVENTEEN

"This is about my fourth trip back into my teens today," Sam said, his head setting in his hands, looking up at a sky full of stars sitting in galaxies he never thought about before.

"Tell me more," Liv purred, curling into the crook of his arm beneath the sheets. It was her idea to move the mattress off the bed onto the deck off her upstairs bedroom.

"I figured you'd slept with him, anyhow."

"With John?"

Sam didn't have to restate it. "I was jealous. I mean school boy jealous."

Liv laughed. "My my. John Boy is a real hunk, isn't he?"

"A real hunk. Yeah, I deserve that, I suppose."

"And so are you. And I know absolutely nothing about you while I know John Boy better than maybe any man on earth, yet here I am, naked under the sheets with you, possibly putting my whole political career in jeopardy. How do you figure that?"

"Why not the senator, then?"

"I think too much of his wife, and their two kids."

A sigh of relief escaped Sam's mouth. "So my plan to see what it would be like to go to bed with somebody famous is alive and well."

They made love again, this time more patiently, tenderly, a long, wet, luxurious hug that moved easily into a peaceful sleep.

Liv awoke first. "Talk to me," she whispered in his ear.

Sam was smiling in a light sleep when she said it again, louder.

"Talk to me, Sam the man."

"What?" He sat up, startled and bracing for a moment. His wife, when she was Karen Parker, would say it just like that, usually when he could tell her even less, usually when all she needed was to be held and loved. He shuttered the thoughts back, let his heartbeat catch its rhythm and grabbed on to the moment, turning one open eye at Liv, noting even half asleep, with one eyed closed, she was one beautiful woman.

She sat up next to him and put her face within inches of his. "Would what I know and feel about you after four days change much if I really knew who you were?"

Sam would have wished to take a lifetime without fielding that question. "What if I don't want to take that chance?"

"Big, brave man like you?"

He cradled her back into him. "Brave. I need to be brave?"

"Very brave."

He looked into her eyes and gently pulled her hair back so he could get a better look.

She stared him back down. "So how long will you be an evasive shit? I'm not saying I need to get you tested, but... well, do I?"

"Tested for?"

"Any number of things."

"Maybe too late for some."

"Okay. Then let me ask you this. You haven't had sex in a while, have you?" Liv asked.

"That would be an understatement. Probably need some work?"

"Lots of it. But we'll get you up to speed. No worries."

They wrestled with each other and she ended up on top, looking down at him, studying his face, touching his jaw line scars. She strummed a finger on his chin. "The way I see it, we are stuck with each other until you stop doing what you do to me or screw up like the rest of your species."

"I see. Probably right. A guy should be a little careful about matching wits with a young, smart woman like you, let alone a powerful celebrity."

"Before you get carried away, this is a pretty small pond I swim in."

"For now."

"For now." She propped her head up on an elbow and tucked the sheet up around her exposed breast. "This would seem to be the right time to ask. Really. What am I dealing with? Married, running away from home? Divorced? Bullshit king?"

"None of the above."

"I do have a theory."

"Which is?"

"I think you were married. Something that didn't end or feel well at the end for you. I get that. When your eyes flash at me and strip me naked at the same time, I can't get my clothes off fast enough." There was a lusty edge to her laugh. "But sometimes I sense there is another set of eyes in there and they are very sad."

Sam wanted to tell her the empty look was actually the extra set of eyes he kept when needed- to watch out for windowless vans, or whatever was coming next or where they were coming from. It was right then he realized a man with a past like his could never expect to outlive it. The best you could do was stay in the moment, like this one, when the only thoughts needed were none at all.

But a mind conflicted could not shut down that easy. "I was married. She was a heroin addict and died of an overdose. Can I say end of story for now?" He shot it out as if that could be all she really needed to know and understand.

"Hardly. Honestly, that kind of chills me. Does she deserve more of an epitaph than that?"

While he tried to keep the mood from eroding, Sam struggled with a collision of thoughts bashing around as if suddenly released from bondage. "I don't know. It wasn't very pleasant for her or for me for quite some time."

"Heroin. God, what set her off in that direction?"

"There are answers which turn into more questions. There was love there a long time ago, no question about that. It's really only been a couple of weeks since she died."

"Oh my God. I'm... sorry." Liv suddenly felt very creepy about having slept with a man who just buried his wife. She sat up and wrapped her arms down under her knees. "You could have told me that."

"I could have. I apologize for that. Being with you these past few days has been like learning to live again. The marriage died long ago. If anything, it was my fault. And her slide was slow but steady and unstoppable. I traveled a lot, internationally, and she couldn't deal with it at some point. I don't know, I suppose a switch flipped and she was off. In the end, I think she was doing some small town, high-class hooker gig to support her habit. But honestly, I never spent a day blaming her for anything. I didn't. She never got what she bargained for. And I never really stopped to consider what would happen when she figured that out, until it was too late."

Liv gave him a strange look to see if there was some possibility he was joking. "Where did you travel?"

"Asia, India, mostly." Sam could feel the grip of regret having allowed the subject to get this far.

"Doing what?"

"Real Estate appraisal, risk analysis, that sort of thing."

"For?"

Sam adjusted on the bed and put his arms around his knees. "Private concerns. Syndicates out of London," he lied. "A lot of Blind Trust stuff where I never had to know much as long as the check cleared at the bank."

Liv studied him a moment and had to make a decision about pursuing this further or setting off the bullshit alarm and asking to know more than he was willing to share at this point. She didn't really want to risk giving legs to the morbid pall that was starting to erode their magic.

"So my stranger…, the future First Man of the First Lady, has some history. I'll get the F.B.I. on it first thing in the morning. I can't risk a closet full of skeletons, you know."

Sam should have at least faked a flinch or at least blinked, but instead shrugged and smiled up at her. "I'll tell you more another time. Honest."

"Honest. Okay. Just tell me you are not wanted by the law or have not committed any heinous crimes I need to worry about. Maybe I'll leave it at that for now."

Sam smiled weakly. "Good."

She resumed a study of his face. Liv was young for the perspectives she carried with her but a great deal could be attributed to the attention she paid to faces. She reasoned both truth and lies took little effort, but when deceit became a habit, the face eventually seemed to become weary of the work, reacting in subtle, involuntary ways. "There are things about you, tall stranger. I hope they are not bad things."

They sat in silence, then eased back onto the sheets and resumed a communion with the sky. Few words were needed to agree making love again was an absolute must. As she clung to Sam as they finished he battled with the voice in his head telling him his secrets were too large to hide. But he battled and won, again, and left the battlefield victorious, silent, and moving forward.

"Are you staying?" Liv asked.

"Would it make me too shifty and dark if I said I really planned on being here, just like this, and nothing more? Or would that be too sappy for you?"

"The thing about me you need to know is, I like sappy, I like philosophical, I like love notes, and I like flowers."

"Anything else?"

"I have a great ass."

"We've covered that."

"I'm smart, tough, and probably downright tenacious about doing something that will make a difference, but my other side, the one close to where your hand is right now... needs and wants love and all love has to offer."

Sam stroked her hair and left his other hand where it was.

"Are you too jaded to love again?" she asked. "You don't have to answer that right now, but I needed to throw it out there... because."

"Because?"

"Be... cuzzzzzz, maybe I could fall in love with you. Maybe I have already."

Sam took her face gently between his hands and kissed her gently, then hugged and rocked her in his arms. "I'm staying."

Her face turned into a wide grin.

"But... given your tender years, I am a little curious about what you might have learned about love and its usual pretenders."

"A fair question. No marriage. No current boy friend. Easy answer. No girlfriend either, for that matter."

Sam raised a brow.

"Figured you would like that," Liv said. "Every man's fantasy. I've been told I would make a perfect lesbian."

Sam winced and looked under the sheets. "That would be a major disappointment."

"Part of me, maybe. Not the sexual part. The part that sees the beauty and sensibilities in other women. I will admit, for the most part, I think most men I have known seem ultimately humbled by a woman with strong... sensibilities. There seems to be something in the species that weakens and pathetically falls back in the wake of a strong woman."

"Fascinating. There you go, turning me on again."

Liv said no more, smiled and ducked her head under the sheets.

CHAPTER EIGHTEEN

It was no surprise to anyone in Kershaw that the obituary of Joshua Gannon made the front page of the Ketchum Gazette and even rated a small photo on the obituary page in the Idaho Statesman. He was supposed be long gone before Christmas, yet here he was with his fresh ashes about to be scattered on a cold, clear day in mid-January.

Livian Gannon looked up at the bluest sky from the promontory point where he first brought her when she was four, gave a glistening wink to Sam Castle standing beside her, then tossed her grandfather's ashes into the light breeze that carried the small gray cloud north towards the snow swept mountains, then down onto a stand of barren aspens and yellow pines.

"Sleep well," she whispered. "I love you." Matching streaks of tears ran down either cheek.

News of Joshua Gannon's passing faded into memory for most around town, but the story about the disappearance of the two odd females living up on Cherry Lane that kept mostly to themselves lingered on. Charlie Talbot, the Kershaw Chief of Police figured they were weird enough to take off in the middle of the night for God knows where, and who really gave a shit anyway. But when Charlie had to deal with the missing persons report filed by the clinic in town where Odessa worked, he ended up prying open the back door to find a quiet, orderly house, kitchen clean, beds made, doors locked. There was no car in the drive or in the old garage. He checked with Lyle Warburton, who owned several small homes like this one and rented most out on six-month leases. The rent had not been paid in all of these months, nor had he been contacted by the women. Charlie stopped short of being able to explain the spoiled food left in the refrigerator, the clothes in the closet, the toothpaste in the medicine cabinet and the massive collection of dildos and sex toys in a linen closet in the hallway, but, as he maintained from the beginning, they were just a couple of odd ducks who could have been very capable of just up and going in the middle of the night on a whim. They had only lived in Kershaw for two years as it was. Kershaw was used to seeing most people come and go, for whatever reason. More moved on than stayed once they had their fill of the majestic mountains and endless green valley views. For those that stayed, the steady movement provided endless hours of speculation and chatter, always kept alive and well by Sarah Johansen. "The usual stuff," Charlie concluded, ending his report with a notation about the three marijuana plants shriveled up under a burned out grow lamp he came across in the basement. "Oggle the mountains, get high, kinky sex, get bored, move on. Nothing new."

As for Liv Gannon, it was business as usual on a Wednesday, that being there was mayoring at hand, an irrigation district petition to consider and a proposal from the county to annex some land.

"Your free lunch is here," came Sam's voice over her shoulder while she was pouring over the county attorney's legalese. God forbid she would find it necessary to be or act or write like a lawyer to further her political career. She put a hand out behind her that waited for one of his. She loved his hands; big, strong and they always felt like they had been warmed over a fire. Sam had set up a small engine repair service in the little ramshackle building that used to be a one car garage at the back of the property behind Liv's office. Word did get around pretty quick that the new stranger that had taken up residence with the Kershaw mayor was a whiz at fixing almost anything. He tinkered with everything from old sewing machines to microwaves. Some nut case had even entrusted him to fix his balky ultra light plane at the risk of limb and life. It worked just fine after Sam Castle reworked the fuel injection system.

He grabbed her hand and folded it into his.

"Still the one?" she asked, still reading, not looking up.

"Always the one," he answered, squeezing her hand.

She didn't have to look up. Smiling to herself, she knew he was standing there in his tan denim shirt, a grease stain or two, filling out the snug blue jean just so and sporting that new tickly soft full beard that set his dark eyes off somewhere she loved trying to reach.

They sat at a small wobbly round table on the back porch eating peanut butter and blueberry jam sandwiches he had made early in the morning. He poured milk into oversized glazed coffee mugs and they clicked and kissed.

"Better than this?" she asked.

Sam shrugged, but did not hesitate. "Saturday mornings, waking up, effing your brains out."

"Okay. Agreed. Other than that?"

Sam just smiled his answer. "Actually, any morning waking up and effing your brains out."

"What a species... ." she lamented. "Amazing, isn't it?"

"Say what?"

"Nothing. In your perfect world, apparently I would be braless and brainless."

"No argument there. And what is with this *species* thing?"

"It explains what otherwise can't be explained." She touched his forearm with her finger.

They kissed again and opened up the third sandwich to share. "So what's the deal on this one?" she asked suspiciously.

Sam's look of innocence was not selling.

"It's not cut diagonally," she said, pointing to the untouched sandwich on the paper plate. "You always cut diagonally."

Sam looked at his own half. "I'll be damned."

Liv was still not sure about the I-might-be-the-new-Jesus look. She thought sometimes it made him look older than when he was clean shaven, and beards usually meant a person was hiding something either in the beard or elsewhere. Sometimes she found herself staring at him until the little girl goofiness came over her and made her laugh out loud. "You eat yours first," she said.

Sam bent over clutching his stomach to accommodate her humor. Not a day had gone by that he didn't think about who might still be after him or who might have thought he was dead, or if, in fact, there was anybody that really cared one way or another. He had not called Dragon again, though he had thought about it many times. On most days, he convinced himself that the bottom line was he didn't officially exist anyway, and long as he kept to himself and kept the demons locked in the closet, he had a reasonable shot at starting a new life. On other days, he awoke to the reality he would always be who he really was.

On days like this, there was just this young, incredible woman to deal with. Who could possibly ask for more than that? But then there was the unsettling, almost manic return of the thought process that insisted he continue to try to figure out what happened to his diamonds. He didn't know how, but he would have bet his life Lomis Walls had more than just something to do with it, and the fact he had disappeared into thin air, though not particularly surprising, gnawed at him and at times turned him into a pacing, ranting lunatic. That was not for Liv's eyes or ears, nor was any of this, but his better side of logic also kept telling him that the better things got, the sooner he would need to level with her. He figured he stood an even chance of losing her either way.

Switching heartbeats, there was doubt in his mind he could simply take off and track down Lomis Walls, settle out his suspicions, and be back in time for lunch.

She smiled as only she could. "Hey, what do you say we take a run up to Sun Valley for the weekend. "There's over a foot of new snow. It would be perfect. Great hot tubs outside. You'll love it."

Sam smiled back at her. "Not much of a skier. I do well in a hot tub though." Sometimes when she talked he could see why she was capable of lighting up rooms, and cities, maybe even a country. "Like I would say no."

"We will be on the black diamond runs in no time," Liv said.

The word "diamond" stuck him like a knife in the gut again and he was sure it showed. "Right. Black diamond...."

"Scared, little boy? Don't be." She put her hand over his, then grabbed hold of it and walked him back to his little shop of parts and bolts. "What are you working on?"

"Mrs. Kendrick's air conditioner."

"It's the middle of winter."

"I know. I think she just wants to watch my ass when I put it back in her window. She's hot."

"She's ninety-one."

"And hot. Just ask her. There's hot old ladies all over this town. Anyway, the compressor went out on it late last summer and she wants to be ready for summer number ninety-two."

Liv's smirk led to that other glimmer in her eyes. She glanced out the window towards her office, considered the large snowflakes beginning to fall, then sank to her knees and unzipped him just as he grabbed a small wrench. One thing led to a lot of things, with tools bouncing around everywhere, and before all was said and done, Sam's little workshop was turned upside down.

As he watched the sway of Liv's gait back up the walkway to her office, Sam wished to think of little else. For him, the unlikeness of it all, the story line that kept unfolding with a precision that seemed to favor him for basically just showing up, also brutally crystallized the reality that could lay patiently waiting. Given Liv seemed to accept his past in generalities instead of demanding the gory details, all things considered, it was an easy deal being this Sam Castle guy; covered up in old denim and beard hair, equal parts slobbering romantic, quiet genius, sexual giant and small appliance repair guru.

Liv opened the door to her office, kicked the snow off her boots and waved back at him. She knew full well he hadn't taken his eyes off her swaying backside the whole time. A little, nonsensical happy melody popped up in her head and she hummed it for most of the afternoon as she got back into the legal documents at her mayor's desk.

Sam flicked a switch on an old Sylvania radio sitting on the window sill, then changed his mind and opted for the 8-track player he had plucked from an estate auction the week before. Broken beyond repair and destined for the trash, he paid three bucks for it as-is, angled up into a cracked plastic paint bucket that also contained cartridges from 1970's artists- Black Sabbath, Vanilla Fudge, Blood, Sweat and Tears and Iron Butterfly, among others dead or forgotten. "You Keep Me Hanging On", Vanilla Fudge style began to blare through his little reworked miracle as he reached under the work bench for the bottle of Jack Daniels. A couple of hefty belts and back under it went. The soldering iron was ready for Mrs. Kendrick's air conditioner.

"Get the damn thing to work and there's one helluva blow job in it for you," Mrs. Kendrick had said with a big wink as he set it down in the back of his pick up truck. Sam had considered a reply but just nodded and piled it into the truck, realizing anything he said would perhaps encourage a more wide ranging promise. It seemed to him there was something wonderfully prowling and ageless about the women in Kershaw.

CHAPTER NINETEEN

"Good riddance to that old fuck," said the grizzled barrel of a man with a painfully whisper thin voice and chest length beard. "Lying bag of bones."

His much smaller associate adjusted uncomfortably on the creaking stool next to him.

Lomis imagined the bearded one could have crushed the little man with a single slam of his gigantic fist. Antsy, out-of-his-mind bored, he found a life spent simply spending money was lacking. There was no smell to his life. Missing was the scent of fear on a woman, the heated metallic sour at his jowls as blood burst through the air of killing, and mostly the smell of heat rising, his own, with the anticipation of the screaming, watching agony play itself out in yet another way unique to his victim. He missed fulfilling history.

"All is I know is Gannon screwed me out of twenty acres when he was mayor," the big man rumbled with a belch.

The shot of Jim Beam wobbled at Lomis Walls' lips. He turned a steady eye again to the bearded one. Guys like that were easy for Lomis to hate. It was immediate. "Hey! Did you say Gannon? You talking about Josh Gannon?" Lomis asked, purposely shouting to be heard loud and clear.

The bearded one turned with contempt for being interrupted. "Right. I was talking. You got that part right. And you got the Gannon part right. But I wasn't talking to you, so I suggest you shut the fuck up, unless I ask you a question."

Lomis Walls almost cuddled up with the potential threat being tossed his way. He usually hung out at another bar off the beaten path in Ketchum, but he had decided to grace Lefty's Short Steer for a change of pace. There were only a few bars in Ketchum where you could get

121

away from the freshly powdered smell of the haughty tourists. He figured Lefty's was one of those and he was right. And it was within walking distance of the room he rented above an old garage on Benardi Road. The twenty-five grand had allowed him a life of undetermined luxury; that of eating and drinking when he pleased, a quiet room, a warm bed, cable television and soft porn channels, and a garage below him where Odessa and Michaelen's car stayed parked under an old tarp he scrounged from the dumpster behind the grocery store. He hadn't killed since Odessa and Michaelen; instead, deciding to stay around in a defying act of courage because Sun Valley and the Wood River Valley just seemed like a quiet place to spend some time and the money until the Gods would dictate his next move. They had always told him what to do, he realized, and in this place, the winds of the Gods came softly, sweetly, and smelled fresh, and whistled a tune when they felt good enough to do so.

He dared himself to remain silent instead of responding to the big bearded man. He challenged himself to still work it on his terms as he sorted through the urges that came natural to him. This was not the longest stretch, but it was beginning to feel like it, especially with the cash dwindling down.

His eyes blinked and a familiar twitch began to work through his cheekbone. But be smart about this, as always, he cautioned himself. Be smart. Bigger men had the tendency to underestimate him and he could literally feel the adrenalin heating up his center in anticipation of a great slaying, an event for the ages, watching the bigger man collapse like crushed foil as he first ripped the arms away from the shoulder sockets before sinking the narrow stiletto blades into each ear until the tips met in the middle of a very small brain. Eyes would bulge, blood would flow and foam from the mouth and nose. Beads of sweat began to form above his lip as he shot the Jim Beam down.

"I think I know the man, is all." Lomis checked his voice back. "No problem, man. Carry on."

"Like I was saying," he said, eyeing Lomis, "That son of bitch Gannon screwed me more than once when he was the fucking mayor of Kershaw. I threatened to kill him once when he made me move a fence line. He told me I would never get around to it before he died and that was the only thing the son of a bitch was right about. The cocksucker."

Christ, he fucked just about everybody in the county out of something from what I hear."

It appeared the little man was going to try to say something but it got caught inside of a cough that choked it off.

"So how is it he got reelected so many times?" Lomis snickered, taking another drink.

"Yeah. Fuck you. So now I hear his little granddaughter is the mayor. How do you like that shit? I hear she's going to run for state senate next year. Yeah, well sure, why the fuck not? Hell. You seen her? I'd nail that little twat in a heart beat."

Lomis waited in silence for a few moments and sipped at his beer. "You the king around here or something? Is everybody like, scared of you or something like that?"

The big man nodded at his little friend. "I believe we have ourselves one smart-ass punk over here." He said it loud enough for the few patrons paying any attention to pay a little more, including Jerry, the bartender, who dropped his bar rag in disgust and walked over to stand firm between the approaching big man and Lomis. "Siegfried. Now you listen to me because I'm only going to say this once. This has got to be damn near the only bar around you can still walk into. Don't cause any trouble."

Siegfried Scharrschmidt grinned widely. "Listen to old Jerry, here. He thinks because he's my brother-in-law I won't take a crack at him. Hmm. What do you think?"

The little man next to him shuttered through a short symphony that sounded like a mix of coughing and laughing that was mostly excess phlegm and gurgled snot.

Jerry tapped his fingers on the bar nervously. He looked big enough to carry himself, but it was a well known fact among the locals that Siegfried Scharrschmidt could fight meaner and dirtier than anybody, and had served time for kicking a man's head in the middle of Main Street in Ketchum some years before. Sig's little sister, Jerry's wife Mary Beth, was a peach, and just as scared of her big brother as everybody else in town.

Lomis was in a feeding frenzy over the fear and uncertainty in the bar at this point. He could feel it, smell it, and the only thing missing was the blood flying around in suspended animation. He could visualize it though. What a way to break out of the drought. Beat some big tough guy to death. Maybe with his own arm? Bloody conquest. A growing stack of bodies decomposing in the earth. It was his destiny, and that of so many others.

"You know," Lomis said calmly, "I had a run-in with Gannon as well not that long before he died."

Sig took a deep breath, rolled his eyes, sucked down half of a Harvey Wallbanger from a red straw in a tall, thin frosted glass and turned to Lomis. "Yeah?"

"Yeah. See, he and I did this business deal and let's just say he likely got the better of it. Fact is, I'm pretty sure he cheated me out of most of it, see."

"No surprise there. Course, you could be just some dumb shit stick."

"Think so?"

Sig shook his head. "Just another ugly ass stranger around here."

"I can go with that, big man." Lomis swallowed back his fiery outrage.

"Hah!" The big man had a laugh in him after all, though more of a guttural spew than a laugh.

The little guy, Charles, said something that Lomis could not make out before succumbing to yet another snot fest. When he recovered, Sig leaned over and began to whisper something into the little guy's ear, occasionally glancing up in the direction of Lomis. They both began to laugh uproariously. Lomis figured it was all at his expense, and began to feed off the gut clenching that was beginning to fire up inside of him.

They both cracked into the same gaudy laughs accompanied by physical noises, slurps and gassy escapes that had Jerry covering his ears and grabbing the remote for the television. "Time for Wheel of Fortune," said Jerry.

Lomis rose and stood still for a few moments before walking to the men's room. He could feel the bands tightening around his head, then his chest and abdomen and down. The springs all began to twist and synchronize, creating a soft humming noise at the middle of his brain. There was sunshine in the meadow, and tiny orange, purple, red and yellow flowers swaying gently over sloping hills of wheat grass that ran off to a never ending horizon. It was his infinity, life everlasting, a world of calm over fear, strong over weak, death over life for the sake of life, holding him tight, bracing for full assault. Thoughts of living a relatively peaceful existence that recently loomed large enough to be considered seriously were sinking into places too far to recall. Instead, the ideas and methodology of causing as much pain as possible, sexual fulfillment and taking life resumed a normal coursing through him, convincing him once again he could and should not play with destiny. Call it some time off for bad behavior. Whatever. He was ready to rock and roll again. Perhaps it would be Gannon that would frame the rage, and others would have to pay. Many others. Right or wrong, a done deal or just a play on his mind, the only thing that mattered was a rightful revenge; a God-pleasing rightful revenge.

Maybe it was time to let old Lomis Walls go. Time once again for a new name. He thought about this as he polished his knife on the cloth towel roll in the men's room. Nah. He liked Lomis Walls just fine. Lomis seemed to be the most powerful of them all. Just a few more moments to plan it out, another quick polish, flicking the sharp edge with the flat of his thumb, giving himself a smiling glance in the mirror before walking back into the bar. He shuffled over and peeked through the orange neon on the front window, looking out at the lights of early evening bouncing off the piles of plowed snow, then moved to the small square window in the front door. He deftly slid one arm down to see how his luck was going to run. If there was a turn button on the dead bolt lock the day was about to get better, sooner. Oh yes! The Lomis Walls show was about to begin. He felt the lock click over as he turned the button with his fingers and began a slow walk back towards the bar, eyes darting around, sweeping for any security cameras. He didn't figure a place like Lefty's would have entered the world of surveillance, but he had to be sure. There was the big man and his little man, Jerry the bartender and a quiet table of three, two men and a woman, over in the corner. Do-able, but the first thing to do was minimize risk.

Lomis edged towards Siegfried and Charles, holding the handle of his knife with the blade running up under his shirtsleeve along his forearm. He quickened the last few steps until he was behind Sig and pulled out the knife waist high. Before Sig could turn to him, Lomis had the blade easily buried into Sig's kidney, withdrew it and plunged it back into the other kidney, then quickly in and out again. Sig straightened and gasped, seeming to hover on his stool until a sound from inside of him began to build into a full screech. He tried to stand but began to crumble sideways into little Charles. "Damm… shit! What the.…" The words fell from bloody spit.

Charles began to stagger under Sig's weight and the ruckus got Jerry's attention. He moved quickly from behind the bar and leaned down over Sig and tried to make sense of his rambling cuss against the backdrop of Pat Sajak's voice.

Lomis took a moment to gauge the three people at the table engrossed in conversation. Perhaps they had become too oblivious to Sig's previous antics to pay any attention. If they did notice, they were probably hoping he really had dropped dead.

Lomis drew the knife back out of his pocket and as Jerry leaned over Sig, he buried the blade into the base of Jerry's skull just above the neck line, feeling the pop and crackle as he sliced in deep enough. Jerry collapsed in total silence over Sig's body. Charles was about to give up trying to prop up Sig's head, and just as he began to catch on to what was happening, the blood coated blade entered his heart. Charles sounded like a balloon slowly losing its air as he looked up at Lomis, one hand failing to grab at the lapel of his open jacket, his eyes rolling back and slumping off the stool while Lomis guided his body down so he could die peacefully against Jerry's back. It was a nice, neat stack, all things considered, a bonus, all that blood mixing and pooling together. A pile of useless flesh the world would never miss.

"What the hell?" A man's disbelieving voice drifted into Lomis's ears from the corner table. Before he could get an answer he was quickly urging the other two up out of their seats and began moving for the door. He turned the knob. Then again, then frantically, banging at the door with a flattened hand as he attempted to pull it open. By the time he figured the dead bolt had been turned and reached for it, he felt the sudden heat and pain that came with the knife entering the middle of his back. The scream came, strong at first, then another, weaker, as Lomis twisted the blade, withdrew it, and plunged it back in. He felt organs ripping loose as he let the man slump to the floor and whirled to face the other two. They were frozen six feet away, stilled at the sight of the blood dripping off the blade and the smile that broadened on the face of their captor.

"Fate, it seems, would have its way with all of us this evening, would it not?" Lomis said softly as they slowly backed away.

"Please, mister. Please!", The woman pleaded before beginning to sob.

"Do not scream. Do not move another inch." They froze and Lomis stopped moving as well, still holding the knife and likewise admiring the dripping blood. "Sit down. Right where you are. Just drop. Those will be great seats, trust me." They dropped to the floor.

Lomis moved back to his pile of death and found Sig was still fussing a bit at the bottom. He figured he would let him suffer plenty before he died, but just to be sure, he grabbed the long beard, and twisted it until he got Sig to look up at him.

Sig's eyes fluttered and his words came weak and breathy.

"What?" Lomis asked. He looked back over his shoulder at his audience of two. "I don't recall asking this gentleman for his opinion? Did either of you?"

They shook their heads.

"Didn't think so." With Sig's focus right where he wanted it, Lomis plunged the knife down into an eyeball until he seated the blade as far as it would go, gave it a five count and withdrew it, then crammed as much of the hanging beard into Sig's mouth as he could and turned back to his audience.

"Do you have a car?" Lomis asked. He craned his formerly broken arm around a few times. Though the bone had healed, he enjoyed the pain that came back to him that reminded him of his extraordinary luck and the mission at hand.

CHAPTER TWENTY

By THE TIME THEY arrived in Sun Valley on late Friday afternoon, another two feet of snow had fallen. Liv looked like a happy woman as she maneuvered the Subaru down narrow streets lined with small buildings with twinkling lights bouncing off of snow piled high on either side.

"Does that say Forty-One Crest hill?" She handed Sam a crumpled piece of paper with some inked scratchings on it.

"Forty-Seven."

"Good. Cause there isn't a Forty-one. Here we are." She wheeled the car up and over older snow and down a long narrow drive that led to a lodge pole home large enough to sleep half of Kershaw. Three decks on different levels ran off the front of the house above a grand double door entrance framed in hand- worked copper and brass. Liv took a house key from a small brown clasped envelope she had in her hand bag and led the way inside to a three-story atrium foyer the took their eyes straight up. Standing on a floor of planked,wood-pegged walnut, the view carried up through a massive, compelling combination of crystal lights and moose antlers to a stained glass ceiling that was side lit to enhance its electric array of colors and shape.

Sam still had the bag straps in his hands. "Somebody owes you one helluva favor."

She considered an answer, or if she should just let him drift around with those thoughts. "Actually, Johnny's daddy would probably like to get in my pants even more than his son. But I figure you can't really hold it against either of them."

"Why's that?"

"They're men."

"So this is a… ."

"A house given to a friend for a weekend. I called. It was available. So was their place in Tahiti, and Cabo. No snow there, though."

Sam had that look she liked to play with; the one where he went back to being the jealous, paranoid sixteen-year-old. "Of course."

"My first time here, too," Liv added quickly. She motioned for him to follow her as they sought out the next most important thing- where, and which bedroom. They chose the loft bedroom on the third floor that overlooked the magnificent snow covered mountain ranges to the north. Raised, king-sized four-poster bed, headboard, walls and ceiling of finished heavy pine with copper trim everywhere. A black marble hot tub surrounded by copper inlays and sapphire stones sat bubbling and waiting on the deck just outside a wall of sliding glass doors. Liv walked over and pulled off an envelope taped to the door with her name on it. Sam was bouncing on the bed and humming some song while she opened it.

> Liv, At least think of me
> in agony thinking about you
> there, without me.
> > Your Johnny
>
> P.S.- The Leer awaits your call

She quickly stuck the note in the back pocket of her jeans and leaped into bed.

❧

Sam hadn't put on a pair of skis in at least ten years, but he wasn't about to use that one on her after he watched her aggressively attack the first intermediate hill of the day.

"Oh shit!" came an echo before the muffling snow caught it. Sam forgot the pole plant on a turn and was headed over a little rise ass first, skis up, poles wherever. "Ohhhhhh shit!"

She spotted him out of the corner of her goggles, stopped and waited patiently as he tumbled on by, gaining speed before finally skidding to a stop maybe fifty feet further down the slope. He looked back up at her, his face covered with snow, ski cap over one ear and eye and a dumb smile on his face evidencing the bruised ego. Otherwise, he appeared intact.

"Are you still alive?" yelled Liv. "I'll go after your poles, Grace." She could see one ski was still attached to his leg somehow and had served as an emergency brake.

Sam rolled to the side and reached out just in time to grab the back tip of the other ski as it was hissing by. "Everything's under control!"

"I can see that," Liv yelled down to him as she dug her edges in and began a sideways trek uphill to retrieve his poles.

There were a few more falls, all his, some worse, before he was ready to surrender, but Sam figured the laughter they shared at his expense was worth the anguish.

"Cocktail hour," he declared just a tad south of three o-clock. He was pretty sure one more body slam against the slope might result in permanent injury.

"Wuss," Liv pointed out without hesitation, as she pushed and pulled him onto the ski lift. He struggled to get organized and sat back for the trip, then looked over at her as she pulled her goggles off and shook her hair loose. The glow coming off her rosy face in the late afternoon sun was astonishing. It seemed she had so many unassuming poses in which she looked unique, impossibly young and magnificent at the same time.

She was aware he was staring at her again. She was getting used to it, and loved it.

He still could not get beyond his extraordinary luck in finding her, let alone falling in love with her, let alone her falling in love with him, seemingly overnight, with neither pretense nor purpose, with such ease and comfort and familiarity as to be unfair. There would be many that would forecast a quick peaking and demise of such a thing, if in fact such a thing even existed; but for the two of them, there was neither time nor inclination to outthink it. The very first time they made love they both ended up in tears; holding each other for fear somebody or something would tell them it wasn't real. And they just sort of went from there, doing and saying and making love, or as Liv put it on occasion, "jungle fucking", a reference to giving in to instant, primitive urges, no matter the time or place.

Sam reached over and turned her face gently to give it an even closer examination, something that had become a bit of a habit. "You are one damn gorgeous woman, you know that?"

"And a better skier."

"And a better skier, that's for damn sure." He pressed his lips onto hers and their tongues met with delicious warmth against the gaining late day chill. He looked her over once more, going weak as her eyes traveled across his face and back. "I love you, Liv Gannon."

"I love you more, Sam Castle." She wiped at his nose and face and gave him the look that understood pain. "You going to bump ski with me or should I leave you off at the bunny hill this time around."

The thought of negotiating that mogul course one more time had his knees screaming up at him for mercy. "What is it with you, anyway? If you really loved me...."

Liv grabbed his crotch with her gloved hand. "Too much material. By the time we got to skin we'd have company."

Sam surprised himself with a grimace. "My balls are even killing me."

"That's what the hot tub is for, silly. No excuses, now."

Moments later she wooshed out off the chair in front of him and waited for him to join up at the top of the mogul run. "Want to race or just follow like usual."

"Okay. That's it." Sam snugged his cap and goggles and got along side her despite the little voice inside of him begging for mercy and warning him of immediate physical harm and a life full of regrets.

"So what do you think?" Liv posed over her poles. "Should I spot you ten, twenty yards, just to be fair?"

"Keep it up." Sam adjusted everything from his head band to the crotch seam of his ski pants. "How about this. How about we race for the rights to the ultimate body massage. I mean the kind you have to give for days, if necessary."

"You must be in a lot of pain."

"You can't imagine. But... I can pull it all together one more time to whip your ass down this mountain."

"No one's ever beat me at anything I really wanted to win," Liv said, winking, but trying to make it come off as a factoid.

"Remind me to ask you to qualify that later when you are cowering in the agony of defeat."

"On your mark."

"Just a damn minute," Sam protested, still not happy where his crotch seam wanted to go.

"You need to go commando next time, sweet. Too much material down there."

"Right. Just a reminder, unlike you, I have parts that might freeze, or worse if left to their own devices coming down the side of a steep mountain. Then where would we be?"

"My guess is I'd find a way to get by, but you, on the other hand, I fear would not do well as a gelding." She readied herself, waiting. "I think I could still love you as a woman, Sam, but the beard might have to go. Then, on the other hand...."

"Shush, you. On your count...."

"Three, two, one, go!" She squealed as she planted her poles and lifted off down the mountain.

The word "Shit" was either repeated a record number of times or it was the repeating echo rising into the pines; in any case, Sam repeated it every time he made a turn and bounced up and around a mogul, fighting and staying even with Liv through the first two hundred feet. Then, surprised at his own speed and getting a warm rush of confidence with each turn, "Shit" began to morph into heavy grunting, then controlled breathing that began to match up to the burst of his body through each turn. It could have been a competitive spirit had risen up inside of him, or that gravity and balance had finally come back to him, but when he looked across for Liv, he found himself a good fifty feet ahead of her. Part of him instinctively slowed but succumbed to the overwhelming urge to make this the best run ever. And no matter, if he beat her badly then so be it.

Sam could feel a smile tugging at him as he got his first view of the bottom of the hill and it added strength in place of pain in his knees as he bent and bounced and turned well enough to recall his old form and ability. Not to be outdone, the mountain seemed to suddenly jump up at him and he found himself at least ten feet airborne and gaining speed down towards a narrow flat landing area. "Shit! Holy shiiiiit!" came the echoes again. The perfect form began to collapse and the landing was mostly ass and hips, bouncing back up and over into a complete somersault and to his great surprise, back up on his skis with both poles still in hand, gliding effortlessly to the trail that marked the bottom of the run. Not really sure what had just transpired, but nonetheless grateful all of his bones were still apparently connected to one another, Sam looked back up the mountain to find Liv had stopped, poles planted, looking down at him, hands in big gloves clapping away. "Bravo!" he heard her yell and the echo repeating.

"Shit," said Sam.

⁂

A welcome respite, the hot water outside the pool at the Lodge at Sun Valley had been there for longer than either of them had been alive, and they were both no less in need of its promise of regeneration.

"Did you fall even once today?" he asked while she massaged his left knee under the churning, steaming water.

"Nope. Really no reason to fall, is there?"

"I suppose not. Of course. Stupid question."

"And you?" she asked.

"Funny. Actually, I look at it this way. How else do you know if you are giving it your all, pressing to your limits? Better one should know that instinctively than suffer the consequences of going over the line unnecessarily."

"Perceptive, I give you that. Flawed, but perceptive."

She moved up and cuddled in under his chin, folding her legs and body in against him while he gathered the rest of her underneath an arm and pulled her even closer.

She stretched up to kiss his neck, then whispered into his skin. "And just for the record? I still haven't lost a race I wanted to win."

Later, after nearly falling sleep and drowning in the intoxicating elixir of warmth from the hot tub and the frigid air above, they sat quietly admiring each other and rubbing tops of hands by candlelight over a late night dinner at Jacques, a six-table French restaurant in Ketchum.

They were finishing a shared duck under a raspberry glaze and sipping the last of a great Pinot. "I can't speak for my legs, which feel like they might be at another table, but as for the rest of me, mid-thigh up, I cannot begin to tell you how spectacular I feel just sitting here, holding your hand."

"Says the silly man with the deep voice."

Sam's voice was a near whisper, but she heard every word, watching his lips move from the middle of that beard and thinking Santa was for real, just a lot younger and better looking than the animated version.

"You keep reaching back there, don't you," she said.

"Meaning?"

"Back to your youth, back to being a kid again."

"That's the way I feel, I guess. Or at least maybe the way it should have felt. It makes no difference for me to know which. I just know how I feel when I am around you is like nothing else I can remember except how a kid should feel when something amazing happens for the very first time. That's how I feel waking up next to you, when I reach over to hold you to make sure you are real. It's how I feel when you walk into my little shop and bring me lunch, and a smile. It's how I feel when we make love." He stopped and threw a big grin her way.

She offered up a toast. "Here's to you never having to grow up again."

"Right. So let's see. Do you think I could be anymore self indulgent?" He brushed his hand over hers and held it there. "How about you? There is that part of me that keeps asking who you are, really. I would settle for what I need to know- probably a little less."

"Not much to know," Liv began, her eyes empty of their usual sparkle. "My parents were killed in a home invasion when I was six. I survived by hiding in my toy chest. Gannon and Gramma Sophie raised me here in Kershaw until I shipped off on a full ride to Boston College." She sounded like she was tired of repeating the news.

"You're serious?" He looked down into her eyes and saw sadness there for the very first time.

"You think I would make something like that up?"

Sam shook his head and reached over for her hand. "I'm sorry." Sam felt awkward; shifting in his creaking chair, thinking as much as he might have wanted to, this was not the time or place to fess up about the real Sam Castle story. But there was no doubt in his mind this was as close as he had come to wanting to tell his story to another human being. Maybe just some parts of it, he thought. Leaving some things out was not always a means of deception. He found himself gently massaging the top soft skin on her hand. Of course it was, he reminded himself. Always. "Did they catch them?"

"No. Never. Nothing ever came of it. They were just gone. But I didn't suffer with it like you might think, so don't read too much into it. Gannon and Gramma Syl were the best things that ever happened to me." Her eyes refilled partially. "What about you. Let. See. You grew up with servants, home schooling, looking up the nanny's skirt?"

"Sort of. Or so I am told." There was obvious reluctance in his voice and eyes. "As the story goes… you really want this?"

"After what I just told you about me? I'm afraid you're stuck, old man."

"So I showed up on the steps of a police station in Chicago one night when I was five days old."

"No making stuff up to top me."

"It gets better. A young Russian couple came to the rescue and kept me off the streets until I was four or five, but they got into drug running trouble and got deported, I was told. Then it was foster homes for a couple more years." Sam seemed to get lost in all of it.

"Then?"

"Then. Then, an angel appeared. Her name was Kathleen Parker. She adapted me, raised me, got me to my eighteenth birthday by three days before she died of cancer. That's the angel part. She told me her whole purpose of being was to make sure I had a life worth living. I think of her often. And I know she has saved my ass a thousand times. Like today, on the slopes. I'm wounded, but not dead."

Both ran out of words and comprehension, not knowing where to go with all the new information about each other. They were both paused by the similarity of their uncertain early years. The quiet was defeaning, but their hands kept working together on the table, massageing, caressing, carrying the message.

"You probably want a rematch tomorrow?" He finally asked.

"Only if I get to see a repeat of that fabulous flip at the end of your run."

"I am announcing right now there will be no rematch." Sam put out his arms to include all in the restaurant as witnesses. There were two couples huddled up over small tables like theirs that could not have cared less.

"I expected as much," she said. "Actually, as good a time as ever to let you know, I got an email from Johnny earlier today and it looks like we are going to get some forum time at an environmental impact symposium down in Denver on Tuesday. Which means I will have to get there early Monday to prepare with the group, which means we will have to cut tomorrow short a bit so I can get my act together back home."

135

Sam was happy to let the short journey into the past die back. He was more curious about the buzzing that hung in his ears at the mention of John Perkins being referred to by Liv as "Johnny".

"And if that breaks my heart, does it matter to you?" he asked, working it as best he could.

"Let's say it matters for mankind. You give up two or three days of great sex for the good of mankind. You would do that, wouldn't you?"

Sam tried silence.

But she would have none of it. "We were told we could get our agenda on stage because the older guard, the gray-haired Gores as we call them, wanted to pitch all of their time-old garbage. So yes, this is very good news. It means our voice can be heard in the right context, against a proper fading backdrop, with millions of eyes and ears watching their future light up."

"Whatever that means, I'm thrilled for you."

"You want to come along, heartbreak kid?"

Sam let it hang there for more than a few moments. "What if somebody's toaster gives out?"

Liv found a deep sigh whistling back out her mouth. "When are you going to tell me why you are trying to so hard to stay out of this part of my life?" Liv asked.

"Hopefully never. Maybe I can just be that part of your life that you'll need and want when you aren't out saving the world."

Liv shook her head a little and bit at her tongue. "You really don't think I would let you get away with trying to minimalize this."

"And I wouldn't. That would be the last thing I would want to do."

"You could become a part of this. You would be a big hit."

"I hope I already am where it counts. What part of me looks uncomfortable just worshipping you for a living."

Liv worked to keep the smile minimal. "Okay then." She sipped the rest of her wine and threw that beautiful hair back onto her shoulders. "So you would have me believe you are this behind the scenes real estate investor guru guy who will be content fixing toasters the rest of your life."

He saluted her. "That's exactly what I want you to believe."

"What if I don't?"

"Then… there is always Mrs. Kendrick's offer."

CHAPTER TWENTY ONE

Lomis GUNNED THROUGH A turn and felt the car grab and hold on like it wanted more. Dabs of falling snow had begun to crash into the headlights. "Only a real asshole would rent a fucking Volvo on a vacation," he said to her, hooting at the looks of the dashboard configuration. According to the rental agreement in the glove box they had picked it up at the airport in Salt Lake City and it was due back in another four days. "Nice big trunk, though."

"Mmmmmftttt...ft!," she screamed out against the duck tape Lomis had picked up at the Circle K. He also bought a really cool flashlight with a glowing NASCAR logo he found on a counter display at the register.

Her hands and feet were bound in tape as well, her lips swollen purple and bursting, but she was in much better shape than her all but dead husband in the trunk. Back in mode, thinking on the fly, they were two blocks away from Lefty's Short Steer when he turned back. The rear door was still unlocked the way he left it, and when he got inside, he found some wadded up plastic sheeting in the back room, walked back into the bar and grabbed the couple's dead friend off the body pile and wrapped him up to go. It had occurred to him he could confuse the hell out of the police by removing the body but leaving the blood evidence of someone else along with the other three in the pile. That would keep them pretty busy while Lomis figured out his next move.

The shadows swallowed up the car as it moved out from under the street lights of Ketchum going south on Highway 21 back towards Kershaw. "Perfect," Lomis told himself, clearly back on track, doing what came natural to him.

"Slpttt fucckr!"

"Yes, my dear, I know. But we need to find the right spot, which won't be easy in the dark. You keep looking on your side though, okay?" Given the amount of snow on the ground, Lomis had to rule out the old Odessa/Michaelen location. There was no way to get a vehicle close enough- and walking up that path was out of the question.

They were around eight miles north of Kershaw when a single light hanging from a telephone pole offered up an amber glow to an intersection with a narrow road that appeared to have been plowed recently. He turned left and made his way up a short incline before the road turned and began a gentle descent beneath tree branches heavy with fresh snow. "Hell, let's see where this takes us."

Certain it was as dark and as far along as he cared to go, Lomis edged the car into the narrow shoulder, turned off the car lights and got out of the car. He swigged at a pint of Early Times while leaning back against the side of the car, waiting patiently until his eyes adjusted to the dark. The Early Times was shit, but it was all the Circle K had in the way of bourbon.

There were no lights in any direction. The tiny flakes hit the top of his nose and melted down over his lips as he swished the whiskey in his mouth, forcing the burn down his throat with one walloping swallow after another.

He was pleased with what he was seeing just ahead on the left; a gentle, short slope down to a stand of darkness that would be a wall of snow covered trees and bramble. He gave his new flashlight a go but didn't want to have it on any longer than necessary. It felt like the right place. Not a porch light, not a yard light in sight. Not a sound, not a whimper of breeze. He could trust his Gods for the rest. He moved to the trunk and opened the lid, peering down as the trunk light illuminated. It appeared the dead one was still dead, but the not quite dead husband was mumbling some high pitched nonsense into his duct tape mask, his eyes all roly-poly, face bloating and crimson. Getting to the work at hand, Lomis grabbed hold of the dead guy and pulled him out onto the ground. The body was heavy but slid along easily on the plastic as he dragged him up along the edge of the road a ways before riding him like a sled down the slope to the bottom. "Wheeee!" Lomis yelped. "Too bad we can't do that again, eh pal?"

Just as he hoped, the snow was at least a couple a feet deep at the base of the hill where it met the trees. He kicked the lighter stuff out of an area eight-by-six, then got down on his knees, pulled off his gloves and began to carve out a deeper basin with his hands and forearms, making sure there wasn't a little stream beneath that could erode the freeze. Frozen bodies neither smell nor show up until the thaw of a spring, Lomis thought pleasantly, comfortably. And spring in the mountains? That could be June with any luck at all. Maybe he would hang around for awhile after all and watch all the fun. If the uninterrupted sleepy months he spent holed up in that room above the garage were any indication, it had been awhile since any law man had to deal with a multiple murder in this tiny town of the stoned and privileged. He never went back over things in his mind much, figuring for the most part his Gods had things under control and served mostly to propel him forward, to keep seeking and fulfilling the mission. It was, however, extremely important he trust only himself for the details. That much they expected from him.

He dumped the dead guy into the snow hole and spun him out of the plastic and carried it back up with him to the car. He ducked inside and took another look at the rental agreement he had thrown onto the front seat. Thomas Soderski. Additional driver- Diane Soderski. Columbus, Ohio. He had forgotten to look inside the dead guy's wallet to see who he was. Not that it mattered in the purest sense of things, but he liked to know who his victims were, if for no other reason, it was a rush to say their name for the last time before they died. There was power there, the final, ultimate power verified and unchallenged.

Mrs. Soderski's voice seemed to be showing signs of strain in her yelping and caroming about in the back seat. "Easy, girl," Lomis cautioned her. "It won't be long now, Mrs. Soderski. I'll be back shortly. I need to finish a conversation with your husband and then, we'll talk. And, if you're real nice to me, I'll give you the fuck of your life before I kill you."

The tears rolled down her cheeks and the corners of her mouth bled from trying to bite through the tape as she shook under the strain of a muffled scream. Her eyes rolled back, looking for him, hearing only the chilling calm of his voice coming from the front seat.

"Given the good mood I'm in, I might even kill you first instead of burying you alive. We'll see. You think about how nice you want to be to me and I'll be back in a jiffy."

Lomis pulled the barely struggling Thomas Soderski out of the trunk and flopped him face down onto the flattened plastic sheet, gave him a series of vicious kicks in his sides and back, and began dragging him along. "Jesus, Thomas, you could stand to lose a few pounds." Sledding was just as much fun with Soderski, though. Atop the plastic, they cut through the snow and dead sticks like a dream. The feint voice of protest Soderski offered at the end of the ride was wasted in the light snow and deafening quiet.

Lomis rolled Soderski along side his unidentified friend with a grunt of finality and watched him wiggle and jerk up against his duct tape bindings. Lomis stood above the two of them, pulled out his flashlight and panned the area, admiring the unique sight; one dead, the other flopping around against him, groaning, moaning, trying to scream. Absurd really, Lomis thought, a grotesque sense of pleasure warming him from the cold. He kicked some snow onto them ceremoniously, then spotted a broken tree limb laying on the ground nearby, and decided to give Mr. Soderski a few solid whacks about the face and head, just in case he had any thoughts of recovery. The tough guy still moaned and jerked around, so Lomis took out his knife, knelt down beside him, reached down to remove Mr. Soderski's LL Bean low-cut boots, then sliced through all the soft tissue and tendons just above his heels. That scream threatened to vibrate the duct tape right off his mouth, but he wasn't going anywhere. A couple feet of snow was much lighter and less suffocating than a couple feet of earth. Lomis had to be sure the bodies would stay put until they froze.

Now for the real fun; the best part of the great expectations that came when he rediscovered his way earlier in the evening. He wondered aloud if a woman could be fucked until she froze to death, what might actually happen if he was inside her right at that moment, but the idea of cold pussy had no real appeal so the curiosity quickly gave way and he began to hum a soft tune instead as he walked back up the incline. He felt a rising in his jeans as he approached the car. It had been too long since the last time. Mrs. Soderski would be well advised to know the back of her head might be flying off. "She has no idea," he delighted in telling himself.

But something unfamiliar began to suddenly grab at him from inside out. Did Gannon con him? Was he duped into thinking his twenty-five grand was the real deal while Gannon pocketed, maybe, millions? And that would mean the little cunt granddaughter would have either the diamonds, the money, or both. He was not used to figuring stuff like this. His figuring skills were made for this killing and raping business; his destiny, his place in history.

He found himself shaking with the thought someone had squeezed into an upper hand position on him- like that damn Riddler tried to do. A few others had tried. He had killed them all ultimately. Which is precisely where he needed his thoughts to be. He would kill them both- the Riddler, which he had figured early on anyway, and the delicious granddaughter, once he figured out what really happened with the diamonds and how to get them back. A warming swirled inside of him, calming him, settling the shakes. He smiled and looked up to his Gods. He was grateful for the reminder of the business yet to be done.

He slowly opened the back door. "Looky what I brought for you," he said, dangling his prized possession. But the back seat was empty. She was gone. Nothing but tangles of seat belts and ripped duct tape.

"Fuck!" he screamed up at the dark sky, scanning around then circling the car, looking down for footprints while he shoved his cock back inside his pants. He flipped on the flashlight and quickly got a bead on the tossed up snowy prints leading from the back door on the other side of the car. The bitch could only get so far, and if she knew the adrenalin rush he was hovering on at that moment, she would know there was no chance she could outlast him. He found her path with the narrow beam of the flashlight and moved with it along the high edge of the road. "Mrs. Soderski! Come back! You're husband is right here with me!" he yelled. The falling snow snuffed out the echo. Nothing. He moved forward, confident and excited for the game, except for the annoying smaller voice of panic begging for recognition that tried to crawl up his throat. Now moving quicker, eyes straining, seeing less instead of more, wiping the snow from his nose and face and stopping once again for a three-sixty turn. Her tracks didn't seem to follow the curve of the road, rather they appeared to end in a tossed up mix of snow and dead plant debris and dirt. The dark shadowing against the white made it all but impossible to tell for sure.

Then it came. A scream so shrill and penetrating he jumped back and fell onto the road. Then again! "Oh gawwwwwwwddd heeeelp mmm...!" Lomis got up and smiled at his luck, figuring the bitch had fallen and broken a leg or worse. He moved quickly in the direction of the scream. It seemed to be coming from pretty close back before the curve in the road. Moving down the hill he thought he could hear moans and grunts that under any other circumstances would have instantly aroused him. As it was, he was mentally already there, figuring he would pound her right where she fell. Pound her hard, then drag her back with the others.

A crunching sound followed by a muffled scream told him she knew he was hot on her trail. He was choking on his own excitement, pushing ahead, flashlight in one hand, pulling branches out of his way with the other. He aimed the beam out at the direction of the noise, freezing it on the thing in the semi-dark, realizing in a moment it was waving a mouth and face full of blood dripping human entrails in his direction. Slipping back and gasping for breath, he turned as quickly as he could while the bear began to follow him and chew angrily at the same time. The heart in Lomis' chest was pounding at his ribcage and he could hear his breath coming in crackling jabs up through the narrowing of his throat. Run, run, run, he told himself. Don't look back! He was aware of nothing until he reached the flat of the road, fell, scrambled back up and sprinted for the car. Falling again as he opened the door he pulled himself up and into the driver's seat and shut the door. He sat inside a symphony of twisting strained sounds coming from his lungs and throat and thought his heart would explode at any moment. His scattered thoughts tried to regroup around some idea of being safe for the moment. He grabbed the steering wheel with both hands, then one hand shook into a coat pocket to find the car keys. Wait, wait, wait, he cautioned himself as he began to turn the keys. You can't leave! You can't leave. He turned the keys and the headlights went on just in time to catch the bear lumbering up to the car. The headlights seemed to startle the animal and he stopped and sat down in the middle of the road, roaring at the beams of light shining on him. His teeth were covered in blood and dangling hunks of flesh. This was something out of a bad movie, Lomis thought. Not possible. But he was safe. And he could just drive away. But he couldn't. So what could he do? The moment the question crossed his frazzled mind, a plan hatched that convinced him once again of his need to tend to the details of the pre-ordained plan.

With the bear still sitting in the beams of the head lights, Lomis unlatched the door handle and slowly opened the door to see if the bear would do anything. He was no expert on bears, but this one seemed as a big as they come; black or a wet dark brown, angry enough, and hungry for certain. The bear didn't move, yet continued to wave and shake its head, roaring its disapproval and dominance. Then, in quick, successive moves, Lomis opened the car door further, reached back in and turned off the car, crouched and slid back along its side to the rear and peered back over the trunk lid. He figured the lights would stay on maybe thirty-seconds. He made a dash to the side of the road, down the hill and began working over to the grave site when the lights went out. When he made it to his friends, he turned the flashlight back on, found the stout limb he had used earlier on Soderski and began shouting. "Come and get me you motherfucker!" he yelled, waving the limb around and pounding up against a nearby tree trunk with it to create even more noise. Then he stopped and listened. Nothing. "Over here, you cocksucker!" He screamed, not caring if anything or anybody else heard him. He pounded on the tree trunk again. Stopped. Listened. The sounds of twigs cracking and breaking. Then a roar. Another. Deafening. He could feel the ground shaking as he scrambled up a nearby tree and climbed up into a crook high enough to be safe for the moment. He shined his flashlight down on his most recent victims. He could feel the tree trunk vibrate as the bear pounced down into the shallow snow grave and sunk his huge head into the abdomen of Thomas Soderski. Lomis moved the flashlight beam up to Soderksi's face and smiled at the luck of seeing his last agonizing moments alive. Flashlight off, waiting a few more minutes until the bear was fully engaged and seemingly happy, Lomis quietly eased down the tree and quickly padded his way back and out over the snow and to the car.

Luck had little to do with fate, Lomis thought as he drove the car back into Sun Valley. He parked the car down the street from his room over the garage, stopped in for a quick, cleansing shower, a change of clothes and drove the Volvo back to the Lodge at Sun Valley where the Soderski's and their friend were staying.

He found himself overcharged by all the excitement of the evening, yet it was woefully incomplete. No complete conquest, no sex. He began to fume and talk to himself incessantly as he wiped the car down for prints and anything that would place him in it.

Maybe that Duchin Room Lounge in the Sun Valley Lodge would produce something. There was still time for a drink or two. And, he was on some kind of roll. Who was to say the night could not offer yet more.

CHAPTER TWENTY TWO

"Maker's Mark, some ice," Lomis said as he pulled up a stool just in time for one-thirty last call. The Duchin Room at the Sun Valley Lodge was still as full and noisy as it should have been this late on a Saturday night in the middle of ski season. This was as unlikely place to find Lomis Walls as there was. What with a shiny black Steinway piano under dimmed lights, a long-gowned black singer out front belting out a show tune, soft laughter at tables full of huddling couples.

He had been in the Duchin Room before, hardly able to finish a drink at the bar before wanting to kill every privileged slob in the place, but he felt the Gods still pushing at him, despite his extraordinary good fortune earlier in the evening. His visions and inclinations always came unannounced, a gifting from the Gods, and though most times he trusted and followed the path they laid out before him, most of his waking hours ended with the same enraging emptiness. The only way he knew to escape the end was to stay away from it; to fill his days and nights with thoughts and acts of violence and depravity; to exact a collective vengeance against the those whose fate included an end at his hands.

He sipped his drink and ran it back through his mind, arguing, questioning his Gods about the need for the bear. After all, he was deprived of the sexual encounter and the credit for the final kill. He misunderstood, perhaps, what his role was to be, yet, maybe there was more to come before he would fight for sleep on this night.

No sooner had he begun to sip at the Maker's Mark and look around when he spotted Livian Gannon leaning over a small cocktail table with her lips just inches from her man's lips. The kiss was brief. They smiled at each other like they were alone in the room, clicked their wine glasses, then kissed again.

Her bearded companion looked familiar, Lomis thought, his mind continuing to race. She was a gorgeous piece, no doubt. He would torture her first, given the situation with the diamonds, then rape her, then torture her again, assuming she would not give them up. Pull finger nails out with a needle nose perhaps, or the ice pick up the nostrils and into the ear canals. It had been awhile since he had done that. Think, think, think. He worked away, sipping, and when he saw Liv's man turn slightly his way, his face catching just a glimmer from a hanging ceiling light, he knew it was Sam Castle and nearly jumped off his bar stool with excitement.

Lomis smiled broadly. If not for the bear, he likely would have been burying bodies for hours. He gave a nod to his Gods and asked them to forgive him for questioning their guidance. He chugged the rest of the Maker's. "Another," he said as the bartender passed in front of him.

"Last call. Sorry, pal."

"I didn't hear it. I just got here. Been on the road all day." Lomis smiled up at him and flipped three tens on the bar. "Have a heart?"

Lomis could not keep up with the thoughts running rough shod through his head, but took the drink and casually moved over one stool so he could keep an eye on his new favorite couple in the reflection of the back lit mirror behind the bar. He knew it. He knew his Gods were not done presenting to him on this great evening. He laughed aloud for a moment and softly tapped his fist on the bar top. Drooling love birds together.

Had he not broken his arm they would have never made the stop in Kershaw, and so on. Just the idea of this was too good to be true, let alone begin the detail work and perhaps the biggest challenge ever now that the Riddler was back on his radar.

"You move over one more stool and you'll be right in my lap," came a liquored up voice from his left.

Lomis craned back and took a good look.

"I mean," laughed the plump older man with a shining bald dome fringed in frizzy gray curls, "It's a bigger lap than some, smaller than others, but it's a good lap I truly believe. You know, testimonials from coast-to-coast, I shit you not."

Lomis hated feeble attempts at humor. He considered it insulting. A polite nod was all he could muster.

The man was clearly more amused and content with his assessment, took a big pull of scotch from a wide bodied crystal goblet, then leaned lightly into an arm that came around his shoulder from the person sitting next to him on the other side. "Don't be getting any ideas on me now, Ike." A completely effected voice lisped into Ike's ear a bit too loud.

Lomis gave a nod of thanks to his Gods. "Robert," Lomis said, shooting out a hand for Ike to shake while he still had his other ear in range.

"Robert," Ike cooed. "I knew a Robert once. Charming man. Wonderful eyes." Ike looked up at he eyes of Lomis Walls, aka Robert. "Positively evil itself," he pronounced flatly, slurring then last word. "You look like a dangerous man, Robert. Are you a dangerous man?"

"Oh yes," Lomis answered flatly. He relished what they might think of his short answer.

"I happen to like a dangerous man." Ike played in.

"Like hell." The brash voice came from the taller, thinner, much older man on the other side. Lomis could see the man was nattily dressed in a white tie and bright red blazer. "You prefer your men meek and submissive if the truth be told. I, on the other hand…." He winked over at Lomis. "I'm your bitch, young man," he said with a breathy easiness.

Lomis let his skin crawl without reacting as these three stretched the final drink into nearly an hour of conversation of double entandres and crude anatomical references while Lomis kept one eye on the mirror watching the love birds pour the last of the bottle of wine into their glasses.

"Seattle," Ike was saying, "and my friend Alan here is from Detroit, but won't admit it."

"Santa Barbara for godssakes," Alan whooshed, clearly annoyed. Robert, I am a fabulously wealthy jeweler, the best in all of Santa Barbara…."

"Yesterday it was best in the galaxy," Ike added.

"Shussh. You sit in your smug little dungeon in Seattle and deal with the low life and you shout at me. Absurd."

"I… make you wealthy." Ike's voice was trialing with vapors of scotch.

"You suck my…."

"And that, too."

They laughed and fussed up about it while Lomis did his best to seem interested, did a little math and shuddered with an evil gratitude. "Did you say Seattle?"

"Yes, indeed."

"You some kind of diamond guy?"

"Some would say that, I suppose." Ike was enjoying the play.

"Would a Josh Gannon say that?"

Ike's boozy eyes tried to focus on Lomis, aka Robert. He searched, but wasn't sure what he was finding.

Ike's silent answer was exactly what Lomis was looking for, but before he had a chance to burrow into Ike, he saw Liv and Sam getting up to leave and the unlikely dilemma froze him. He watched as Sam draped an arm around that lovely young thing. Shouldn't be a problem, he mused. They weren't going anywhere, certainly not back to Kershaw on this snowy Saturday night, and all things being equal, they would likely head back to their room for the obvious until they fell asleep on each other. They would wake in the morning and do it again; then, being a Sunday and all, shower, dress, get brunch at the lodge and head back to wherever they came from, which he figured had to be Kershaw. It wouldn't make much sense to be mayor of Kershaw and not live in Kershaw, and any betting man would put all his money on Sam Castle living within a stone's throw of wherever she was, if not in the same pile of stones.

Ike and Alan shared a short, whispered conversation between them and surfaced smiling. "Would you care to party with us, darling?" Alan asked in an assured, but tingly-all-over voice.

Lomis quickly figured he could let it all ride and follow along. He followed a short distance behind as the pair stumbled their way a short distance back to their villa. When they insisted on playing around like neither had the room key, Lomis resorted to chewing at the insides of his gums to keep from strangling both of them with his bare hands.

"If you would have let me carry my purse, but no, not to make a scene, you said," Alan mocked, posturing and waiting as Ike dug through his pockets and weaved in the cold, trying to keep his balance.

Once inside, more drinks were poured, classical music was set to a mood inducing volume and oversize pillows were tossed into the middle of the sitting room in front of the gas fireplace that lit up with a quiet roar at the flick of a light switch. Alan cleared some magazines from the glass coffee table, then began to hum and study Lomis while he produced a small plastic bag of white powder. He shook out a little mound onto the glass and used a razor blade to make a series of lines.

"That should get us jump started," he announced, shooting a wink at Lomis who tried to look reasonably interested while he cased the place with his eyes.

Ike returned from a trip to the bathroom dressed in a white terrycloth robe and flopped onto the overstuffed couch. He pulled himself up at the sight of the cocaine and took the short straw Alan readied for him. One line up one nostril, one line up the other, lick the straw and settle back. Alan eyed Lomis with a glowing, sneaky smile. "I believe it would be your turn."

"You know," Lomis began, starting to walk across the room, "don't mind if I do." It all shuddered down through his body and lifted twenty pounds from his center and feet, but his mind was still right where it needed to be.

As Alan took his, Lomis resumed a slow walk around the room. "Ike. You know, Gannon mentioned a diamond guy in Seattle by the name of Ike. Ike the Kike, I think is how he put it."

Ike's eyes nearly jumped off his short wide face.

"So how many guys named Ike deal in Diamonds in Seattle you suppose?" Lomis asked, stepping closer to Ike.

Ike's head bobbed to the Mozart CD Alan had begun to play. "Robert, as you can imagine, the diamond business is very confidential. We never discuss our clients."

Ike looked at Lomis and gave Alan a puzzled look that might have bordered on fear. "What are the odds," he repeated, turning the sentence into a laugh.

"So you are the one?"

Ike's alarm system was on off. "I guess I am the one. You know, he died recently."

"No, I didn't know that."

"Yeah. Cancer got him."

"Sorry to here that."

"Yeah, well," Ike quickly changed his tone in a clearing moment. "Beyond that I don't discuss my clients or my business dealing with them. Isn't that right, Alan?" Ike bent down over another line.

Alan nodded and put his hands up. "Not a party topic darling. I'm going for a quick shower. Fresh is best, I always say." Lomis watched him sashay off as if he had an extra hip joint in the middle of his ass.

Ike took a deep breath and watched it go back out along the point of his nose. "Enough already. Now come on over here and let's see what you might have in store for us tonight."

Lomis walked over and stood in front of Ike, taking in the boozy, sheepish look as Ike loosened his robe. Ike reached for him, but a slow blink later found his forehead leaning into the tip of a knife. Lomis moved his face to within an inch of Ike's nose. "Okay you fucking fagot, you start telling me everything you know about the diamonds Gannon brought you last year and make it fast. I swear there is nothing better than slicing up an old fucking fagot. Nobody will miss you. Nobody."

"Oh, we are playful, are we," Ike giggled. "You are the evil one, aren't you?" Ike lowered his voice and added some spice to it. "Is that a real knife?"

Water running and Alan's baritone could be heard from the bathroom. "Feel free to start without me," he yelled. "My wife thinks I'm in Johannesburg. Can you imagine?"

"You heard the man. Take that damn coat off and act like you want it for godsakes," Ike added, but as he tried to move back from the knife point, Lomis leaned down and clocked him across the face with the back side of his hand, and the force knocked Ike back and bounced him off the back rest. Then he grabbed a handful of the curly frizz on one side of Ike's head and roughly pulled him back and put the blade of the knife across his throat. "Tell me about the Gannon diamond deal. Now!"

Ike's playful mood changed abruptly. He wasn't sure if his throat had been slit already or not. "Okay, okay. I won't even ask why you need to know about it, but put the knife away. Jesus. Please!"

Lomis backed away a few feet but dangled the knife at his side, massaging the blade with his tightly gloved fingers. "Let's hear it."

"Okay, so as I recall...," Ike began, trying as he might to shake loose of the booze and cocaine coursing through every blood cell in his body, "Gannon called me and told me he had come into a mother load of small diamonds. He joked about them being in a coffee can. So I never saw the can, but the diamonds, yes, they were good enough to move along. So I did my job. That's about it. Why are you so damn interested?"

"How much?"

"Oh come on, you can't expect me to compromise my integrity. People come to me for secrecy. It's how I make my living for god's sake."

"How much?" Lomis moved a step closer and tightened his grip on the knife.

"You are beginning to scare me. Stop it."

"You should be scared for your life, fudge-packer. How much?"

"More than a million. That's all you're going to get from me. You kill me, they kill me, what's the difference, right? Anyway, why does it matter to you?"

Lomis felt the trappings of rage building as he slipped the knife into his coat pocket, but as he launched his full weight at Ike, he caught his right leg on the edge of the glass coffee table, causing it to flip and crash to the hardwood floor, splitting it into jagged, cocaine coated pieces. "You fucking curse," Lomis murmured. "How much?" He gripped the lapels on Ike's robe and tightened them around his neck.

"Four. Maybe five million. In layman's terms, The best small diamonds that I have seen in a long, long time. Are you happy now?" Ike's voice began to quiver as he started to sense the return of an ugly reality he spent most of the evening trying to escape.

Lomis recognized the feel of the heating bile of hatred rising inside of him. It was flame-tip hot, finding its way up through his insides until it rushed into his temples, just like it had the first time his father had beaten him, and every time after that. In more recent years it was no less than a call to action, a remand to inflict and strike back not for the single moment, but to exact and carry out the punishment required of his life and his right to a judgment. "Twenty-five thousand?" Lomis was asking his Gods for an explanation.

Ike began to mumble and struggle against Lomis, thinking he would let go but when he only tightened his grip he stiffened and tried to clear his throat. "Twenty-five thousand what?"

"Those diamonds were *mine!*" Lomis began to tremble, his face twitching uncontrollably, the heat unbearable, his mind on fire. With a roar and one motion he lifted Ike off the couch and threw him in the air. "I want them back!" he screamed at him.

Ike landed awkwardly and struggled to get back up, the laugher beginning to pour out of his mouth. "Yours? You fucking moron, we never did the deal. He took his diamonds back with him. I don't have a clue what he did with them." His laughter cranked up off the ceiling and bounced back down through the middle of Lomis' head. He was going to try to explain why this was so absurd when his nose met with a perfectly landed fist that turned it into a spray of blood. Lomis followed with a vicious upward punch through the solar plexus that sent Ike careening backward until he lost his footing and collapsed back across the broken coffee table. As he lay there, an odd squeal began to expel from his lungs and his face went slack and still as he tried to look down over his chin at the jagged shard of bloody glass sticking up through his stomach. One hand tried to reach for it, flopped and missed, while words at his lips puffed out into silent streams of blood.

Lomis hovered above him and looked down at the jagged glass glistening with fresh blood. He tried to comprehend the moment and the unfinished expression etched into Ike's face. He wanted more, needed more. It wasn't time for him to die. Not yet. A cable of steel began rolling up inside of him, all but choking off his ability to think. Once again, in the same night, his rage unfulfilled, the final moment denied, the conquest given away. Then he heard the water stop running. Killing Alan was an immediate, easy thought, but he had a quicker sense this was all very sloppy and he needed to get out quickly, leaving Alan to explain to the police how this all had happened.

Alan was primped and powdered, donned his stiletto red high heels and a new pair of his wife's thigh high black silk stockings from Paris as he entered the room, humming to a Mozart concerto, and opening his robe for all to see.

But Lomis Walls was already making his way back down the path to the lodge. He was much too tired to find out what room Sam and Liv were in. He was weary indeed, weary of his Gods who seemed to be pushing him to the edge for some reason. One moment they were placing him in position, the next denying him the moment. He reached up and cupped his ears with his hands and pushed in as hard as he could, trying to squeeze out the fog. Instead, a scream shot out from his lungs that echoed and repeated into the mountains. He waited until the echo dissipated, then screamed again, louder, dropping his hands and clenching them into fists which he raised in protest. He stood motionless, spent, chin dropping onto his heaving chest, long strands of saliva dripping to the ground.

He walked the three miles back to his cozy little room above the garage, cracked a beer, flipped on CNN and waited for sleep.

CHAPTER TWENTY THREE

THEY HAD BEEN UP for two hours, showered, made love, showered again, but in the midst of a hysterical naked chase around the room, an insistent knock at the door broke the cycle.

"Room Service."

The best eggs Benedict on the planet made up for cold rye toast and undercooked hash brown potatoes, washed down with champagne and orange juice. Then the love making got serious. Sam and Liv were holding each other the way they did that first night, amazed, speechless, hanging on and dropping a few tear drops on each other.

"How could this be happening, Sam Castle," Liv whispered as she kissed away the bead of sweat running down the front side of his ear. "My plan was to meet you when I was thirty-two."

"So sorry," Sam lamented. "I really mean that." He was enjoying the feel of his head sinking back into the pillow.

"It's going to get complicated," Liv said flatly."

"Complicated. This? How so?"

"Loving you will be very complicated for me." She stroked and played with his chest hair. "Everything I do from now on will be framed by my loving you. Everything."

"Am I supposed to apologize."

"In a way. You need to keep making love to me the way you do. Like forever." She grabbed at his face and shook it around playfully. She smiled to herself and could not remember ever thinking she could be this happy. Even when she would dream of such things as love and marriage when she was just a young girl, she could not have imagined loving somebody would feel so completing, so overwhelmingly simple, small to hold and so large to keep inside once it was there.

"Idea," she said with her usual brighten-up.

"We already did that."

"Why don't I fly right out of Hailey for Salt Lake City later today? Then we don't have to go back to Kershaw and then back to the airport tomorrow morning. I'll catch a flight down to Denver from Salt Lake City. That way, we can spend the rest of today right here... just like this."

"Clothes for Denver?"

"I'll need two outfits. I'll buy them when I get there. It will be worth it."

"I'm buying." Sam rolled over on top of her and held her face still in the cradle of his arm. "You are...."

"What?"

"You have to be tired of me saying it."

"Never. Never, ever."

"Each day, I see something in you I didn't see the day before. It might be your hair, the way you carry it, or it might be a button left unbuttoned that on any other day should have been buttoned. You wake up amazing things inside of me, Liv."

He stroked her damp hair and smoothed it in along the edges of her face. Her legs shot out beneath his and locked on to his calves.

"Idea?" she asked.

"You got the floor," Sam said.

"What do you say we move to the bed? One more rug burn on my ass from this carpet and I'll have the funniest walk in Denver."

By the time they emerged for a late check out there appeared to be an unusual gathering of squad cars in a cul de sac that bordered the walk way to the main lodge. Sam spotted two Ketchum squads, one Kootenai County, and three Idaho State Police cruisers. A Ketchum ambulance was parked as well as two Sun Valley Lodge vans. A few uniformed police huddled outside of a villa smoking and just then another man in jeans and a cowboy hat joined them and lit up.

"Looks pretty ominous," Sam said, walking and holding Liv's hand. A bellman with a carriage full of luggage approached them going the other way. "Hey! Any idea what's going on?" Sam asked.

"Don't really know for sure," the bellman said. "Seems some guy got all drugged up and flipped out or something. Anyway, he died in some kind of fall I guess. Apparently he was by himself, so who knows."

"Lots of squads."

"Pretty weird for this place, for sure. And even stranger is I heard there was some kind of multiple murder in some bar in town last night as well. I mean, you got to be kidding me. Not here." He thought of going on but kept pushing his cart forward with the job at hand. "Dude. We'll be on CNN before the end of the day. You watch."

Sam and Liv looked at each other and hustled up to the lodge to check out and leave for the airport. They moved quickly, jumped in her Subaru and held hands the entire trip to the airport like two kids secretly going steady. Just before they got there, Sam drew his hand back, reached inside his coat pocket and put his hand back over the top of hers, then flipped her hand over and dropped something into it and closed her fingers around it.

"What?" she asked, enjoying the play.

"Something I spotted in the gift shop at the Lodge. Just something silly."

Liv opened her hand and brought the delicate ring closer to her eyes. There was an exquisite miniature ivory carving of a woman's face surrounded by flowing hair. It had a curious three dimensional look to it. Unique and beautiful. "Is this supposed to be me?"

"In oh so many ways. It's Marapolis, the daughter of the Greek God, Zeus, the one who controls the fate of life- those we meet, when, where, why…. I thought it was a nice fit."

"It's beautiful." She leaned over and kissed him on the cheek, then turned him and kissed him gently on the lips. "You can't imagine how grateful I am to you for making me feel like I will miss you so badly."

They got out of the car and walked together arms hooked as far as the security would allow. "No words… ," Sam said softly. "There just aren't the words. So go."

He waited and watched her get checked in at the small counter. It was only minutes before they motioned her and the others aboard, escorting them out a ground level door for a short walk to the small, twin engine plane. She turned and waved before getting in, not sure if she could really see him or not, then ducked inside.

❧

The drive back to Kershaw alone was sweet with the longings bubbling up inside of him. The two of them had been virtually locked at the hips since their chance meeting, and sending her off on that little twin engine airplane felt like saying goodbye forever way, way too early. It actually hurt- set up in the pit of his stomach and sent stingers out in all directions. He could smell every bit of her in the Subaru; her hands on the leather of the steering wheel, her hair behind him on the headrest, the scent of her perfume etched into the fabric of the seat itself. He tried to shake it all loose with a laugh as he pictured himself at the side of the road, knees in the gravel, a steep drop off and certain death a few feet to the left, sniffing and caressing a car seat.

The car moved around a tight curve and just off to the left was a little bar and road stop along the highway that looked just too inviting to pass up, but when he walked inside and found it empty except for its lonesome owner who appeared to be half-in-the-bag, he settled for a six-pack to go.

Another moment of truth was quick to follow as he drove ahead and cracked a beer between his legs. Sure enough, the scraggly looking guy leaning on one leg standing on the side of the road had his thumb out. Sam smiled and shook his head slowly. The grand irony was lost on him as he hit the accelerator. "Wonder what that crazy son of bitch is doing these days?" he said aloud, recalling the gangly, goofy-looking Lomis Walls. Probably trying to cash in those diamonds, Sam thought again, front and center. He would find him when the time came. It would need to be soon, he figured. But then, even thinking about going back to being Colonel Jake Parker for a short time thrashed around in his head and left him swearing off and moving forward. Screw the money. Wasn't meant to be, he would tell himself. He *stole* the diamonds from a dead man. How was something good to come of that anyway? The hell with it. Yeah. The hell with it. Millions. Yeah, right. Strange, conflicting, a mess of wasted thinking. Then there was being in love again. Strange. Nothing better. Not ever. But it sure was strange to be crazy in love again.

No less strange was pulling into the drive of Liv's house where they had set up light housekeeping. He walked inside to the quiet and dark of a Sunday night, flipped the living room light switch and froze. Every object in the room had been moved, ripped, torn, overturned and there were dinner plate sized holes in the walls and ceiling. Sam cautiously moved ahead into the den to find the same situation, then on to the kitchen and back bedrooms, all disheveled and disassembled in an obvious search for something. His heart pounded at him relentlessly and moved up to a dry throat where he began forming the words that described what he thought he had put behind him. They had found him again. And there was no reason to believe they were not close by, waiting to make another move. Worse, he had brought this to Liv's doorstep, literally, which was the very last thing he had wanted to happen. He carefully walked up the stairs that led to the master bedroom, trying to figure out another option other than getting out of there and taking his mess with him. It was his only move. He knew it.

He swung the door open at the top of the stairs and turned on the light. In matching rockers by the bay window sat two figures in black ski masks and sleek black body garments. The one rocking gently spoke first. "Dr. Parker. Where are the diamonds?"

Sam hadn't heard himself referred to as Dr. Parker in so long his mind rejected it at first. But it only took moments to go back; only moments to bring back the life he was trying to leave behind.

He swallowed hard as it all settled back in and leaned into the wall. "You are after the *diamonds?*"

"Yes, you know the ones. Tiny, uncut, rare diamonds, five million American dollars worth? Those diamonds?" Sam was guessing the accent was Russian. "The ones belonging to our friends back in Pakistan. The ones you managed to steal when you escaped."

"I don't have them anymore."

"Not here. We are quite certain of that. Yes. Then where?"

"There was an accident."

"We know all of that as well. Where are the diamonds? Let's not waste any more time."

"That's the point. I went to get them after the accident and they were gone. I suspect they were stolen."

"Most amusing, my friend. If that were true, it would mean the diamonds were stolen from a thief, that being you..., and, of course, the crushed man you took them from had also stole them from the central treasury. And, of course, they were likely stolen in the first place." The one rocking laughed heartily and the other joined in on cue. "You are but the next greedy fool in line, Dr. Parker. But enough of this. Obviously we checked out the same car at the bottom of the same canyon. You were supposed to die in fiery car crash, by the way, I am told. But there was no body, no diamonds. And, we weren't going to read about the fiery death of a man who never existed, were we? So we went back to the house in Iowa. Surely you can surmise we did not find you or the diamonds there either."

"So how did you find me again?" It was Sam's nature to assume a conversational tone while his mind was grinding out a plan. Buy a little time here, he was told by a little voice inside.

The laughter coursed higher to raucous. "Why don't you turn that overhead light out, Dr. Parker. That big window to your deck faces the mountains, and who knows what else is out there. Big, bad American boogyman, perhaps?"

Sam flipped the switch off which left them to continue their discussion in the shadows of the light from the hallway.

The voice was that of an educated man, a professional seemingly accustomed and quite enamored with the deep resonance of his own voice. "We let things settle down for a few months, then we returned to the scene of the crime."

"But how did you find me? Just curious."

"Of course. Your curiosity for such things is most understandable. That's the best part of the story thus far. We stopped in to, I believe it is called, Gert's Grub, for a coffee, and as we were enjoying what was a surprisingly bold and pleasant brew, we could not help but listen in on a talking magpie of an old woman telling two other old women the story that had us on the edge of our fucking seats."

Sam could have finished this part for him, but kept thinking through his plan instead.

"It seems this dashing, good looking man just dropped into the Kershaw midst and next thing you know there is a whirlwind of love and romance with none other than the town's good mayor, a young, beautiful woman most think has a bright political future. She was a great story teller, Dr. Parker, perhaps needlessly loud, a bit repetitive, but full of information and most willing to share her knowledge. The others referred to her as Sarah, I believe. Anyway, moving on, finding the mayor's real office, then your little workshop in the back was child's play, and picking off this address from a couple of utility bills from the honorable mayor's desk was a cake walk as well. And, as it worked out, here you are. What are the odds?"

"I wouldn't bet them."

"Yes. By the way, perhaps key for us may be paying more attention to that girlfriend of yours. Where is she?"

Sam's sense of being began a dizzy back spin that took him whirling quickly through all the guilt over what had happened to his wife, their life together, the ending, the cemetery, and now Liv. "I can think of a thousand reasons people would be after me. But the diamonds... ." Sam laughed quietly and stared at the empty irony that should have been written on the wall. He watched the two men rock in silence.

"Enough, then, Dr. Parker. The fact of the matter is we collect if I can prove you are dead, but there is much more in it for us if we retrieve the diamonds. I am inclined at this point to call it even as long as you come up with the diamonds. Or five million dollars in cash would do, I suppose."

"Five million! Really? Five million?"

"How about until noon tomorrow. Will that be enough time for you to figure your end out?" The one doing the talking rocked while the other took out a large revolver and screwed a silencer onto the barrel end.

"A smart guy like you. Where do you suppose I might find that kind of money in Kershaw, Idaho?"

"No matter. Should we just shoot you now, then?"

"Too messy."

"I am told you are a man who can summon great resources at the highest levels. So let's get on with this, Dr. Parker. We will return tomorrow at noon."

"For the record? Fuck off."

"Until noon tomorrow then?" He looked over at his counterpart to be sure he was ready, cocked his revolver and pointed it straight at Sam. "Your call, Dr. Parker."

Escaping a sure, slow death in Pakistan only to have the quick sort of death pop up as an option in the mountains of Idaho. "You win," said Sam.

"Right here. Noon."

"So be it."

They rose immediately and Sam followed them down the stairs and through the kitchen towards the back door. "And one more thing, Dr. Parker," the talker shot back over his shoulder. But before he could get to that, Dr. Jake Parker had circled his neck with a powerful flex of an arm and with a quick, perfectly executed jerk, broke the spinal chord away from the base of his skull and dropped him to a lifeless pile on the shiny kitchen floor. Moments before, Dr. Parker had done the same to the silent one as he reached the base of the stairs. He looked down at his hands as the adrenalin caressed his insides. It had been so easy. So effortless. And he felt the nothingness that came upon him after a righteous kill. A job done. As it should be. The expected result, nothing more, nothing less.

He panned back and forth between the bodies while spending too much time wishing this had happened anywhere but in Liv's house. Finally, his mind clicked into gear and he began dragging his dead outside.

The pickup truck gathered speed as he headed south of town, its driver numb to the world except working hands on wheel, eyes on the road that he traveled northbound just hours before in the Subaru. He tried to decide just how far out to go, which unmarked road leading off the highway to take, knowing he could not get rid of his cargo in the truck bed soon enough.

The cell phone on the front seat next to him buzzed and lit up. He knew he had to pick it up.

"Hi baby doll," he said without breathing.

"I'm missing my man."

"You can't imagine how he misses you."

"Ridiculous, right? Two people can't love each other this much."

Not grown-ups," Sam stuttered out. They both took a breather into the phone. "So, who is this?"

"You sound like you're going on fumes. What are you up to?"

"Just... sitting here, thinking about you. You being down there with that guy, Perkins. Something about him, I don't know, a little puff of lie dust coming off of him when he talked." Even as he said it, Sam disliked the echo of irony he was tossing out.

"Listen, I'm keenly aware the man thinks each time he sees me is going to be the time my jeans magically drop to the floor, but it actually works to my advantage."

"Okay."

"Okay? You alright, baby? You really do sound kind of strange to me. You're forcing the funny."

"I'm fine."

"A woman knows."

"Just didn't realize how much I will miss you."

"Will...?"

"Would. Would miss you. Sorry. Just tired. You're right."

"Get some sleep then.

"Okay."

"I'll call you in the morning."

"Okay."

Sam thought the silence was just that, but when the dial tone sounded off in his ear, he was relieved she had hung up.

CHAPTER TWENTY FOUR

It was not like Lomis to hang around after the fact. But the fact was this time around demanded not only that he stay, but reclaim what was his at all costs. He bought a reasonably good fake beard from a second hand store in Hailey that made him look like an integral part of the deliberate human landscape in and around Sun Valley and Ketchum.

This had been anything but a sleepy week in this mountain community. The local paper and radio stations were buzzing at the firing line with the triple killing at Lefty's Short Steer Bar, and to a much lesser degree, an odd and ugly death at the Sun Valley Lodge that left many questions unanswered. The authorities insisted there were many clues and leads being pursued in both cases, but admitted nothing seemed to link them. They were looking for anyone who had been in Lefty's and had reason to believe two or maybe even three people besides the victims were inside the bar at the time of the murder. In the Sun Valley Lodge incident, it was confirmed the condo had been rented to the victim but also widely reported another man from California had been sharing the room with the victim and had vanished afterward. Bit and pieces ran off over the radio, in the papers and off the tongues of patrons in local bars, all tuning forks to the ears of Lomis Walls, who was surprising himself with this delight in the aftermath. He was usually so far down the road when his work had been discovered that he rarely heard or read anything about the actual goings on that were now tickling him into muffled laughter over a beer in a saloon in the middle of downtown Ketchum on a Thursday afternoon.

"I heard the whole thing at the Steer was cult stuff, triple suicide thing or something like that," one down a few stools was adding to the fuel.

"You know those damn white supremists from up north hate this town. We know that for a fact. Wouldn't surprise me a bit if they was involved somehow."

"Gotta be outsiders for sure," said another older guy, wanting to hear himself be part of the conversation.

"They ruled out anything gang related, I guess," said a woman on short days and last legs, as her brittle thin fingers shook a shot glass of cheap vodka into her mouth. "But it scares the bejesus out of me, Wally."

"It's Bob."

"Sorry. Bob."

"No big deal, Wanda."

"Nothing surprises anymore, does it? Everybody yelling and screaming and shooting for goddsake. Everybody demanding to get theirs. Makes me glad I only got a few bottles left to guzzle down," she said.

Bob gave Wanda plenty of room at the bar. Bob always gave her plenty of room at the bar so she could wave her hands without smacking him around.

Lomis sat alone. Lomis always sat alone, fidgeting with a beer label or twisting a straw, thinking, mumbling out of range, debating, occasionally offering himself a chortled grunt to acknowledge a running summary of his own work to date.

He needed to get on with the unfinished business in Kershaw with the love birds. This would take another plan, carefully thought out, unlike anything he had attempted before. After all, the underlying reason for all of his success had been the inability of anybody to link him with an event, place or time. He had always been under the radar and understood how to remain there. This was a risk with familiarity of event, place and time. Going back, as it were, and adding risk in the face of reason. Maybe the money wasn't important. Maybe it was. Senator Perkins had suddenly stopped sending money to the P.O. Box Lomis had set up under the name of Johnson Industries in Ketchum. Despite the phone threats Lomis continued to make, it was obvious to him Perkins was trying to call a bluff, and maybe the P.O. Box thing was a mistake. Maybe the Senator would come after him. But that wasn't likely, Lomis figured. At this point, with the larger issue at hand, and just the idea of someone scamming him out of a rightful fortune he literally held in his hands at one point was adding a topping of growing anxiety to the risk and necessity.

Lomis popped a few Xanax, finished his beer and left. He would catch the Andy Griffith Show and Sanford and Son, catch a nap and be ready to go after dark. Hands jammed in his pockets, cursing the cold, he headed towards a dead end street two blocks from his apartment. An old Chevy pickup truck sat angled on the side of the road just past the last house on the street and before the road demised to a fenced pasture. He had been casing it for months. As best he could tell, it had never moved. To wit, a mound of snow the size of an igloo snuggled into the truck bed. And it had current Idaho license plates.

As things worked out, Lomis was asleep before Aunt Bea had finished scolding Andy with a wagging finger for not finishing his vegetables at dinner. He awoke energized and eager for the work to be done, filled and swelling with the confidence of the roll chosen for him to play. When he pulled the tarp off of Odessa's car in the garage, it was as if he had unearthed hidden treasure no less important than the raising of the Titanic. He had taken the license plates off and disposed of them long ago, and began humming as he put on the set he had just borrowed from the old Chevy.

The car groaned reluctantly at first but then started with a grateful rush that brought a wry smile to his face and a little twitch to his cheek just above the jawbone.

By the time the speedometer read fifty-five on the highway, he had to suppress an urge to wave to the darkened, pathetic world around him that seemed at that very moment so small, idling by in the blackness, sapped of its vitality and significance. There was only his world, his rules of life, the fates of all decided by his Gods imbedded clearly in every movement he made. And there, deep down beneath the base of his skull, a haunting of sexual urgings screamed out for attention. His mark, the Mayor of Kershaw, had blossomed into a wonderful fantasy over the past few days. Extraordinary circumstances. A perfect storm of blending his outrage about the money with his fermenting sexual depravity. And to think he could possibly settle both scores, then toss in a fitting death for the Riddler, and walk away with a fortune left him without the words or thoughts to thank his Gods enough. Never had such opportunity been laid at his feet. Lomis glanced over his shoulder to make sure he had tossed his gym bag of utensils and knives onto the back seat. He had, but with all the commotion going on in his head, he couldn't be sure until he reached backed and felt for it.

Just when he thought the delirium of feeling just lucky to be who he was might cause him to run off the road, Lomis heard a voice on the radio cutting into a Toby Keith song:

"FBI agents in California reportedly have taken a Palm Springs California man into custody for questioning in the recent mysterious death at the Sun Valley Lodge. At this time there are no indications as to whether the man is also being questioned regarding the triple homicide at Lefty's Short Steer Bar in Ketchum on the same night. More on this story at the top of the hour."

"Praise the Gods!" Lomis yelled out, opening his window and waving at the people in the dark again. Convinced now, beyond a doubt, his short lay off was for a reason. This was to be the biggest moment for him ever, a reward from the Gods for past services rendered; A laying down of the gauntlet to see if he was up to the challenges that would surely lie ahead and beyond.

Immortality and living forever. He began to play it back and forth in his mind. What would his place be in history when in fact he would continue to add to the history with each day and each conquest. This would go on forever. He would go on forever. It was a luscious thought, too big and overwhelming to think about for very long.

As he reached the outskirts and the quiet that was Kershaw, a gripping chill set into the small of his back and rose up to fill him and bring a cold sweat to his forehead. With fame came the end, did it not? For most, at least those with some degree of an infamous note beside their name, a death of their own, or a life behind bars being quietly observed as some sick icon with a growing price on his head.

His Gods would see to it this would not be his fate.

Lomis wiped the sweat away and tried to shake himself back into a reality that worked for him. The spinning and weaving continued inside his head as he drove around town to get a feel of what might be going on, if anything. Suddenly a complete change of thought set in, shifting and lightening the load considerably. He hadn't killed or raped for nearly six months, the longest stretch he could remember in his adult life. The only thing different was having the money, the twenty-five thousand, which had dwindled down to less than a thousand. Rent, food, liquor, and cocaine had eaten it up far quicker than he could have imagined. He could never afford cocaine before but he had made a nice little connection at a Laundromat in Ketchum. He never kept track of what he spent, but he knew the pattern. If he drank enough, he would go from there and neither cared or remembered much after that.

Just the idea of having any money at all brought him sleep in the night, skin that crawled less, jaws that twitched less. The typically uncontrollable urges inside were nothing more than tiny flat pebbles skipping across the glassy surface of a small pond. What would life look like with millions? What would he be like with millions? What would he do first? Whatever and wherever his Gods led him. There was time for all of that.

He eased back and pulled the car over to listen closer to his own conclusions. Kill the bitch for sure, right or wrong, diamonds or no diamonds, she was to die. Maybe he would then be Lomis Walls, a man of means. Perhaps a new name, something befit of money. He would work on that after. Maybe Florida. Miami, or South Beach. Play the women with a different angle; a life with an angle he never dreamed possible.

He drove to the little office building across from the clinic where his Kershaw story really began. He looked for Sam's pick up truck, not expecting to find it and didn't. Small town, but damn near everybody had a pick-me-up truck. She had that brand new Subaru though, he recalled, and matching the two of them up shouldn't be all that hard unless they sat in a garage. Lomis spent the next two hours driving around while sipping off a bottle of Jack Daniels held between his legs, becoming more irritated with everything from the infernal darkness to the ridiculous number of detached garages in Kershaw.

"Fucking people. People are just fucked," he announced to the world, spitting out the window he had cracked open to keep it from fogging up, and to try to rid the car of the feint, nauseatingly sweet odor of Odessa, Michaelen, and the house they used to live in. In an annoying departure from the matter at hand, his mind began to list all the reasons he should really be a thousand miles away from this place right now. The list started with bodies and ended with bodies. It wasn't hard to refocus on millions, to the point he sneered in the rear view mirror at the little voice of a suggestion that he had forgotten the diamonds were not his to begin with. He was reaching too far for the big money. He had already made twenty-five thousand on the deal; more money than he had ever seen in a lifetime.

As he turned another corner and rumbled down a gravel road with darkened houses scattered on either side, he brought back the conversation he had with the senator from a couple of days before. It was the first time he had ever talked with him direct.

"So I could use another five thousand. Not to be greedy," he had said. He smiled into the phone and waited.

"What if I was to say you weren't going to get another dime?" The Senator's voice had tumbled back slowly.

"I would say that would be bad for business. Yours, particularly," Lomis said.

There was bolder, more educated laughter from Senator Perkins. "Yes, I was told you seemed a very witty guy over the phone. Not really the rapist/extortionist type."

"I'm just a business man, senator. I might go about my business in just a little different manner than you, but then maybe not. You think?"

"I will tell you what I think. I think it is time you pay for your crime."

"What the hell is that supposed to mean?" Lomis was clearly enjoying this. What the good senator did not realize was Lomis didn't even need his money anymore. This was all just for shits and giggles. "You sound all official and ominous. I can't even vote for you, you sick fuck. Nor can all those little girls you cram your dick into."

"What you don't understand, Mr. Walls, is that I have related the problem with my staff, shared it with the authorities in a manner more flattering to me than you, of course, and I have employed certain operatives whose sole reason for living is now tracking you down and killing you in a most vicious and painful way."

Lomis found it difficult to believe, but Perkins did not sound like much of a player in this game. "Well, I do admit I love it when your little faggot ass talks shit, Perkins." With the new opening, Lomis launched into a diatribe that covered every known despicable attribute a man can put on another man.

There was silence at the other end. Lomis thought the senator may have hung up. Then the senator sighed and cleared his throat. "By the way, you should know in case you try to peddle your sweet little tale, the wonderful owners of the Pine Bluff Hotel have recently sold the place for an extraordinary amount of money and let's just say part of their keeping all that money is a golden silence for the rest of their born days. "Again, good luck, and thanks for the trace, dumbass. Don't call us. We'll call you."

Lomis tried to rip the phone set from its metal bound cord, but it only bounced back and smacked him in the chin. How could he have fallen for that? How sloppy can you get? He spent the next few hours pacing in his room, then walked down to Albertson's food store in Ketchum to get a bottle of Jack. He had his route from there, circling back and across town to a side street and the laundromat, a rundown, one-story building that hadn't been painted in fifty years. He went inside and grabbed a red sock from the cardboard box marked "Lost and Found", slipped five twenty dollar bills into it and clipped it to the center window lock on the front window. From across the street, or from somewhere he was told never to seek out, the red sock was spotted and within fifteen minutes a little Mexican boy no older than fourteen walked inside, grabbed it and walked back out. Another ten or fifteen minutes later, the boy reappeared with the sock and dropped it back into the Lost and Found box. Lomis had his gram. There was a note in with it this time- "Next time $200." Fucking little shit. Started out at fifty bucks a few months ago and now two hundred?

He screamed out for his Gods and took another swig from the bottle in his lap. "Fuck this shit," he said disgustedly, turning another corner and thinking he might be better off coming back and casing it out during the daylight hours. "Town's too fucking small, goddamit," he swore. But just as he was about to call it quits, a car coming from the other direction pulled into the driveway ahead on the left. It was the prettiest little Subaru he had ever seen.

CHAPTER TWENTY FIVE

"Interesting," said Liv, admiring the new couch and furniture. "He redecorates, too."

Sam was quick to make the drinks, a Bailey's Irish Crème for her, a brandy for him, but for the first moment since he had met her, he was uneasy and certain things were about to change for the worse. He struggled to think of a way to reel things back, but nowhere in his vast arsenal of tools and skills was there a way to keep this conversation from happening.

"I know we have our little agreement about the past, Sam," she said. "You are going to have to tell me what's going on with you if I am ever to trust those eyes again."

Sam took a deep bolt of the brandy and waited until Liv settled in among the pillows on the oversize couch in the den. He looked out the back window into the darkness and turned to her, smiled and leaned up against the wall and took a deep breath. "My real name is Jake Parker. Dr. Jake Parker in some quarters, Colonel Jake Parker in some others, both in yet others. The doctor part refers to an MIT engineering degree, the Colonel part refers to my Navy Seal years and subsequently various contracted assignments as a CIA operative and a mercenary of sorts for the State Department. In my last assignment, I was operating as a lone wolf and closing in on Osama Bin Laden in the border mountains along the Pakistan/Afghan border when I was captured by a band of Bin Laden loyalists and thrown into a jail cell to rot. I got an opportunity to escape and I did." Jake stopped for a moment to gauge how this was sitting with her. Not well, he thought, but felt he should go on anyway. "It seemed, rightly, most everybody had me for dead, including my wife. You know that part of the story." Sam walked over to refill his brandy. He knew Liv would nurse hers and likely leave an inch in the glass to be poured out. In the glances up at her eyes, he could tell she had prepared herself for something, maybe even assuming a politically correct pose of sorts to help her keep her true feelings and expected reactions in check. "So…, I just got into a car I had hidden in my garage and took off. No destination in mind."

Liv walked up and poured herself another full glass. "What question should ask I first, you think?" She thoughtfully ran her tongue around her mouth and looked up at him, giving him a look of under whelmed innocence. "So let me assume you are telling me some version of the truth because if some of what you say is true you really couldn't tell me anyway, Sam. Or I guess we go with *Jake,* is it?"

"It's Jake. It's the name the nurses gave me when I showed up at Cook County Hospital one morning some thirty-eight years ago. Not much more that really matters right now, I guess."

"How heartbreaking. Then, what was is it? CIA? Foreign Legion by the age of five?"

"I get the sarcasm."

"I should know better. There's no such thing as what we had. I hate the role of playing the fool."

"I…, I can't tell you much more."

"Jake can't. Sam could."

"I guess you could say that."

"Actually, I liked Sam, Jake. I was in love with Sam. I still am." She steadied herself. "But then, I'm young, naïve, and obviously in need of some schooling in the wicked ways of men and their multiple ways to break a heart."

"I deserve this."

"Yes, you do. One minute you are a good guy, good looking, adoring, masterful in bed. I could go on about Sam. You would even like Sam, Jake."

It was as if they did not know where to take the conversation as silence fell on them and their eyes refused to meet. When the doorbell rang, it was almost a relief. They both looked at the front door as though it was a total surprise it was there.

"Constituency calls, more than likely," Liv said, easily changing her mood as she walked slowly to the door. She looked back at the old Sam to make sure his eyes were on her ass, then turned to look through the peek hole. "Vaguely familiar." She pressed her face up to get as good a view as she could. "Take a look."

Jake moved to the door and took a look. "Christ. It's Lomis."

"Who?"

"Don't worry. You'll remember him," Jake said as he opened the door.

"Riddler!" Lomis said, opening his arms to the sides to present the unlikely in full.

"What in the hell are you doing here?" Jake asked, leaning into the door and crossing his arms.

"You'd never believe it," he said with an evil grin, the one the Riddler remembered well and didn't like. "You going to invite a guy in for a beer or what?"

"Not my house." He turned, but Liv was gone from the room. "But then you might know that."

"Hey, I was just passing through, reliving a memory or two about falling off the side of a mountain and stopped into Big Al's for a beer. I'm puffing up about the guy who saved my life and all and Big Al tells me you were still in town and shackin' up with the Mayor. He told me where the place was and thought I would take a shot before I disappeared forever."

"I'll be damned." Jake gave up a short laugh and shook his head. "You just come from there?"

"I know it's a bit late. I figure you might have some of that good brandy around you like so much."

Jake stiffened against the door and stared a whole through Lomis. "Big Al is in Vegas. Been there for two days."

Lomis began to laugh. "Gotcha!" he laughed and quickly pulled a silver revolver from his coat pocket and trained it between Jake's eyes. "You are one nasty motherfucker, Riddler, and I never liked your ass. Now, what do you say we get inside and you can get me that fucking brandy." His jaw twitching away, Lomis nearly thanked himself out loud for deciding to bring the gun along he picked up through his coke connection, delivered in a large white, unmatched Nike tube sock.

"Why not leave this outside," Jake said. "You want money, I got money. Let me get it and you can be on your way."

Lomis motioned Jake inside with the tip of the gun. "Not your money I'm after, smart guy. Inside. Now."

Jake turned and walked inside. Lomis stayed safely back but kept the gun pointed and his finger on the trigger. Once Jake was half way across the room, Lomis peeked through the crack at the door's hinges to make sure the woman wasn't hiding there with something to bash his head in, then ducked inside quickly and circled his eyes around the room as he shut the door behind him. "Where is she?"

Jake shrugged. "Actually, we were just in the middle of a rather touch and go moment when the door bell rang and I would not be surprised if she wasn't calling the police right at this very minute." Jake's voice was as loud as it got aiming for one set of ears wherever they might be.

"Cute, motherfucker. Real cute." Lomis could see the walk-up bar set up on the other side of room that led to the kitchen.

Liv appeared in the doorway of the first floor bathroom. "What is all the commotion...." She saw the gun, looked up at Lomis, then over at Jake as he poured brandy into a glass.

"You get over on the couch. Sit." Lomis waved the gun at Jake, then at Liv. "Hate guns. I really do." Jake walked towards Lomis with the drink. "Just set it down on the table there," said Lomis. "Then take a seat next to your little whore."

Jake did as he was told and sat down next to Liv as Lomis picked up the glass in one hand and took a chair across from them. He waved the tip of the gun a little, overplaying the aim at one, then, the other, pretending to be perplexed by the decision making process.

Jake started to put an arm around Liv. "None of that shit," Lomis warned. "Both of you keep your hands out front on your lap where I can see them."

"It's been a very interesting evening," Liv said softly, but coldly. "Which one of you would like to fill in some more blanks for me?"

"Oh, listen to her highness, the mayor of fucking Kershaw. "Yeah, I'll bet you are one smart cunt, alright."

Liv turned to Jake. "It's coming back to me. This is the guy who was with you when you came to town."

"Oh yeah," Jake shook his head. "The last life I saved."

"For a reason," Lomis added. "For tonight."

"Why the gun?" Liv asked.

"I'm deciding that right now. I mean, I can kind of see up between your legs there and I'm getting hard as a rock."

Liv squeezed her legs together and pushed her jean skirt down as far as the material would go."

"I mean, we have things to discuss, but it's been awhile for me. I can see that now. See, I got this cock the size of the Riddler's left forearm there.... Yeah, I can see that's got your attention."

"Enough, for godsakes," Jake blurted, trying to cover up whatever Lomis was going to say next. "Lomis, you crazy fuck, tell us what you want and then get the hell out of here!"

"And listen to the big man over there. I suppose you think I wouldn't shoot you or your bitch?" Lomis aimed the gun at a mirror above a credenza across the room and the explosion from his shot echoed through the room, followed by a silence only Lomis seemed to enjoy. "Better." He sat back in the chair and got himself comfortable, crossing his legs, preparing to enjoy the drink. "Damn it was easy to get in here. You know I had all these thoughts about the how and when, then when it came right down to it, I rang the fucking doorbell!" His laughter was madness, unabashed and evil.

Jake studied Lomis' every move, calculating, trying to stay even or get ahead, but he had seen this kind of insanity emboldened with a gun before; it was universal and global and unpredictable, and more often fatal for some or all involved. As Liv's look went from stoic to anxious, her eyes pleaded with him to do something, or to tell her what to do.

"Shall we get down to business?" Lomis asked, double checking to make sure the safety was off the gun. He preferred knives absolutely, but it seemed time to change up on some of that, modernize, upgrade the old Lomis Walls into a speeding world requiring increasing agility and adaptability. He liked the warmth coming to the cold steel in his hand, the way in which the gun seemed to dig in and press to his skin like a big hug.

"You can leave your wallet in your pocket. My guess is your lady here knows what I am after."

Liv's eyes widened. "What are you talking about?"

"Let me run the story for you. You might know parts of it, or all of it, for all I know, but it really doesn't matter."

"Try me," Liv shot back.

"Actually, it's too bad your granddaddy couldn't be here right now to hold your hand while he explains it to you."

"Gannon? Oh, please." Liv shook her head and shot the pleading eyes back at Jake.

"So tell me, little Miss Mayor. Did he give you the diamonds in that old coffee can? Or did he dress it up a little and give them to you in a gift box from J.C. Penny?"

Jake's body nearly launched from the couch, but Lomis waved him Back with the gun.

A tight smile tried to work its way into Liv's face. "What diamonds?"

Jake was bursting inside, but an instinctive voice, the one that had kept him alive in the face of certain death a dozen or more times told him to hang on to his thoughts for now. He shrugged and tried to ease back closer to the back cushion of the couch.

"This could get more interesting than I thought," said Lomis. "Maybe we should let you tell her about the diamonds, Riddler. I think she's a lying bitch, but let's play along for awhile until I get bored." He looked over at Jake, and waited.

Liv's face drew long and pale as she turned to Jake with a wet mist of confusion in her eyes.

Jake stared Lomis down. "Are you sure you want me to do that, Lomis? I mean, after all, if I do that, your claim for the diamonds goes in the crapper and your very reason for being here goes right back out the door."

"What are you talking about, Jake?" Liv barked. The name fell oddly from her mouth.

"Jake?" Lomis inquired. "Who's Jake?"

"And I don't know all of that story either," Liv shot back.

"Lomis, please, put the gun down. There's no need for the gun." Jake's tone was one of final settlement and a foregone conclusion. "You know the diamonds weren't yours, so why do this?"

"That's not the way I see it. Not the way I see it at all. Far as I remember, I found those diamonds in an abandoned, burned out car. Could have belonged to anybody, I suppose. Maybe somebody killed in that car wreck. I was just after something I thought might still be in the car when I came across a couple of sparkly little guys on the ground and found this old burned up coffee can laying on the ground. What luck, eh?"

Jake smiled and nodded at Lomis. "You are one lucky guy, Lomis. Luck comes and goes, though. You figure yours is coming, or going?"

"Fucking Riddler," Lomis mumbled.

"Truth is… ," Jake began, "The diamonds weren't mine. At least not to begin with."

Liv shot him a look. "*You* owned the diamonds?"

"Sort of."

"Shit almighty!" Lomis bellowed. "I thought you didn't know anything about the diamonds, sweet thing."

Jake sighed deeply and watched as Lomis moved up a notch on the chair and Liv leaned forward to make sure she wouldn't miss a word. "At one time I thought they would be sort of a back pay thing for me. But, as it turned out, they were more like an insurance policy. I just kept them and I let my mind play with what I should do with them for a long time. Never cashed one in, never used one for as much as a cup of coffee. But I knew they were there. That was interesting."

"Your ass!" Lomis yelled out.

"Actually, just recently, the rightful owner, or at least two representatives of the rightful owner, showed up to reclaim them. Nasty guys. Even nastier than you, Lomis."

"So this explains the new furniture?" She glared at Jake.

"So what did you tell them, Riddler?" Lomis was on the edge of his seat.

"I told them the truth. I didn't have them anymore. Of course, when they told me what they were worth, I shit a brick."

"As if you didn't know. Fuck you!" scoffed Lomis.

"I didn't. I didn't want to know. Not really."

"God, you are a horse's ass. I oughta just kill you for being fucking stupid, Riddler."

Even if you kill me, Lomis, that's all I can tell you. It's all that matters anyway."

"I knew there was something about you," Lomis said, clearly amused by the story. "You are of the dark side, Riddler. How did you get the diamonds, then?"

"I can't tell you that."

Liv's anger was turning to disgust, as though time had been wasted, and maybe more than that. She looked up at Jake and contrived a smiled that didn't last.

Jake felt like a sheet of ice had coated her and could not stop the Colonel Parker from bubbling up through his middle. But he welcomed him back because his instincts were telling him he might need to rely on the Colonel taking over to survive once again.

"That's some real bullshit," said Lomis.

"You can call it about anything you want, but you still stole the diamonds from me, out of my car," Jake added quickly.

"Call the cops!" Lomis offered, then laughed hoarsely and got up to refill his glass. Jake's head swiveled to every move Lomis made, waiting, watching, anticipating a misstep or mistake. "See, I figured you were on the run just like me the way you handled things after the crash. No cops. You just sort of taking care of everything like it didn't really happen."

"None of that has any bearing on this," Jake was quick to point out.

"Sure does. Sounds to me like I lucked into finding those diamonds the same way you did, and maybe back pay for my whole fucking life, Riddler." His voice grew somber as he poured and returned to his seat, aiming the gun with a finger heavier on the trigger.

"Give this up before it gets out of hand, Lomis," Jake said.

"Then you have the wild card, the wild thing there," he wiggled the gun tip in Liv's direction. "She comes along on your end while I just happen to buddy up with her old, lying, dying grandpappy. I give him the diamonds to fence- let me know if I'm going too fast for you, Riddler- and he gives old grateful Lomis Walls twenty-five grand and a big smile which I have to tell you made me the happiest man on the face of the earth at the time."

A reluctant smile tried Jake's face on for size, but a glance at Liv's stone exterior chopped it off. "Twenty-five grand."

"Yeah. Cheap bastard, eh? But you know what? My Gods were still with me through all of this. Brought me here to you tonight to get what's owed me from your little sweetheart here. She's ends up with the diamonds, dog. Go figure."

Liv's face broke into a knowing smile. "Gods? I must admit that is an amazing spin on all of this and my heart is just breaking for the both of you. My guess is you are in this together and this is some thinly veiled attempt to try to extort money from me. You'll never see any money, diamonds, or anything else."

Jake studied her to see if she was putting out a signal for him to pick up on.

"Okay." Lomis got up, cheeks twitching and pinking up with a rush of boiling blood. "I'm bored with this already. Let's cut the shit."

Jake's eyes tried to meet Liv's, but hers were somewhere else. It had only taken days to unravel everything he had tried to put behind and in front of him. Hours really. Unrealistic, he supposed, to think something that felt so pure and right could remain disconnected from the rest of the world. By most reports, even outer space was full of floating junk. He pushed his hair back and rubbed at his beard. He could not detect any body language to figure where she was going with this, but he figured he would play along until his time came. Maybe she was smarter than he was giving her credit for. Of course she was.

"Well then," Lomis said, rising and reaching into his jacket pocket. He brought out a roll of silver gray duct tape for observation. "Your time has come."

CHAPTER TWENTY SIX

"Riddler, if I use any more of this on you I might not have enough to hold that wildcat down." Lomis had taped Liv's arms and wrists to a chair next to Jake, one piece across her mouth, but the single layers were just temporary. He had tied Jake's hands behind his back first thing to make sure he couldn't outmaneuver him in any way. That being done, he positioned Jake into a high-backed dining room chair and lashed him to it with the duct tape, doubling and tripling the wraps. Lomis stood back and took another look at his work, using his hands and fingers to frame the picture of the two of them sitting side by side, looking up at him, regaled in silver gray duct tape. "Boring," he pronounced. "Excuse me a moment. I will be back in less than a minute, but if you want to give everything a good try while I'm gone, feel free." Lomis flipped a winking smile at Liv and went out the front door, leaving it open a crack.

Jake looked over at Liv as both struggled against their bindings. Jake was sure he could get out of his if he could be left alone long enough, but before he could get one wrist cocked and working, Lomis was back in the room, a long hank of thick nylon rope over his shoulder and what looked like a new, carved handle hunting knife in a sheath strapped to his belt. An unfamiliar self doubt began coursing through him, suggesting it was possible the rust in his game had him waiting too long to make a move on Lomis.

Lomis looked up and studied the large wagon wheel light fixture hanging down from a black steel chain. The chain led up to a huge eyebolt at the apex of the high ceiling. He began to fashion a loop at one end of the rope. When he was satisfied he had what he wanted, he pulled off some line and began twirling the loop and gave a throw at the large hook that held the chain of the big light fixture. "Damn," he said, louder when he missed it a second and third time. But on the fourth try he got it. "Yo, baby!" He got the rope to move freely back and forth through the loop of the hook, then pushed the dining room table over beneath the light fixture, climbed on top of it and reached up to feed and pull the rope through the spokes on the wheel until he got the rope to hang straight. He got back down, pushed the table aside and jumped onto the rope and let it swing with all of his weight. "It'll hold," he said. He went around the room and killed the lights, then fashioned the other end of the rope into a noose. "Gotta make things interesting, Riddler. Right? Kill you, fuck her, kill her, fuck her, whatever. Let's have some fun with it! I mean, since nobody wants to give up the diamonds, let's make an evening out of it. Whaddaya say?"

"Give it up, Walls. You can't get anywhere with this game," said Jake.

"We'll see. I have been known to take my time with these things. I want everybody to have a good time, particularly me." The evil sound that came from Lomis was more of a chant than a laugh. "So, here is what we are going to do." Lomis slipped the finished noose around Jake's neck and pulled it tight enough to bring up a reluctant groan from his suddenly restricted throat. "That should be about right. Now don't you move, big boy." Lomis moved and pushed an ottoman from in front of the couch along the wood floor until it was directly underneath the wagon wheel. "Really nice that these wheels underneath work nice and smooth."

Jake could see what was going on and stepped up his wrist work at the back of the chair.

"I know you are working on that," Lomis said, pulling the rope tighter and walking behind Jake's chair. He took out the hunting knife and cut the binding that held Jake to the chair but there was still a triple wrap holding his wrists together. "Follow me," Lomis said, pulling the rope tighter and pushing Jake into place, letting him choke just enough to know it was nearly over for him. "Now step up there. That a boy." As he pulled tighter yet, Jake had no choice but to step up onto the ottoman. "Stand tall. Stand straight!" Lomis commanded as the ottoman moved slightly back and forth under Jake's weight. Once he had Jake centered and perfectly vertical, he gave the rope another hard tug and watched Jake's eyes widen. "Like a bobble doll, sort of," Lomis chuckled. He slowly moved away and let out rope gradually until he got to the front door, looped it around the wrought iron handle to get some extra leverage and pulled until Jake's feet were pushing at the ottoman to keep contact. Then he doubled the rope back over and tied it secure.

Liv's eyes were steady and trained on everything that was going on, her body still, nostrils barely flaring above the duct tape.

"No, I'm not going to kick out the ottoman, Riddler. "You're going to do that." With that pronouncement, Lomis walked over and cut the duct tape holding Liv to the chair, pulled her up roughly, and threw her face down at the couch. "As for you, sweet thing, show me a woman who won't lie through her teeth to get what she wants. You got money. Plenty of it. Diamonds or no diamonds. What time does your bank in this butt hole little town open? Eight? Nine? At any rate, we have a long night ahead of us. I don't know what will be more fun. Fucking you in the ass or watching the Riddler watching me fuck you in the ass. I guess we'll see. Like maybe right now."

Liv could hear him unzip and felt his long, bony fingers begin to move up the inside of her jean skirt. "Wait!" she cried out. "I have internet banking. We don't have to wait until morning. I can wire you money anywhere you want! Right now!"

"Oh, a thong girl. Nice," Lomis said softly, closing his eyes and connecting her warmth with his anxious fingertips and every answering nerve in his body. "How nice for you, my dear. But, you see, I am at a complete loss as to where that might be. I don't really exist, you see, except that finger going inside of you right now has to feel pretty real, eh?"

Liv swallowed hard and forced calmness into her voice while trying to block out what was happening to her. "I can make arrangements. I have connections everywhere."

"You need to relax," Lomis said calmly. Just relax. The wetter, the better. For you, anyway."

"Stop. Dammit! Please, just stop and listen to me for a minute."

Lomis withdrew his finger, rubbed it around his lips then stuck it into his mouth. "I'm listening."

"I have money. I have the diamonds, for whatever they are worth. I can give you either. I could give you a million dollars in cash in a day. Think about it. It would be worth trusting me."

Beads of cold sweat began to gather in Jake's brow as he scanned the room and tried to think it through. There was just enough light in the room to make everything out. Everything. It was implausible to think someone like Lomis Walls could so easily get the upper hand on him. It was unthinkable to consider what he had brought into Liv's life trying to leave his in the past. The haunting memory of his dead wife popped in and out of his mind as he wiggled the ottoman ever so carefully. There were so many brushes with certain death, the thought of actually dying had long stopped triggering original thought. But having loved only two women in his life, and having created a hell for them they would have never known otherwise was certain to follow him into his own afterlife, wherever that might be. Maybe he should just get it over with and let his eyes close from the inside on their own before someone else flipped the lids down for the last time. Going meekly, neutralized by a lost street soul like Lomis Walls. Somehow fitting. He continued to listen to Liv plead and bargain with Lomis, wishing he was as deaf as he was helpless.

Liv was breathing hard, pleading. "You don't want to do this."

"Sure I do," Lomis replied easily. "Those diamonds anywhere close by?"

"Yes! Just let me up. And please, please cut him down! I'll do anything you want."

"How close by?"

"Very close."

"Sounds like you are playing me, little one. I can be merciful, you know. Actually, that's a lie. I wouldn't know anything about that. Let's just do this and get it out of the way so you'll know what will happen if you double cross me. "Nothing like show and tell, I always say."

Liv could feel him getting in position behind her and struggled and stiffened back up against him, but she was no match for the duct tape.

"Fucking bastard!" Liv gasped as she felt him fumbling around against her flesh. He pulled her hair back tight with one hand and took a moment to study the glorious terror in her eyes as they shot back at his. "Jake!" she cried out.

Jake was too enraged to feel anything more, and his pleas and threats aimed at Lomis got no further than the duct tape across his mouth. The adrenalin surged and wracked through his body while his bloody wrists continued to twist against their bindings at the small of his back. Lomis had added two more layers with a knowing smile before he put the noose around his neck. As his ears filled with Liv's muffled screams, he could only wonder how it had all come to this. His head hanging, gagging for air, he became only vaguely aware of the flashlight beam on his forehead, then flooding his face. He looked up suddenly and the light of the chandelier above him came on full blast.

"What the fuck?" came a voice. "Holy shit. Freeze asshole. Get off of her now, jag off!" Another, deeper voice came as Jake focused in on two darkly dressed men that looked identical to the two he had killed less than a week before. There were more, just as he thought. They were back. And he was almost glad to see them. They both brandished small semi-automatic weapons and wore black full face masks.

One shoved Lomis off the couch onto the floor. "Shit, Bennie, did you see that! Look at that fucking thing." The man looked back up as Liv tried to gather herself into a corner of the couch huddled up against the cushions.

"Gotta be him, no doubt, Vin."

"Okay, okay....," Vin continued, obviously rattled. "What the hell is going on here?" he asked, shining his flashlight in the face of each of them, pausing for a ridiculous moment on the equally puzzled look on Jake's face while he tried to recall if he was missing something in the directives. He brought the beam of light down into Lomis' face. "We never got a real good look at your face but that GPS we put on your car couldn't of been on there an hour when you started moving. A real stroke of luck, except, of course, you interrupted our dinner."

The red laser beam of Bennie's weapon kept bouncing around the room. "Nobody makes any quick moves," he said.

"Which one of you guys or girls is Lomis Walls?" Vin asked.

Liv's glazed eyes drifted down in Lomis' direction as she tried to get her breath and cradled her legs together in her arms.

"Who the fuck are you?" Lomis asked, hopelessly trying to look inconspicuous.

"Hilarious! Just like he said," Vin interrupted. "Donkey dick mothafucka. How do you like that, Bennie? His fucking cock gave him away. I don't know or give a fuck about the rest of this mess, but this is our guy, for sure. Let's go motherfucker!" Lomis went for his gun laying on the coffee table but the two men grabbed him and pulled him to his feet. Bennie pressed the barrel of his gun into Lomis' temple while Vin worked the flashlight and waited for a mesmerizing moment until Lomis got himself all tucked back in.

"What the hell do you assholes want with me," Lomis asked carefully. "Nobody knows me and I sure as hell don't know you."

"We are a present from your good friend Senator Perkins," Vin announced. "He suggested we might take you to a nice dinner."

"Perkins. What the hell, man. Hey, I'm okay with all that now. I got me a different source of income."

"We can discuss it over dinner. Let's go." Vin nodded and Bennie nudged Lomis back a few feet with the gun barrel before turning him towards the opening that led through the kitchen.

"This is some fucking bullshit...." Lomis tried to run Bennie into a left-hook roundhouse but his arm dropped like a limp noodle when the but of the gun whacked him with precision across his chin, dropping him to the floor. Lomis summoned the strength of ten men and arched back up with a roar only to be floored again by a thudding kick to the groin by Vin and another whack across the face with the gun by Bennie. Lomis moaned and rolled over before coming back up with a roar louder than before. This time he managed to get a stiff arm into Bennie that sent him flying across the room and caught Vin's next steel-toed kick in his hand and flipped him over the couch as Liz scrambled away into the dark. Steadying himself and wiping the warm gusher of blood from the side of his mouth, Lomis pounced on Vin but caught a fist to his jaw that cracked loud enough to echo off the high ceiling. Lomis screamed in pain but his anger rose up with a growl and he lurched forward with a flurry of fists into Vin's throat and face.

Bennie stood back up, found his gun and quickly moved to the backside of Lomis, gauged, and swung the gun with everything he had. Another crack resonated across the ceiling courtesy of the skull bone of Lomis Walls, just above the left ear. Lomis went slack as he fell off Vin with a moan and appeared to be out.

"This mothefucka," Vin spit and bubbled up a mix of saliva and blood of his own that was about to drown him as he took Bennie's arm assist to get up.

"I'll kill the cocksucker right now, Vin."

"No!" Vin shot back. "The man said slowly, painfully.... And anyway, not here, like this. There's weird shit going on here. Too fucking complicated. Get his hands tied up and we'll get him out of here. Let's go."

CHAPTER TWENTY SEVEN

THE FULL MOON WAS up over the mountains and threw a blue haze of light down through the sky lights. The razor precision of Jake Parker's mind was no better than a mish-mash of anger, fear and befuddlement, but when he felt the ottoman suddenly give to one side and flip away, it boiled down to a one-on-one battle with the nylon rope that begin to sink deeply into the skin of his neck. A muffled half-cry came from his mouth beneath the tape and he began to swing slightly. With perhaps a final pinch of his shoulder blades and a grinding twist of his bloodied wrists, the tape around one hand broke free, then the other. He tried to pry the ring of nylon rope out of his neck but it was already in too deep. Reaching up and flailing his arms about him, one hand found the wooden rim of the wagon wheel light fixture. He grabbed and pulled with a muffled scream and got just enough weight off the noose to swing his other hand up to get a grip, missing the first time, but on the second attempt he found another hold and had himself balanced on the rim of the wheel as it tilted under his weight. Getting his breath, it was as if all of the blood inside him was rushing around trying to find a way out. His hand shook and wavered as he tried to decide whether to swing or just hope by all rights the hook at either the fixture or the ceiling would give out. Still, he knew one bad move would be the end. He figured if he started to swing and went too far, the taught rope could pull him free of the fixture and he would have nothing but his neck to hold on to. He reached one hand down and ripped the layers of tape off his mouth, tearing what felt like most of the skin off his lower lip. He got the hand back up and tried to think through various moves that some way might hook a leg or just a foot onto the chandelier. "Liv...," he coughed out, barely audible.

Liv didn't answer. He had experienced the ominous silence of death being close by before, and it had once again come to visit. It was all but over unless he took a chance of swinging up to get his legs somehow hooked onto the light fixture. He regripped carefully, not having any feeling left in his fingers tips, and began a controlled swing sideways, thinking he would get a rhythm and swing his stronger left leg up on the count of ten. The middle of his head spoke to him, loudly. Seven, eight, nine. Ten! He swung the leg and it caught something, but the noose pulled tighter and slid back into the crevice in his neck it had created earlier. He let go with one hand to grab at it, then his other hand came loose, his foot dropped and he was a dead man hanging just like the stick character was drawn up.

Jake felt the air being sucked from his lungs as he tried to wedge his fingers into the noose. Suddenly there was a crashing sound, a flash of light bouncing around in his upturned eyes and he was falling. He was near unconscious, lying on the hardwood floor, grabbing at his shoulder, coughing and spitting up blood and everything else, but in the small recess left of his aching brain it occurred to him that someone had opened the front door.

Jake's head bounced back up off the floor and he became aware the lights in the godforsaken chandelier were on except for the one he had kicked out trying to get a foot up on the wheel rim.

Blinded, he looked up and away from the bright lights, but caught a blurred, but growing image of a tall, familiar man in an all too familiar olive green trench coat. "Dragon?"

"Don't look so surprised, Jake. Sorry we got delayed a bit. Carter's prostrate, as usual. Had to stop to let him pee about every fifteen minutes."

"What in hell are you talking about? What in hell are you doing here!" Jake's voice cracked, he coughed up more blood and his throat closed up on him as two young men in ski jackets with small black medical bags began to check out his various wounds. "Not that I'm ungrateful or anything. I'm just glad you broke in the front door instead of the back." He pointed to his throat and shut up, but his eyes looked up at Dragon, loaded with questions.

"When you disappeared without saying anything we got a little concerned. Not very Colonel Parker like. So after a few months went by, one of our people reported you were seen in Kershaw, Idaho. We got a GPS on your pick up at that point. We checked into things a little further and we find you are cavorting with one of those pretty, young and ambitious environmental types. And the mayor of Kershaw, no less." Dragon looked around the room and decided lighting a cigarette was no big deal. "You want more?"

Jake grimaced and flinched as they fit him with a make shift sling for his shoulder, dabbed at the gashes in his neck and forehead and gingerly brought him to his feet. "More? That's nothing. More than nothing? Yeah. I want more."

"Your girlfriend is probably okay, it would seem, but we had a bead on two guys who were sent over by your former Pakistani landlord to wipe you out." Dragon leaned back against the banister of the stair case and took a long pull on the cigarette.

"And so, my protector, any idea where might they be now?" Jake asked, rubbing at his neck.

"Hell if I know. We lost track of them. I thought it best to just come and find you, thinking, of course, that we find them as well."

"Right. Well, while I am grateful, you are a little late to give the Colonel Parker death squad a go.

"You've seen them?"

"Oh yes. They paid me a visit just recently."

"And?"

"And... nothing. Let's just say I should have been on the payroll, Dragon. Mission accomplished."

Dragon gave his head a little shake and peaked out the front window to see what his staff was up to. "No doubt. You know, the strangest damn thing, though, we would have let this thing go a few more weeks but we kept getting our GPS signal jammed with another GPS signal. Never seen it happen before. Anyway, our tech's thought somebody might actually be trying to jam the signal because it was like two GPS signals sort of on top of each other, or maybe you might have even been sending a signal back at us. Impossible to know right now. They'll get to the glitch. Anyway, I decided to move now, just in case, being how flaky you had become and all. Finding you at the end of hangman's noose was my eye candy for the next month. Not much of a fitting end for a man of your distinction, Jake. Besides, We still need you."

"Which is the real reason you are here. Fuck me."

"Multi-tasking, Jake." Dragon said with a laugh. "We aren't here. You aren't here, either, for that matter."

"Not existing is really fucking hard sometimes, Dragon. Not all the shits and giggles it's cracked up to be."

Dragon pretended to play a tiny instrument next to his ear. "World's tiniest violin, playing just for you."

"You should never try to be humorous. I've told you that before. You suck at it."

Jake's mind began to slow into it's methodical sequencing to sort out what had happened. He couldn't believe it took him this long. "Where is Liv?" He jumped up. The two men attending to him were no match to keep him down. "And what about Lomis!"

"Who's Lomis?" Dragon asked.

Jake kept moving forward towards the front door, snagging the slackened nylon rope with one foot before kicking it away. "Never mind. What about Liv?"

"Easy, Jake. Easy," said Dragon, pressing his hands into Jake's chest, trying to hold him back as he listened to the chatter coming into his earpiece. "Assuming she was the one running from the house, they have her in the van outside. She's quite safe for now."

"What are you going to do, shake her down, Dragon?"

"Just being careful, Jake. Come on, we don't take chances like that. What's happened to your edge?"

Jake eased back. "I've been trying to lose it. She's been helping me."

Dragon put a hand to Jake's shoulder and tried to square him up eye-to-eye. "How about... not just yet. We have a situation. It's close by. Mexico. Eminent. Your ball park, completely. And a handsome reward. Trust me. You know that's all I can say for now."

"Trust you." Jake managed a smile at Dragon and shook his head as he began making his way out to the van. He had trusted Dragon with his life countless times. "If she's in cuffs, all bets are off and I kick your ass instead."

"By the way," Dragon called after him, "we got some chatter about some stolen diamonds in this mix of all of this. You know anything about that?"

Jake stopped dead in his tracks and thought for a moment before turning back to Dragon. "What if I did?"

"Just curious."

"You are never *just* curious, Dragon." Jake turned back and headed for the van. "I don't exist," he said, just loud enough.

The closest house to Liv's was still as dark as the night surrounding it. When he opened the side door of the van, a small overhead light came on and beneath it sat a disheveled but otherwise dark haired beauty anybody would proudly parade in front of mom and dad, then sneak upstairs into the guest bedroom. She looked up at Jake and offered a tired smile under eyes that glowed with either defiance or pure shock. They said nothing to each other as he sat down on the floor of the van and leaned his aching back into the door frame, then he reached over and grabbed her and held on as tightly as he could without breaking her.

"My God, what just happened, Sam?" She whispered into his chest."

"Are you alright?" He tried to touch her everywhere to make sure she was in one piece. "God, I am so sorry, Liv. *So* sorry."

"Tell me... who are all these people, Sam?"

"Jake," he whispered into the top of her head. "It's Jake. Sorry, baby. I am so very sorry for all of this. I hope you can believe that."

"God, don't ask me to believe anything right now. Okay? I was nearly raped and likely would have been killed tonight. I believe that." She pulled away and wrapped herself up in her own arms.

Jake tried to pull her back, but she would have none of it. "Okay." He tried to gather what thoughts he had. "Let me just recoup a little." He took a deep breath and let everything settle back. "So I guess I understand why you would run away. I mean, I didn't much think of anything other than trying to get the rope from around my neck."

"Truth is... I started to run. I thought you were either dead or going to die. I was running for my life. I was no match for those goons. But when *whomever* they are grabbed me outside and put me in this van, I was actually running back to see if I could save you somehow. I didn't care what happened to me at that point. I wasn't going to leave you... ."

"You weren't."

"No. I could never... I would never leave you." She eased back across and leaned into him, her eyes dripped against his chest, she began to shake and the tears came freely. She sunk into his arms and he held her as tightly as he could. "Thank you for being alive," she sobbed.

There weren't many moments in his life when Jake Parker had to work to keep it together, but this was one of those. "Liv. I love you more than anything in this world. But, as much as I love you, I cannot tell you certain things about me. I can just tell you that I do work for our government. Not in the same way you do, but I do good things, nonetheless. Necessary things. And because of how I do what I do, very little can be said about it. Jake Parker technically does not exist. He died in some God forsaken tunnel in the mountains of Pakistan. And, even what I just told you puts you at risk for knowing. I have lived in a very dangerous world, and obviously, I still do." Jake stopped to gauge her softening, but puzzled look. "When I fell in love with you, I really felt I could maybe escape who I was and become what you wanted me to be- part of you- part of your wonderful grand scheme to save the world from itself. And I love your scheme. I love your approach a hundred times better than mine."

Live sensed the opening and shot back into his arms. "Then come and join me, you idiot. You know how much I love you."

He closed his eyes and drank her in as he felt her arms go around his waist. "God damn, I wish it were that simple. As you can see, the danger of my life has followed me. Even here. I have managed to put you in danger as well."

"Why so complicated. We can just love each other. That would be okay with me, too." She kissed him on each cheek and their lips met and held.

"If I were to tell you I need to go away for awhile, that it was business, would you just be okay with that?"

"Maybe. I can't say for sure. I think so." She shuddered and closed her eyes. "I would do anything for you. You know that."

"Would you keep the shop for me?"

"Depends on who drifts into town next. What if you really are this other guy? The dangerous one. I might never see you again. I probably won't ever see you again." The tears started again.

"I promise. Just keep the shop for me- just like it is."

"How long?"

"No more than a couple of months," he said, guessing badly.

"I guess we'll see." She managed an uncertain smile. "Best offer. The best I can do." She stiffened her resolve a bit.

Jake pulled back and studied her. A face to never forget. Not for a moment. "I will come back to you."

"If I ask you if this is the last time you will do this, would that be fair?"

Jake knew the answer now. "Probably not. Unless I screw it up again."

Dragon approached, buttoned up his trench coat, lit another cigarette, and watched them devour each other in another embrace. "Done?"

"Dragon.... . I'll call you in the morning," said Jake.

"No later than seven. We need to be on the way, directly."

Liv and Jake watched as Dragon and his crew snuck away back into the dark. "And *your welcome*, by the way," Dragon yelled.

The quiet returned as Jake and Liv stood there under the stars and moon. She molded herself into him and they held each other without saying anything for a long time.

"Can you still be Sam for me?" she asked.

"I think you are going to have to put up with Jake. But I can guarantee you he loves you even more than Sam did yesterday, or even than Jake did an hour ago. Nobody will ever love you more or longer than I will." He kissed her deeply. "Do you believe that?"

"I believe." The tears were coming again as she sensed their parting, but she was smiling beneath it all. "I need to believe that."

"That's a good start. Hold that thought."

CHAPTER TWENTY-EIGHT

LOMIS GOT HIS INDEX finger wedged into his back pocket and was able to inch the tiny Swiss Army knife up until he could get a fingernail into the slot on the narrow blade and pulled it out. He continued to watch and listen to Vin and Bennie laughing away in the front seat while he began cutting at the heavy nylon cords that held his hands behind him.

"Comfortable, hot shot?" Vin shouted back over the seat.

"Where we headed?" Lomis asked.

"Damnation. Now how would that information be of any use to you?"

"We'll get you a brochure. How's about that?" Bennie asked.

"Always interesting listening to guys who think they are tough trying to be funny. Brings out the real stupid in you. I mean, sorry, but that was just too easy." Lomis almost had one hand free. "You know, I could get into this gig. How about you call your boss and tell him I'll come and work for him. I could run circles around you fucking guys."

"We'll pass the message along a little later," Vin said.

"Hey how about I give you a little bit of shut the fuck up," Bennie said as he turned to give Lomis a fist to the bridge of the nose.

"Easy, Ben, easy. Save the pieces, man." In the rear view mirror, Vin could see some blood trickling from one of Lomis' nostrils. "Goddamit, Bennie, no fucking blood in the car, you fucking moron. How many times I gotta tell you that? Fucking moron. Christ."

"Sorry, Vin. I'm just letting him know who's in charge is all, you know."

"Yeah. Gee, thank God you are here to get that all squared away for everybody."

"Hey, Bennie," Lomis began, "you a fag boy or what? I smell fag perfume in here. I'll bet you spritz it on your balls, eh?"

Bennie shot over the back seat and put his hands around Lomis throat and dug his fingers in. "You piece of shit. I"ll gut you... ." His words stopped and caught in his throat as Lomis sliced him open ear to ear. He tried to draw back but Lomis held the back of his head with one hand and began to slowly pull him down over the seat back while Bennie grabbed at the gaping wound pounding blood out of his neck. "Acckcck,,, acckcck ckk."

"Bennie! What the fuck are you doing, asshole?" Vin slowed the car and tried to pull Bennie back into his seat. "Come on. We're almost there."

Lomis slithered to the side of Bennie as he struggled for his final breath and popped up right behind Vin, reaching up and adeptly digging the small point of his knife up tight against the biggest artery he could find in his neck. "Actually, and very carefully I mind you, pull over and turn the car around. You're going the wrong direction. Can you imagine? GPS and all."

Vin's eyes widened and he tried to get a glimpse of Bennie in the rear view mirror, thinking he would get the cue and collar this asshole.

"Bennie's toast," said Lomis. "So much for the rule about no blood in the car. Sorry about that, chief."

Still, Vin looked. "This is some kind of bullshit," he sighed. "Take it easy, now."

"Yeah. I'll take it easy. Don't you worry. You just keep driving, fuckhead."

"No problem. You know you're right. Maybe you would be good at this. Bennie? Bennie was a fuck up. I could get a good word in with the big boss for you."

"Gonna be my best pal in the world now, eh Vin? Let's get real. I figure on calling your boss and tell him I killed the dick wad and I'm standing at your death bed watching you bleed to death. He's got two choices. Send more meat, or figure he needs to pay me twice what he's paying you guys put together. That's what I figure."

"Yeah. And who's going to give you the phone number, asshole?" Vin tried a laugh on for size.

"Nobody. Sure as hell not you while I'm dissecting you. But my guess is your cell phone has a recently dialed number or two in it. I'll take my chances. Don't worry, Vin. I won't need you. You won't have to worry about going out like a pussy. We'll go for the slow, full suffering treatment, kinda of what you and Bennie were talking about when we first got in the car. You know, the laughs were on me? All that?"

"Come on. Don't be a sick fuck. We are two of a kind, you and me."

"Really. Looks to me like you're a fat slob that probably hasn't seen your dick in ten years. My dick stands up and takes a picture of me every morning."

"It's a good life, I'm telling you. You would fit in like family, Walls."

"Except I've never needed family, Vin. And family has never needed me."

"Okay, Okay. You need to think about what you are doing. Where the hell are we going now?"

"A far better place. Trust me." Lomis dug the bloodied blade into Vin's neck skin just enough to mix some of his blood with Bennie's. "I've made a living handling knives, Vinnie boy, so don't try anything quick and nasty."

Driving through mountains in the dark was much the same as driving in circles for most, a feeling of encroachment on all sides, and just the loneliest of street lights was a welcome reconnection with reality. "Turn right here," Lomis said.

"What the fuck, man." Strands of sweat were running down Vin's neck, mixing with the blood, and Lomis could feel the moisture gather against his hand. He smiled in the dark. "Keep going."

"You gotta believe me, man. There's big dough in this for you. I can arrange it. I can make this all good."

"It's all good. You are right about that. Now, pull over just ahead on your left." Vin pulled the car over and put the gear shift in park as he felt the pressure of the blade increase against his skin. "Now, ease that gun you have out of your pants and hold it up in front of you by the barrel, handle down," Lomis said.

Vin was hoping maybe Lomis had forgotten about the gun. Not a chance. He eased the gun up in front of him and gauged his chances of making a quick move before Lomis could bury the knife into his artery. Better to wait it out, he thought, and watched anxiously as a hand came forward and took the gun back.

"What now?" he anxiously asked.

"Easy, Vin boy. You have some work to do." Lomis got out of the back seat and used the gun to direct Vin to do the same. "Now walk around to the other side of the car and get your friend so we can give him a proper burial. Then we'll talk."

Vin did as he was told and slung Bennie's fresh bloodied body up over his shoulder. "Cold as hell out here, man. Let's get it done."

Lomis directed Vin ahead and down an embankment. In moments, Vin sunk to his knees in snow and fell forward, launching Bennie's body to the bottom of the incline.

"That will work," Lomis said. "Get the fuck up and keep moving."

Vin pulled himself up and shook off the snow. "Hey, I'm with you. Bennie out of the way, I move up and you move in. It's a beautiful thing, Lomis."

"Shut the fuck up. I said we'll talk later. Lomis looked up and smiled as his eyes adjusted to the light blue glow being thrown down on the landscape by the full moon. He could see exactly where they needed to go. His insides flooded with a surge of heat as he thanked his Gods and quietly mumbled about the turns of his fated destiny. No matter the twists and turns, he would move on. He played that out for a few moments and had to force himself to focus back on the stumbling big man in front of him trying to get Bennie's body back onto his shoulders. "To your right. Head up between those two big pine trees."

"A man with a plan," Vin said. He had a compliment in mind but it came out as a breathless whimper.

There was perhaps an additional foot of snow on the ground since he had been there last, but Lomis was certain they were in the right place. "Put him down. Sit down, and don't move," Lomis said as he moved his boots through the snow and tried to locate the depression in the ground where he dug the grave. The moon wasn't as bright in the shadows, but he was thinking they had to be close when his right foot suddenly gave way and he tumbled sideways into the snow.

Vin leaped to his feet and flew across the ten feet of ground that separated them and landed full forced on top of Lomis. The gun went off and Vin shrieked in pain as a bullet tore through his upper thigh. "You fuck!" he screamed and got one hand on the gun arm and another around Lomis' neck. The gun went off again, this time straight up to the sky between their clenched fists. Lomis began to spit and cough as Vin found and tried to rip out his vocal chords through his neck. Vin got a knee up on Lomis other arm, the one broken in the car accident.

"Fuuuuuck!" Lomis screamed as the recently healed bone snapped crisply under the weight of Vin's knee. Lomis heaved up against him and with a scream summoning his Gods, managed to push Vin off and away from him, but the gun went flying as well.

Vin struggled to his feet, his bleeding leg nearly numb and barely dragging along but he was no match as Lomis gathered up and swung his foot directly into Vin's face, landing it to the sound of crushing cartilage and bone. Vin screamed in pain and his face dropped into the snow. The blow had forced Lomis back off his feet and he fell onto his rebroken arm yelling and cursing the Gods of another.

He struggled to gather himself, crawling and sifting through the snow for anything that would finish Vin off- the gun, his knife, a rock, stick, anything to kill the son of a bitch so he could get the hell out of there. He came across a sturdy short piece of a fallen limb worthy of using to open up the back of Vin's skull, but stumbled and lost his footing as he lunged forward. As he steadied and got a good grip on his weapon he realized what he held was actually a bone, a long bone, perhaps a femur, perhaps a human femur. His shrill of evil cracked through the air and strands of saliva flew and dangled from his lips. The broken arm dangling uselessly, he was standing, weaving, looking up at the sky, asking for the strength he needed when a searing pain shot up his leg as it collapsed beneath him in an instant.

"Yeah, baby!" The blood from Vin's throat spit out like a fountain as he grabbed for Lomis' other leg. He could not see anything through the twisted mess left of his face, but as Lomis cried out into the night, Vin moved his hand from the twitching leg he had just cut, then grabbed the other leg and took the knife he had found in the snow and sliced it through the tendon at the back of his heel. Lomis lurched out and tried to pull himself away, but his legs had been taken away and he had but one arm left to try to pull himself from Vin's reach. With all the strength left in him, his legs dragging helplessly through the deep snow, leaving a trail of blood, he managed to free himself of Vin's weakening stabs at his calves.

"You stupid fuck!" He screamed. "You worthless, stupid fuck!"

Vin was in a delirious laughter, feeling something of a lift from the pain, sensing the possibility of survival. He was on one knee when they both heard the first roar and the ground begin to vibrate.